Sunshine & Rain:

Triple Crown Collection

Sunshine & Rain:

Triple Crown Collection

Dawn Desiree

www.urbanbooks.net

Urban Books, LLC
97 N18th Street
Wyandanch, NY 11798

Sunshine & Rain: Triple Crown Collection
Copyright © 2007 Triple Crown Publications LLC

This title is published by Urban Books, LLC under a licensing agreement with Triple Crown Publications LLC.

ISBN 13: 978-1-62286-990-9
ISBN 10: 1-62286-990-7

First Mass Market Printing March 2016
First Trade Paperback Printing (July 2007)
Printed in the United States of America

10 9 8 7 6 5 4 3 2 1

This is a work of fiction. Any references or similarities to actual events, real people, living or dead, or to real locales are intended to give the novel a sense of reality. Any similarity in other names, characters, places, and incidents is entirely coincidental.

Distributed by Kensington Publishing Corp.
Submit Orders to:
Customer Service
400 Hahn Road
Westminster, MD 21157-4627
Phone: 1-800-733-3000
Fax: 1-800-659-2436

Sunshine & Rain:

Triple Crown Collection

Dawn Desiree

Dedication

Dedicated to Aunt Pam -R.I.P.
(Beautiful Queen)

Acknowledgments

Oh my God,
I thank you first and foremost.
To you I give the praise and all the utmost, for allowing me to pursue this dream I treasure most. To have my thoughts and feelings expressed in books from coast to coast.
Thank you for answering my prayers and planting this gift.
I thank you more for paving a way out of no way to go about this.

Thank you to my Triple Crown family for making a vision clear when it was only just a dream to me.

And now . . .

To Andre (Earthquake): Big, big love for all your support and dedication. You sure held me down. You're a true soldier with the strength I need and I'm so glad I found you.

And to you, Jacqué, my big li'l sis, for always having faith in me, even when I was without it.

India (Peanut), thank you for being my angel and bringing out the softer side in me. May you rise to the top like I know you will and be all that God wants you to be.

Dazia (Day Day), thank you for "playing mommy" when I needed some "me time," and for supporting me when light was dim. Now we gonna watch it shine.

Keith (son-son), when I look in your eyes, you inspire me to rise, through the tears and the cries; it's what makes me wise. Keep gaming, son, for soon you'll be football faming.

Malachi (baby boy), I told you that if you worked with me, this thing would happen. You had my back and I got yours. Now you can get ALL the wrestling men.

Mommy, our road was bumpy. I got out; you kept driving. I came back, and now we riding.

Mamma Rita, you're "all up in it," and this would not be without you. At a time I really needed you, you pulled through.

Big luv, Tony. Wow! I can't even express it 'cause it's so deep. Thank you, thank you, thank you, for EVERYTHING! Did I say thank you?

Tou Tou (Toutie), I always prayed for God to send me a true blue. In case you didn't know, it's you . . . it's you.

Mr. Walter Ficklin, thank you for helping make this thang legit. Your belief, faith, and encouragement helped me not to quit.

Kevin Hinton (lil' bro), thanks for the last minute help. You're the BIZOMB! When things looked doubtful, you helped reverse the wrong. Keep your heart in S.W.O.W.L. sounds. Take to the sky what you built from the ground.

To Mrs. Hall and the entire Big Mamma's Crew, for upholding my family and keeping it true.

To all my haters: I'm not trippin off you, cuz. We all have a gift that we can use it or lose it. Once you put your shit out there, it'll be one to refuse it. You don't get it twisted, and I won't confuse it. I'ma keep coming, and you can't diffuse it. Hate me if you will, love me when you won't, I still and I will, even if you don't.

ONE

"Listen, Sunshine, I need to talk to you."

Sunshine looked over at her mother. She could tell by the way her mother fiddled with her fingers that she felt uneasy. Ayanna always had a nervous habit of fidgeting.

Sunshine moved closer to Ayanna's bedside to comfort her fragile mother. Ayanna had been battling her disease for over two years; now she was fighting for her life. Her condition had seemed to worsen within the last two weeks since she caught pneumonia.

Ayanna's illness was a battle that Sunshine had been fighting with her mother every step of the way. In her heart, Sunshine willed her mother's pain and suffering to end. This disease was much too evil for even the devil to endure.

When her mother called and told her to come to the hospital, Sunshine knew something was seriously wrong. Ayanna remained in critical condition at Howard University Hospital for over a week, and this was the first time that she not only allowed Sunshine to visit her, but asked her to come.

Sunshine missed her mother desperately during their time apart. They hadn't been separated this long since the time Sunshine spent a weekend at a sleepover with some friends, way back when she was still in elementary school. That was the first and last time she spent time away from her mother. Sunshine missed Ayanna so much that weekend that she wet the bed. Her friends told everyone at school, and Sunshine was ridiculed for weeks.

It pained Sunshine to see her mother this way. Ayanna looked nothing like her usual self. She had once been the most beautiful Hershey chocolate woman to walk the streets of Washington, D.C. In her prime, Ayanna had been advantageously blessed with the thickest pair of hips and deep-set curves that made her the envy of the town by all the women and the talk of all the men. Her smile was so big and bright that she could lighten the darkest midnight hour.

Sunshine looked down at the woman lying in the hospital bed now, and she barely resembled the strong, sexy woman who had been singlehandedly raising her daughter for the past fifteen years. Now, this teenager stared at her dying mother with a heart that cried out at the reality of Ayanna's rate and with eyes that told Ayanna to finally leave this miserable illness behind and find peace.

Ayanna's frail and deteriorating body was slowly surrendering to her disease. Without the same vibrant glow that masked her only one year ago, even her skin seemed to be two shades darker. Protruding cheekbones, the same ones that had always dominated and enhanced her facial structure, now made her look like a breathing corpse.

Sunshine despised seeing her mother this sick. Who had done this to her? Why did she have to endure this torture? As Ayanna lay on her deathbed, Sunshine finally understood why her mother kept limiting her visits. She tried hard to stay composed while still continuing to support her ill mother.

Ayanna took Sunshine by the hands and looked deep into her eyes. She the fought tears that were anxious to escape, in order to avoid making this conversation harder than it already had to be.

"What is it, Mama? You know I'm strong enough to handle whatever it is you have to say to me," Sunshine offered in an attempt to make the conversation easier.

It was hard for Ayanna to continue to look into her baby girl's big brown eyes. *She's too precious to have to go through this, Lord. Please be with her, Father,* Ayanna prayed while focusing her sunken eyes on her busy fingers.

"I know you're strong, baby, 'cause you just like your mama. You got fight in you," Ayanna replied. "It's just that this is a little more difficult than I expected it to be. Sunshine, you know that I like to keep things real with you. In this life, you have to deal with a lot of fake people, and I want to be the one person you can always trust and believe in. When I tell you this, please know that I have looked into all of my options. I have prayed, and there is not much else I can do," Ayanna confessed with a heavy heart.

Sunshine squeezed her mother's hand to let her know that whatever it was she had to say, Sunshine already understood.

Ayanna spoke slowly and deliberately. "Sunshine, you have always been my motivation. I've done a whole lot of bad things in my life. I don't claim to be perfect, but I provided the best way that I could for you. I raised you, even though it was hard for me. I kept you in school even when we were homeless with nowhere to go. I made sure you learned how to read, because I know how important it is to get ahead in this world and because I didn't want you to end up like me. I'm not a bad person, but I lost my chance at life a long time ago. I could never get the kind of job I wanted to get us out this ghetto because of my illiteracy. Without the skills, you can't pay the bills. So, I did what I had to do. I stripped at those nasty clubs to feed us, and I sold my body at the after parties to pay the rent."

Sunshine felt overwhelmed with emotion as she sat and listened to her mother express herself. She had always respected her mother for taking care of her the best way she could. At the same time, Sunshine had always secretly blamed herself for her mother's ways, because if it weren't for Sunshine, Ayanna wouldn't have to trick and lick to pay the bills.

"Sunshine, I don't want you to blame yourself for any of this. These are my mistakes, and it's not your fault." It was as if Ayanna read Sunshine's mind.

"I made my own decisions in life. I chose this road, and I'm only sorry that you have to suffer with me," Ayanna confessed.

"Sunshine . . ." Ayanna paused, inhaled, and finally said, "I'm dying." Her eyes began welling up as she spoke. "The doctors urged me to contact my family and to say my good-byes now.

You are my only family, Sunshine. You are all I've got, and I want you to know that I love you with all my heart. I put my all into raising you to be a good girl, even though I was bad." Ayanna couldn't fight back her tears any longer.

"A social worker will be coming to get you in the morning to take you to a foster home, where you'll be taken care of until you turn eighteen. No matter what, baby girl, I want you to remember to always keep your face to the sunshine so you don't see the shadows."

Sunshine held onto her mother's frail, shaking body. "It's okay, Mama. Everything will be okay, Mama. I'm going to be okay."

The two ladies rocked each other in a seesaw motion until Ayanna fell asleep. Sunshine stayed the entire night at the hospital with her mother, determined to be by her side until the very end.

The next morning, Sunshine was abruptly awakened by a loud, non-stop beeping noise that sounded almost like an alarm clock. Realizing that the long beep wasn't a wakeup call but the devastating sound of death, Sunshine trembled with panic and sorrow. Doctors and nurses swarmed the stark hospital room. Their attempts to revive Ayanna were hopeless. She was now gone to rest in peace.

Sunshine waited patiently for the commotion to calm down, and then she asked the doctors for a moment alone with her mother. She wanted to say a proper good-bye. The doctors obliged her request and left the room.

Sunshine walked over to her mother, grabbed her hands, closed her eyes, and prayed.

"Heavenly Father, you have called for your angel, my mother, to come home. She was everything to me, Father. She was my mother, my father, my best friend, my provider, and I don't know how I will go on without her, Father. However, I trust and believe that your will has been done. My mother's life was a struggle, and because of her, I can come to you this day and pray that you allow her now to rest in peace."

Sunshine stood up and allowed the presence of God to fill her with peace. As she turned to leave, Sunshine promised herself that she would always remember her mother as the beautiful woman she was.

"Rain, come here for a minute, *puh-leez!*" Jody screamed. Rain ran downstairs to see what all the yelling was about this time.

"What do you want *now*, Jody?" Rain screamed back.

"Could you please tell Daddy that it's Jerome's turn to do the dishes and not my turn?"

Rain looked at Jody with an expression that said *Are you for real?*

"Listen to me, Jody," Rain began. "You've got to stop calling me down here for stupid stuff, and stop worrying Daddy. Just do the damn dishes! Jerome can't clean all that well anyway. He always leaves stains on the dishes," Rain added.

Jerome sat smiling, satisfied as Jody stormed into the kitchen to wash the dinner dishes.

Jim, Rain's father, stood to go into his bedroom. "Thank you for handling your brothers," Jim said to Rain before retreating into his daily hideout.

Rain stared at her father with shame as his bedroom door closed. What went on behind those doors was no mystery to Rain. She knew that her father was getting ready to inhale all the crack his money could afford for the evening.

Rain had grown accustomed to her father's crack habit since the death of her mother, Evelyn, three years ago. Days like this were all too familiar to Rain. She could hear the constant clicking of Jim's lighter as he lit his crack pipe, and she could smell the sickening, perfumed aroma of incense that he used in an attempt to conceal the drug's pungent scent. This predictable scenario made Rain ache with a deep anger. It hurt her heart to watch her father go downhill this way.

Rain knew her mother would have never condoned her father's behavior, but in a strange sense, Rain understood her father's habit. It was as if he was slowly killing himself to be with her mother again.

Jim blamed himself for his wife's death. She had a nervous breakdown and had never recovered after learning about her husband's affairs with several different women. Secretly, Rain also blamed Jim for her mother's death, but she would never let him know it.

Rain ran upstairs to her bedroom to finish reading the book she had started before Jody had rudely interrupted her.

Downstairs, Jim sat on his bed and placed huge amounts of crack on his pipe, trying to maintain the surreal rush that he got from the first hit. He inhaled the narcotic, swallowing deep breaths, exhaling only when he felt his heart pounding heavier and his head getting lighter. He relished the trip. Jim no longer had worries in his heart or burden in his soul; only the anxious feeling of wanting a stronger, more crucial rush. He wanted to keep the guilt and shame gone forever.

Jim was on his fourth hit. He had to light more incense so that his children wouldn't smell the smoke. Usually, Jim would take his time and indulge, but tonight he had a large supply, a result of finding a stash outside of his dealer's home.

How lucky, he thought. Since he had such a great amount, he could smoke as much as he wanted, as soon as the urge hit him. The urge seemed to hit him every couple of minutes. Jim knew he should slow down. He'd seen so many movies where people overdosed on drugs. But as quickly as the thought entered his mind, it left.

Jim decided to turn on some music to enjoy his moment a little more. He turned to the slow jams and listened while they played one of his favorites, "Love and Happiness" by Al Green.

Briefly, Jim was transported back to many years earlier, during the good times when Evelyn was still alive. Jim stood up to dance with an imaginary silhouette, pretending his lost love, Evelyn, was right there with him. He swirled around and around on his bedroom dance floor, until he began to feel nauseated. He sat down and let tears fall down his face.

"I'm so sorry, Evelyn. I did love you with all of my heart. I just had so much temptation, baby." He said this aloud as if Evelyn sat right beside him.

Jim turned, in search of the pipe he'd placed on his nightstand. Ready to be rid of the tears and hurt that had managed to resurface, he loaded the pipe with a huge rock and struck the lighter to flame. He took in a deep breath, but this time he was unable to exhale. He could feel his heart racing so rapidly that it shook his entire body, pounding so hard that his pulse thumped to the rhythm of the music like a drum. Sweat began to pour down his face as it turned the deadly color of blue. Within seconds after his fifth hit, Jim Concise was dead.

Sunshine had packed all of her personal belongings, and some of Ayanna's as well. For sentimental reasons, she made sure to pack her mother's favorite lucky dress that she wore every time she went to Las Vegas to try to win them some money. Sunshine also packed Ayanna's photo album, which included tons of fly pictures of Ayanna from childhood up to adulthood.

Just as Sunshine was closing her suitcases, she heard a knock at the door. *I wonder who that could be?* Sunshine asked herself. She dragged her luggage to the door with her as she answered it.

Much to her surprise, the social worker who stood before her looked more like a young, hip diva. This woman looked nothing like the old, withdrawn senior citizen that Sunshine had expected.

"Hello, Miss Sunshine. I am Ms. Waters. I'll be working to get you stabilized in your new foster home." Sunshine felt at ease as she shook Ms. Waters' hand.

"Is this all you?" Ms. Waters asked as she eyed Sunshine's limited luggage.

"It's all me," Sunshine replied.

After the luggage was situated in the trunk of the car, Sunshine felt an emotional pain in her heart. She wasn't ready to leave home. Sunshine stood by the car and couldn't help but to glance back at the small, cozy apartment where she had built so many special memories with her mother. "What's going to happen to the rest of our belongings that are still inside?" Sunshine asked Ms. Waters.

"Well, baby girl, to be honest with you, I believe your landlord has the rights to all those riches, unless one of your distant relatives surfaces and claims the prize."

Sunshine grinned at Ms. Waters' sweet sarcasm.

"That sure is one beautiful smile you're wearing, little Miss Sunshine," Ms. Waters complimented. Sunshine's smile grew even wider.

"Well, is it okay if we leave now? Or would you rather linger around here feeling sorry for yourself? Don't get me wrong. I understand that what you're going through is rough, but it won't help you to try and hold onto everything that you must leave behind. You feel me?" Ms. Waters asked.

"Yes, Ms. Waters, I feel you," Sunshine answered. Sunshine could feel herself beginning to like Ms. Waters already. It was as if she genuinely understood what she was going through.

The ride to Sunshine's new home was peaceful, with only light conversation on the way. Sunshine felt that it was best not to get too much information about her new foster home before she experienced it for herself. Although she was leery, she would rather wait to form her own opinion once she got there. She couldn't choose where she wanted to live or who she wanted to live with anyway. All the arrangements were already made and organized for her. Her new life was in the state's hands.

Ms. Waters took it upon herself to inform Sunshine that her new foster parent was a single woman just as Ayanna had been. "She lives in a quiet, well-kept neighborhood close to Georgetown. She's been caring for children for a little over six years. She is a wonderful woman, and I know you'll like her," Ms. Waters added.

Sunshine liked the idea of being parented by a single mom. Maybe it would resemble being raised by her own mother, although no one could outdo Ayanna.

Sunshine was almost tempted to ask more questions about her new home, but she held back. Instead, she asked Ms. Waters' permission to turn on the radio.

"That's cool with me," she answered, "just as long as we don't have to hear about how somebody shot their mama in the back to get a stack, or stole a bankroll to get a little gold in their mouth." Ms. Waters began to wave her hand from side to side in a hip-hop motion as she bopped her head to an imaginary beat. Sunshine had to laugh at the woman's weak attempt to criticize rap music.

"Okay, I'll keep the music nice and clean, so as not to disturb the senior citizens in da house," Sunshine teased.

"Oh, this kid's got jokes. I like it. I like it a lot," Ms. Waters mocked.

Sunshine reached over to turn up the soft R&B tunes that lifted the air. The music helped

Sunshine relax. She leaned her seat back and hummed to the smooth melody of Chante Moore.

"Did you have breakfast already, or shall we stop and get something?" Ms. Waters asked as they rode past a strip of fast food restaurants.

Sunshine's stomach yelled, *Please feed me!* but her heart cried, *No, I'm not ready to eat!*

"No, thank you. I ate something before you came to get me," Sunshine lied.

"Well, if you don't mind, I think I'll stop and get me a bite." Ms. Waters pulled into a small diner on the corner and went inside. She ordered two blueberry muffins and two orange juices. She had a feeling that Sunshine wasn't being honest about having eaten breakfast. She couldn't let the poor child starve.

While Sunshine waited for Ms. Waters to come back to the car, she briefly took inventory of her surroundings. She wanted to keep up with landmarks, so she would know how far away she was from her old home.

They were still in Northwest D.C., but it seemed like a whole new world from Monroe Street, where she had lived. Her neighborhood was a majority of Blacks and Hispanics, with a few Caucasians. The part of Northwest they were in now seemed to be filled with mainly Caucasians and a few upper class Blacks. Sunshine wasn't familiar with this part of the city, but it wouldn't be too difficult to find her way back home if need be. All she had to do was walk backward until she saw the first group of Latinos posted up by the big playground.

The aroma from the diner battled Sunshine's previous denial of hunger. She was relieved when Ms. Waters came back to the car and handed her the warmest, fluffiest blueberry muffin she had ever tasted and some ice-cold orange juice to wash it down.

Ms. Waters watched in amazement as little Miss *"No, thank you. I'm not hungry"* Sunshine demolished the poor muffin before they pulled out of the parking lot.

"You know I could go back in and get you a value meal or a couple of number threes. Money is no object," Ms. Waters joked.

Sunshine blushed, feeling slightly embarrassed. "No, thank you. I'm all right," she said quietly.

As they pulled back onto the highway, Sunshine focused her attention on the shiny, silver jewelry that dangled from Ms. Waters' wrist and complimented her fingers. It matched perfectly with the sky blue pants suit and silver heels that made her look like an official diva.

"Do you enjoy your work?" Sunshine asked, trying to make small talk.

"I am devoted to what I do, and it makes me feel good knowing that I make a difference in children's lives. I have a caseload of twenty-seven children, and every so often I like to gather them up, five or six at a time, to go hang out for a day. We might have a picnic, go swimming, or tour the city down by the Monument. That's if they're behaving and following their house rules. So, I hope that encourages you to do the right thing, so you can join in the events. However, I don't see that being a problem for you," Ms. Waters said.

Just as Sunshine was about to inquire about Ms. Waters' other clients, she turned the car into the driveway of a huge two-story home. Sunshine was instantly impressed by the home's curb appeal. A pure, white picket fence wrapped around the home to mark its territory. Perfectly manicured bushes stood proudly along the walk leading up to the front porch. Cream marble rocks sat along the path, adding an eye-catching flair to the home's exterior. The front porch was adorned with a white outdoor loveseat and a patio table engraved with gold leaves. It could seat two people comfortably. All the curtains on the windows were open, allowing the sunshine to light the home's interior.

The scenery was so inviting from the outside that Sunshine almost felt guilty for being anxious to get her bags inside. This extravagant house was like heaven compared to the run-down apartment from where she had just come.

Ms. Waters noticed the look of sinful enthusiasm on Sunshine's face. "This is a brand new beginning for you, Miss Sunshine. Your mother and I talked frequently before her unfortunate death, and she made it clear that I put you in the best home we have in our system. I put in a lot of research, and your mother and I decided this would be a good home for you."

It brought tears to Sunshine's eyes knowing that her mother had actually helped in deciding this new home for her. Sunshine quickly wiped away her tears, determined to be mature and strong, as her mother would have wanted her to be. She closed her eyes and said a quick prayer.

Father, please bless me in my new home, with my new family, and please let her like me.

She slowly opened her eyes, unsure of what to do next. In a way, she wanted to jump out of the car and run back to the neighborhood where she had grown accustomed to the trash littering the grass, the familiar stray cats strolling the sidewalks alongside the dope fiends begging for money and the determined drug dealers patrolling the streets, trying to get paid. Did she really want to leave all that? She wasn't sure if she was truly ready to unload her belongings and go into the picture-perfect home with its unknown lifestyle.

Ms. Waters made the decision for her. "Okay Sunshine, enough stalling, girl. Let's go get 'em."

Sunshine forced a small smile on her face.

The two ladies exited the car and dragged all the luggage to the front door in one trip. Ms. Waters rang the doorbell that sang the popular baseball anthem, *"Take Me Out to the Ball Game."* The scene made Sunshine feel as if she was in a movie, a ridiculous movie. Who would have that silly song playing just to announce visitors? A simple *ding-dong* would do.

Seconds later, the woman Sunshine assumed to be her foster mother answered the door. Sunshine was caught off guard when she saw that the woman was white.

The lady reached to shake hands.

"Hello, Ms. Waters," she said. "And this pretty girl must be Sunshine." The white woman cheerfully greeted Sunshine and Ms. Waters while gesturing for them to come inside her home.

Cathy's house smelled like a rose garden, like there were PlugIns plugged into every outlet. Sunshine inquisitively sized up Cathy, slowly looking her from her short, black, shag haircut all the way down to her Armani pants suit. *Nice.*

It didn't take long to size her up. She was every bit of five feet tall. Cathy was petite and shapely, and flawlessly fit like Halle Berry. Her frame was shaped like a work of fine art, as though someone had chiseled each and every voluptuous curve to make a masterpiece. The two-piece suit she wore fit almost like a body suit, emphasizing her curves even more. The outfit was stylish and looked like something Sunshine would like to own once her own body blossomed a little more.

The lady continued talking. "My name is Cathy Stone. Please call me Cathy." She looked at Sunshine as she spoke. "Let me show you to your bedroom so you can situate your bags. Are there any more bags I can help you with?"

"No, this is everything," Ms. Waters answered.

"Well in that case, follow me," Cathy said.

Sunshine followed behind the two women, noticing all the creative decorations and furnishings along the way. She was so entertained by it all. Finally, they arrived at her new bedroom.

"Just set your things down, and you can unpack while Ms. Waters and I discuss some business, okay?"

Sunshine nodded her head in approval and was relieved when the two women left her alone in the room. She needed a minute to take in this new scenario.

Sunshine glanced around the unfamiliar room. It was huge. Her old bedroom couldn't compete with this one. Back home, her bedroom was only big enough to fit her twin mattress that lay on the floor, and a small nightstand.

This bedroom was refreshing and much more appropriate for a nearly sixteen-year-old girl. The walls seemed to reach heaven. They were decoratively splashed with soft, mint green paint. All the accessories inside the bedroom complemented the paint color. The mint green rug felt so soft, Sunshine needed to take her shoes off. *Ahh, this carpet feels good enough to sleep on.*

When she looked at the queen-sized bed covered with a light green Ralph Lauren comforter set, it looked even more inviting. She was overjoyed when she noticed the miniature entertainment center, which proudly displayed a 32-inch Sony flat screen TV with a five-disk DVD player. It sat above a five-disk Sony CD player with dozens of unopened CDs.

Sunshine suddenly felt very fortunate to be there. She decided to get comfortable with her new surroundings. She eased herself onto her new bed, lay back on the soft, silk comforter, and felt as if she had been swallowed whole. She decided to rest her eyes before unpacking. All these changes were starting to take their toll.

Just before she dozed off, she joked to herself, *Was that woman really white? This can't be Constitutional.*

Sunshine strained to hear Ms. Waters and Cathy conversing, but all was silent. She closed her heavy eyelids and began to think of Ayanna.

"This place is nice, Mama, real nice, but I'd still rather be back at home with you," Sunshine whispered. She let her mind drift back to when her mother was alive and well. Recent memories floated through her mind until she fell asleep, and the memories became a pleasant dream.

Sunshine didn't hear Ms. Waters come back into her room to say that she was leaving. A warm smile spread across Ms. Waters' face as she watched the peaceful, angelic expression the young girl wore as she slept like a newborn.

Noticing the unpacked bags, Ms. Waters assumed that Sunshine must have had a restless night and decided against waking her. Instead, she walked over to the dresser and set her business card in plain view for Sunshine to find when she awakened. On the back, she scribbled a short message: *Call me any time.* Quietly, she exited the room and walked downstairs.

"Is everything okay?" Cathy asked Ms. Waters, surprised to see her returning downstairs so soon.

"Yes, she is fine. Fast asleep actually," Ms. Waters answered.

Cathy shook her head in a sorrowful motion. "That poor child. She's going through a lot right now for such a young thang."

Ms. Waters nodded. "I couldn't agree with you more," Ms. Waters responded.

"She'll be fine here, though," Cathy reassured her. "I'll even prepare one of my special meals for dinner: sweet barbeque meatloaf and my famous baked macaroni and cheese. You're welcome to stay, too, if you'd like," Cathy added.

"Thank you. The invitation sounds delicious. However, I really must be going now. I have two other clients that need to be relocated, and I'm already behind schedule. I'll call later in the week to check on Sunshine and to see how things are working out with the new arrangements. This is her first transition, so we should expect some type of withdrawal behavior."

"Not if I have anything to do with it," Cathy responded.

Cathy followed Ms. Waters as she headed to the door to leave. "Will you be able to find your way back to the highway?" Cathy asked.

"Just as easily as I found my way here," Ms. Waters said, smiling.

As Cathy prepared dinner, she couldn't help but feel excited. It always made her feel good to cook for other people, especially children. Just as she began to mix diced onions into the ground beef with her hands, the telephone rang.

It never fails. She giggled to herself. *Someone is always trying to reach me while my hands are full.* She quickly rinsed and dried her hands.

Cathy answered the phone and was surprised to hear her partner, Caesar, on the other end.

"What's up, Cee-Cee?" Caesar asked, using Cathy's nickname as if it were a casual friend-to-friend phone call. Cathy was instantly irritated.

"Hello, Caesar. What are you doing calling me on my home phone? You know that all business calls are handled on my cell. So, what's up?"

"My fault, Cee," Caesar apologized. "I didn't realize that I had dialed your house number. My mind is somewhere else."

"Yeah, well you need to find it," Cathy said half-jokingly. "So tell me, what's up?"

Caesar hesitated for a short moment. "I don't know. You tell me," Caesar began. "I'm sitting here in my car in front of the Penthouse waiting on your man, Tee, and he's twenty minutes late, so his grace period is up. I'm about to leave this joint. I wanted to know what you want me to do with this situation."

Cathy picked her cell phone off the kitchen table. She dialed Caesar's cell number to get him off her home line. "Pick up your other line, that's me calling you."

Never handle business on your home phone, she reminded herself.

"Okay, listen to me," Cathy began. She knew she needed to say something convincing to put this man at ease. He probably thought the spot was hot and that Tee had something up his sleeve. Tee was a newcomer, which meant that until he showed true loyalty like everyone else, he was still considered hot and needed to be watched and observed.

"I don't know what's up with Tee. He's usually on time when it comes down to business. Maybe he ran into some traffic or something. You know they doing roadwork on Florida Avenue. He probably got caught up in it. Give him another five minutes. If he doesn't show, then you call me back on my cell, and I'll meet you out at

Lakeland in front of the basketball court to get that load up off you," Cathy assured.

"A'ight, Cee, but you know I'm not feeling this, riding around with all these dirty clothes."

Cathy liked his choice of words. Street codes were important and almost mandatory when talking over the phone. You never knew who could be listening, and you never wanted to get caught up. Cathy read between the lines and understood that Caesar didn't like riding around with the 18 ounces of pure cocaine he had hidden under the bumper of his car and the loaded nine millimeters he had posted on each hip.

"Don't get paranoid on me, Caesar. The feds are not gonna fuck with you, if that's what you're trippin' about. Why would they? You are driving the Honda, right, and not that hot-ass El Dorado with the midnight windows?" she asked.

"Yeah, I'm in the Honda, and I'm not paranoid. I'm just trying to make this move so I can get on top of my game. I've got peoples waiting on me, too, you dig?"

Cathy had to respect that. "I hear you, Caesar. Just give the man five more minutes. If he's a no show, then it's his loss, and we'll move to Plan B. Call me back either way to let me know."

Cathy slapped her cell phone shut. As she washed her hands, she thought about calling Tee herself to find out what was going on.

On second thought, he should be calling me. I don't need his money; he needs mine.

She continued making dinner, speeding up her pace just in case she had to meet Caesar herself.

Cathy managed to get the meatloaf in the oven within five minutes. Ten minutes later, the noodles were boiling for the macaroni, and her extra cheesy sauce was in its pot, ready to be poured all over the pasta.

Fifteen minutes later, Cathy was beginning to get concerned. She hadn't heard from either Tee or Caesar yet. She picked up her cell phone and dialed Caesar first. Relief set in when he answered on the second ring.

Before Cathy could say anything, Caesar spoke. "Yeah, Cee, everything is all good. Tee is right here looking at the clothes, making sure it's all here."

Cathy was satisfied. "That's all I needed to know," Cathy said. There was no need for her to talk to Tee unless he wasn't pleased with the product. She knew that wouldn't be an issue, because she sold the best butter in town. She had been in the game for too many years and had put in a lot of work to become who she was today: a low-key, certified hustler.

Only a few cats knew her name, and she liked to keep it that way. She didn't need every nigga on the block who struggled hustling nickels and dimes knowing that she was the one putting bread on their tables and in their pockets. She liked watching them on the sideline, stacking their dough to re-up, so they could try to be on her level.

Sunshine could smell the delicious aroma of a decent home-cooked meal in her dreams. It was so real she could almost taste the food. She woke up with soaring hunger pangs. Once she realized that the tasty aroma was actually coming from downstairs, she jumped out of bed and rushed to the bathroom to freshen up. She peeked at her watch and couldn't believe that two hours had passed. Just as she was about to unpack her belongings, Cathy appeared in the doorway.

"Well, Sleeping Beauty has awakened."

Sunshine rubbed the sleep from her eyes. "Yes, and I believe my Prince Charming awaits me in your kitchen, if my nostrils serve me right. And he smells like a loaf baking in the oven."

Both ladies laughed at themselves and their silly sense of humor.

"That would be correct, princess," Cathy said. "Now let's go devour the prince. Let's eat!"

Sunshine followed Cathy downstairs to the kitchen, where the scent of dinner was now in full effect. The dining room table was divinely set for two. Sunshine noticed that Cathy had even made the atmosphere soft and cozy by lighting a scented candle. The entire spread was impressive.

"Is all this for me, or do you have a hot date?" Sunshine asked.

"This is for us," Cathy boasted. "I figured that since this is your first night here, I would like for us to comfortably get to know each other. I know this is a hard time for you, and I just want to be there for you, if you don't mind. We can just sit back, eat good, and get to know each other."

Sunshine sat down while Cathy prepared their plates.

"Well, let me start off by telling you a little bit about myself first, and some things I expect from you. Not much, just some basic house rules. Once I'm done, I'll pass the mic to you, and it's all yours," Cathy said, initiating the conversation. "If I bore you, just grin and bear it. You know, pretend you're interested, so I won't feel so dreadfully old and dull. However, if I do interest you, that means I definitely have to get you out more."

Sunshine giggled and was already amused by the way Cathy carried herself.

When Cathy finally sat down, she reached for Sunshine's hands so they could bless the food together.

"Heavenly Father, thank you for this food. Please bless it in our bodies, and please put it in all the right places. Amen."

Sunshine observed how dignified Cathy looked as she ate her meatloaf, gracefully using her knife and fork. Not once did she show the food in her mouth when she spoke.

"I have one biological son of my own. Right now, he's in Miami staying with his father for the summer. I made the decision to become a foster mother because I was raised by a foster mother. I saw how much she enjoyed helping children in need, and that's what motivated me.

"My mother is gone now; she died from breast cancer when I was twenty years old. I'm thirty-eight years old now. I use to be married, but I'm not anymore, and that's by choice. I ain't found a man who can handle me yet.

"People tell me I have an urban soul. I love children, and I have been a single foster mother going on eight years. You are the only foster child living with me for now. I have two extra bedrooms upstairs prepared, so you might get some company if a worker decides to place another child here with us. And for the record, I don't play that favoritism mess." Cathy continued eating gracefully while she spoke.

"Let me see . . . what else? Oh, my rules are simple and sweet. I know you're not a little girl, so I'll be lenient with you. I will give you a To Do list for chores around the house. I promise not to be a slave driver. You'll mainly only be responsible for your bedroom, the bathroom in your room, and the dishes, which you only have to place in the dishwasher. I really don't like nobody cleaning up my house. That way things are always where they are supposed to be."

Sunshine let out a small laugh.

"Oh, you think that's funny, do you?" Cathy asked. "Well, let me tell you. I've been called a compulsive neat freak by some of my best buddies. They only say that because the way they livin' is so trifling. They'll come over here and treat my living room like their own personal trash bin, leaving belongings everywhere like it ain't nothing. I find myself exhausted by the end of their visit, because I'm constantly picking up behind them as if they were my kids. You wouldn't believe how messy grown folks can be. They're worse than y'all," Cathy added.

Sunshine didn't say a word while Cathy rambled on. She just shook her head when she needed to show that she was keeping up, trying not to be rude. Truthfully, though, she was paying more attention to the tasty food on her plate than she was to the conversation. Sunshine attacked her food like a wild animal devouring its prey. She couldn't help it. Dinner tasted better than any meal she'd ever eaten at any restaurant.

"Help yourself to more, sweetheart," Cathy said. While Cathy continued on about enrolling Sunshine into the local high school and summer jobs, Sunshine stood up to load a second helping onto her plate.

"Okay, with that all being said, is there anything you would like to ask me?"

Sunshine thought for a brief moment while she dug into her second helping of meatloaf, using just her fork.

"How long can I live with you?" she asked.

"If things go right, you'll live with me until you turn eighteen, which is only a few years from now. Once you're eighteen, Social Services expects you to be in a position to take care of yourself. They offer an independent living program through which they'll help you pay your rent and utilities in your own apartment."

Sunshine stopped chewing. "My own apartment! Picture that," Sunshine said excitedly.

"I can picture it," Cathy stated, "and it's a bright, clear picture, too. Now, tell me some things about yourself, Sunshine."

"Well," Sunshine began, "I'm fifteen years old, and I'm currently in the tenth grade. I'm from Washington, D.C."

"Hold up. Hold up," Cathy interrupted. "You don't have to speak to me as if you're on a job interview. This is your home, baby. Relax and tell me the juicy stuff."

Sunshine smirked, half embarrassed, as if she had something to hide. "Well, I'm not sure what it is you want to know. I don't have much to tell. As you already know, my mother died yesterday. She was only thirty years old. She died from AIDS. She had been living with the disease for over twelve years, almost my entire life. She didn't bother to tell me about it until late last year. By then, it was obvious, but I wanted to hear it come from her.

"My mother was all the family I had and all I needed. I don't know my grandparents, but I think they live in Upstate New York somewhere. My father was just a sperm donor whose only concern was to do what it took to get me in this world. I heard he was a player and dated lots of different women. After he sexed my mother and got her pregnant with me, he didn't bother keeping in contact with her. As far as I know, he doesn't even know that I exist," she said.

"And I don't have a whole lot of friends," Sunshine added.

Cathy interrupted her again. "I find that very hard to believe. I was under the impression that you were the outgoing type, the head of every clique."

Sunshine gave Cathy a soft, pathetic look. "Far from it," Sunshine continued. "I'm pretty much a stay-to-myself type of girl. Most of the girls I went to school with weren't into the same things that I'm into. They are into clothes, gossiping, boys, and partying: all the things that I don't care for—well, except for clothes, but it's not a life-or-death situation if I can't get the latest Dior dress or the new Jordans."

"That's very interesting. Different, but interesting. What kinds of things *are* you into?" Cathy asked curiously.

"My favorite things to do are read, sing, and write poetry," Sunshine answered proudly.

Cathy was amazed, to say the least, by this young girl. Sunshine had endured a lot of mental trauma at such a young age, more than any girl should experience, yet she managed to keep her pretty little head up.

"Not much to tell! Hmmph! I don't think I could handle what you'd consider a lot. May I hear one of your poems?" she asked.

Sunshine wasn't shy when it came to reciting her poetry. Ayanna used to enjoy listening to her, as Sunshine would read her writing to her mother all the time. She was more than happy to oblige Cathy.

She wiped away any food crumbs from the sides of her mouth with her napkin. Then, she sat up tall in her chair, as if she had an audience of a thousand people awaiting her. When she spoke, her words flowed in a smooth, soft rhythm:

"I'd rather not be born rich, but poor; For the riches of a dream mean so much more. When you strive to achieve the goals way beyond your reach; And all of your efforts eventually come to be. For you worked so hard to receive; The true riches you deserved from the very beginning." She smiled at Cathy and said, "I hope that's not too deep."

Cathy's jaw fell to the floor. Sunshine even thought she spotted two cavities. "Wow! You go, girl! Are those your own thoughts and your own words?" she asked.

"Yes, my very own," Sunshine answered proudly.

"You have a special gift, Sunshine. At such a young age, your work is so profound. You may very well be the next Emily Dickinson."

Sunshine shook her head. "No, thank you. My dream is to become a top-of-the-charts music producer. Besides, Emily Dickinson's poetry didn't get noticed by anyone until after her death. I'm still alive and kicking," Sunshine reminded her.

'Well, go 'head, girl. You've got the drive and ambition, and obviously the right mind for it. I'll tell you what," Cathy said. "Once you finish school, I'll see what I can do to get you to follow your dream, if that's what you want to do." Cathy had a good feeling about Sunshine. She had never offered any of her children tuition for college before.

"Now, if you're done with that plate, I have the world's best gourmet dessert prepared for us."

Sunshine rubbed her belly. "Ooh, what is it?"

"Root beer floats!" Cathy announced.

TWO

Rain was surprised to notice that her father's bedroom door was still closed when she woke up the next morning. *Boom! Boom! Boom!* She banged on his door as if she were the law.

"Daddy! Daddy! Wake up. It's eleven o'clock and you're late for work!" she screamed at the top of her lungs.

Boom! Boom! Boom! Rain knew he was still inside because his radio was playing. He would never leave anything electric on intentionally. He was always crying about the bill. Rain felt like they lived in a deep, dark cave sometimes when all the lights were off inside the apartment at night.

Maybe he took off work today, she thought, *probably a hangover from being high all night.*

Rain started into the kitchen to make breakfast. Opening the refrigerator, she was disappointed to see that all the eggs and milk were gone.

"Shit! I forgot to go to the grocery yesterday." She began searching inside the cabinets to see if there was something she could whip up real quick.

As she opened the worn wooden doors, roaches fell onto the counter and began scurrying, trying to make a fast getaway before crawling safely into their new hideout. Rain stomped her foot hard on one huge bug that was unfortunate enough to miss the counter and landed too close to her foot. She smashed it until it was stuck to the bottom of her flip-flop. Rain took the shoe off and banged it against the kitchen sink until the flat, dead insect fell into it.

"Yuck!" she spat. She quickly washed her hands and went back to search for anything they could eat. She reached into the cabinet and pulled out some oatmeal.

"Nothing like some good ol' hot, sticky oatmeal on a hot, sticky morning."

As she poured warm water into the pot to boil, the telephone rang. She placed the pot on the burner and started the fire, taking her time moving toward the phone.

It probably isn't nobody anyway.

Finally, she answered the phone on its fifth ring. "Hello!" Rain shouted loudly into the phone.

"Good morning," a pleasant voice began, "This is Bernard Smith, and I'm calling to speak to Jim Concise."

"Bernard Smith, who?" Rain asked boldly.

"I'm his supervisor at Smith & Company, and Jim didn't report to work today."

Rain straightened up her demeanor real quick. "Oh, I'm sorry, Mr. Smith. I thought you were one of those telemarketers. My dad's not feeling well," Rain lied. "He tried calling in earlier, but he said that he didn't get an answer. He took his medication, and it makes him real drowsy. I'll have him call you when he wakes up," she said.

Rain hung up the phone. She began to feel butterflies in the pit of her stomach. Something wasn't right. She contemplated getting a butter knife and using it to unlock Jim's door to check on him.

On second thought, he's probably just in a deep sleep. She would let him rest.

Rain continued with breakfast. She turned on the clock radio that sat atop the refrigerator, and hummed along with Mary J. Blige's tune. She thought about Terrance as Mary sang "Real Love."

Terrance was the neighborhood small-time dealer who lived two buildings down from Rain. He rocked fresh, long cornrows, caramel skin, and a midnight blue Crown Victoria that rode on spinning wheels. He was hot!

Rain reminisced about the other night when Terrance had picked her up and took her out to eat at Checkers. She giggled aloud when she thought about how she sucked him dry while they were in the drive-through line. He wanted to take her to the hotel afterward and go all the way, but Rain was too afraid for all that.

She had never actually made love before. She liked fooling around, though. She had already kissed and rubbed on four boys and three girls. She liked being with girls, but she enjoyed boys a lot better. Girls were whiny and foolish, while boys were thorough with money.

"Jody! Jerome! Come and eat!" Rain yelled loud enough to invite the neighbors to breakfast. The boys ran downstairs sounding just like a herd of hungry elephants.

"Stop stomping! Daddy is trying to sleep!" she screamed.

At the command of their big sister, the sound of their footsteps quickly changed into those of mice. After all was quiet, Rain ran upstairs to shower while her brothers ate. She didn't like to eat breakfast, especially not nasty oatmeal. Her father always referred to oatmeal as jail food for jailbirds, and he'd been in enough times to know.

Rain turned on the radio inside the bathroom, damn near blasting the music. Every room she entered had to have tunes. She locked herself in the bathroom so neither one of her playful brothers would barge in.

While she waited for the shower temperature to warm to her liking, Rain pinned her shoulder-length hair in a bun, admiring her budding body in the mirror. She appreciated her deep-set curves, voluptuous breasts, and her phat-to-def J. Lo ass that God had blessed her with. Her body was shapelier than some grown women out there who she observed in the streets. Grown men even noticed and were always eager to get her attention. Too bad for them that Rain wasn't into old meat; she liked her meat fresh, like Terrance's, and one day when she was ready, she would give him some.

The steam from the shower blurred her vision. She hopped into the shower and began singing every song that played while she bathed. Showering was always time-consuming for Rain. Once she was behind the closed door, everyone in the house knew it would be a good thirty minutes or more before they could get in. They would make sure they used it before the lady of the house took over.

Rain would wash her body repeatedly, using different fragranced soaps each time. She loved the smell of all her favorite soft soaps mixed together. If they sold it in a bottle like that, she would be the envy of all girls.

Rain was so caught up in her bathtime boogie that she could barely hear the loud banging on the bathroom door. At first it sounded like it was part of the song, but as she strained to listen, she could tell that it was Jerome trying to get her attention. Rain pulled back the shower curtain and reached for the radio to turn down the music.

"What?" Rain yelled.

"Rain, open the door. Daddy's bed! Daddy's bed!" Jerome screamed.

"Daddy's *what?*" she yelled, irritated. She didn't want her father to wake up and be upset by their yelling match, so she got out of the shower, covering herself carefully with her towel. She pulled the bathroom door open to see what all the fuss was about this time.

"What is it?" she asked Jerome

"Daddy's dead! Rain, he's dead!" Jerome was hysterical, grabbing and pulling on Rain.

"Calm down, Jerome. What do you mean, Daddy's dead?" She trembled, confused and bewildered by her brother's words.

Jerome grabbed Rain by the hand and dragged her down the steps. Jody sat at the bottom of the steps, shocked and pale. Jerome didn't stop; he pulled Rain past Jody and hauled ass to Jim's room.

"Jody told me to do it!" Jerome cried.

"What did Jody tell you to do? Why on earth is he just sitting on the steps looking all crazy like that?" Rain asked, still confused.

Jerome continued on with his plea. "Jody told me to use the butter knife and sneak into Daddy's room to get him a nasty book and . . ." Jerome shook his finger in the direction of their father, who lay slumped over and lifeless on the floor, blue in the face.

Rain could feel her own blood dry up, and she suddenly felt dizzy. She didn't feel her head fall backward, pulling the rest of her body to the ground.

When Rain came to, she was no longer wrapped in her bath towel. Someone had dressed her, and a uniformed man was dabbing a cold, wet rag all over her face. Her vision was blurry at first, but once she saw that the man was a paramedic, she realized what had happened.

"Stay calm, ma'am. You're okay," the gentleman reassured her. "You just fainted. You'll be okay in a few minutes."

Rain looked around and saw cops and detectives everywhere. *Please let this be a bad dream.* She saw Jody and Jerome sitting on the couch, being comforted by one of the officers. *Wake up, Rain. This is not real.*

"Are you able to stand?" the gentleman asked. Rain gazed sadly into the eyes of the paramedic as the truth started to sink in. She slowly pushed her body upward to stand, as two officers helped her walk to the couch, close to her brothers.

"Where is my father?" Rain asked, ready to hear the truth be told.

"I'm sorry to have to tell you this, baby girl, but they have taken your father's body down to the city morgue. It appears that he died from a serious drug overdose." It all made sense to her now: her father's locked bedroom door, his silent response to her calling, his not showing up for work. Life had taken its toll on Jim Concise. He had finally escaped from his self-inflicted pain and guilt.

Rain didn't know whether to laugh or cry. She felt numb. She didn't know whether to weep at this tragic loss or to find peace in knowing that her father received his wish of being reunited with her mother.

Rain looked over at her little brothers. With a puzzled look on his face, Jerome was calm now as he leaned his head back on the sofa. Jody looked deep into Rain's eyes.

"I didn't know that Daddy was in there. I wish that we hadn't found him like that." His eyes welled up with tears. He held his face in his hands to conceal his sorrow, and he began to shake and sob loudly. Rain moved over to comfort him.

"It's okay, Jody. It's not your fault. You did a good job handling all this, you and Jerome. You both are heroes when you think about all that just happened. There is no telling how long Daddy's body would have rested in that bedroom if you and Jerome didn't find him. You called the police, and you got me dressed before they came, so you are a superman," Rain encouraged him. "You did get me dressed, didn't you?" Rain asked, making sure she hadn't been exposed to any of the male authorities.

She could barely hear Jody's answer through his cries, but he managed to spit out, "Yes."

Rain felt more pity for her twelve-year-old brother, Jody, and her seven-year-old brother, Jerome, than she did for her dead father.

How could he do this to them? She thought hard for a moment about what would happen to them next. They already had endured so much living without a mother for so long, and now they were orphans.

Rain's thoughts were interrupted by the sudden presence of a stout, oversized black woman standing in front of her and her brothers, nearly blocking the view of everything else around them. Rain looked up curiously at the huge woman. Her face was as black as midnight, and she radiated a golden yellow smile. Her facial features would never win her a beauty pageant crown; a sash wouldn't even fit across her cumbersome figure.

Rain was almost afraid to shake her hand when the woman extended it to greet her. She was admittedly disgusted by the encounter. Rain gave the woman a limp handshake with the tips of her fingers.

"Hello, children. My name is Bertha Lee." The woman spoke like an angry man trapped in a fat woman's body. Rain caught her breath in her throat to keep from busting out in an embarrassing laugh.

Did her parents really name her Bertha? If you added Ug to her last name, it would be Uglee, which fits her perfectly.

"I am a case manager for Child Protective Services. I am so sorry to learn about the sudden death of your father. My report tells me that your mother is also deceased." She said it as if she were asking a question. Rain nodded.

"Well, I'm responsible for ensuring that the three of you are placed in a suitable home. I will try to keep you all together, but I can't make any promises."

Rain looked over at her younger brothers and was unable to fathom the thought of not being with them. As she turned back to Bertha, she said in a slight panic, "Please try hard. My brothers need me right now." She knew they would be no good without her. This was going to be hard for all of them.

"As I said before, I will try to keep you all in the same home. However, the system is very congested right now. We have an excess of children and not enough space to house them. I'm going to make a few calls to see what's available."

Rain couldn't believe this was really happening. Seemingly in slow motion, her world was turning upside-down right before her eyes.

"I need for you kids to go pack some of your belongings so we can go and get you situated. You don't have to pack everything. We can always come back for the rest later. You just need to pack enough to last you for a couple days."

Jerome reached out for Rain. "Where are they going to take us?" he questioned.

If she could, Rain would've hawked spit on the one who was responsible for the lost, confused look she saw in her baby brother's eyes.

"I'll explain it to you when we get upstairs." Rain took Jerome's hand in hers and led him upstairs. Jody followed closely behind them.

Rain looked down at the chaotic scene from the top of the stairs and wondered for a moment if she should take her brothers, jump out the window, and run for their lives. They would run as far away from the apartment, the RoboCops, and Ms. Uglee as their feet could carry them. She realized, however, that her fleeting urge was hopeless. Where would they run? How would they eat? What would happen to them if they were caught?

Rain left those thoughts behind her and proceeded to do what she had been told, starting first with Jerome's room to help him pack. While she patiently explained to him about what she knew of foster homes, she quickly grabbed items from his dresser and closet. He asked a thousand questions, making it difficult for her to concentrate.

"Why did Daddy die? Where is that lady gonna take us? Did the police take Daddy to the graveyard? Is Daddy in heaven with Mommy now?"

Rain couldn't keep up with all the questions. She gave one answer: "I don't know, Rome. I don't have the answer to everything. Now, go downstairs and get me some empty grocery bags from out of the kitchen. We've gotta get packed, and then I'll try to answer your questions later. Hurry up."

Jerome stopped his interrogation and ran downstairs to get his luggage. Rain walked into her own bedroom and began to pack her belongings. She made sure to pack the one and only picture that she had of Terrance. Despite the current situation, she still had Terrance on the brain, and the thought of him actually put a little smile on her face. The idea that she still had one person to turn to added light to the dark situation.

She looked at her watch and noticed that it was well past noon, and Terrance hadn't called her yet. If he was awake, she was sure that he would have noticed all the commotion with the police cars congregating outside of her building. Surely, he would be concerned about what was going on and would want to find out if she was okay. Rain assumed that he was still sleeping, and she kept grabbing items to pack.

Her mind was darting from the current moment back to the events earlier that morning. She couldn't focus, so she impulsively picked up the phone to call Terrance. Since they were being escorted out so quickly, she needed to make him aware of what was going on. She had to let him know that she was moving away.

Her mind drifted for a moment to thoughts of Terrance. She thought about him swinging by before she rolled out to give her a quick slob down with those big, juicy lips that his face wore so well.

She dialed the number to his cell phone and waited patiently for him to answer. After the seventh ring and still no answer, she almost gave up. She was about to hang up when someone answered.

"Hello?" the voice said.

Rain paused. The voice wasn't Terrance's; the voice belonged to a young girl. Maybe Rain had dialed the wrong number, because only Terrance answered his phone.

"My bad. I think I dialed the wrong number," Rain told the girl and hung up.

Rain dialed his number again, this time pressing each number very slowly to make sure every digit was correct. The phone rang, but this time someone answered on the second ring. The voice that answered was the same as before, but this time she sounded more irritated.

"Hell-o?" the girl screamed into the phone.

This time Rain was certain that she had dialed the right number, so she boldly asked to speak to her man.

"Hello, can I speak to Terrance?"

"Terrance is busy." *Click!* The bitch hung up right in Rain's ear.

Rain could feel her hormones catch on fire. This was the last thing she needed right now.

"Who the hell was that?" Rain shouted. "I should go over there and find out." She gave the thought an enormous amount of consideration.

She didn't mind whooping somebody's ass over her man. In light of the current circumstances, she welcomed the thought of unleashing on whoever had just answered her man's phone. Unfortunately, she knew it would be impossible to escape big Bertha, who was probably downstairs, huffing and puffing right now, waiting on them to pack.

Rain picked up the phone. She was determined to talk to Terrance, so he could explain the identity of the hood rat who answered his phone. This time, the rat answered almost immediately. She sounded like she was beginning to have fun with Rain's insecurities when she answered the phone.

"Hello," she said in a soft, raspy tone that made Rain want to slither through the phone and inject her ass with some venom.

"Put Terrance on the phone, bitch!" Rain screamed in her ear.

"Sorry, sweetheart. Maybe you didn't hear me well the first time. I told you, Terrance can't talk right now. His hands are still wet from playing with my puss." *Click.*

Rain slammed the phone down, almost shaking with rage. She didn't have time for her shit right now. She might mess around and get a life sentence before she even made it to her new home, so she decided to deal with Terrance later.

Jerome entered her room just then with the plastic bags. "Are you okay, Rain?" Jerome asked. He misread her look of anger for a hurtful gaze.

"I'm okay, Rome. Just trying to hurry up so Ms. Barney doesn't come up here and get us." Rain snatched a handful of plastic bags from his hand and threw her load of belongings inside.

"You go take the rest of these bags and put your stuff in it," she ordered Jerome.

Rain stuffed as much of her things inside the grocery bags as she could, even the picture of Terrance.

Although she had more pressing matters to tend to, Rain couldn't stop thinking about how she just got carried like a sucker by a smelly hood rat. She couldn't let that rodent slide away so easily. It might tarnish her track record.

Rain picked up the phone and dialed Terrance's number one last time, just to see if she could recognize the girl's voice. That way, she would know whose ass to kick later.

It better not be Simone, either, 'cause she don't want it. Rain had heard rumors that Simone had been all over Terrance's sack at India's house party last weekend. Yet, when Rain had stepped to Simone in the parking lot, Simone quickly denied the rumor, probably trying to avoid the beat down she would've received had she confessed.

This time, the phone just rang. No answer.

"Oh, now they're playing games," Rain thought out loud.

Bertha appeared at her bedroom door just as Rain was hanging up the phone. "Are you guys just about done? I've got to get you kids placed, so we need to get a move on."

Rain admired the way Big Bertha stopped to take short breaths as she spoke. She sounded as though she had just run ten miles. Rain assumed that the hike upstairs wore the poor woman out with more exercise than she could handle.

Rain gave Bertha a hard look. "We are coming," she said. "With such short notice, it's taking us some time to get ourselves together, if you don't mind."

There was no mistaking the hint of sarcasm in Rain's voice as she spoke. If looks could kill, Bertha would be saying *hello* face-to-face with Jim Concise. Rain didn't necessarily have any good reasons to dislike Bertha at first meeting; she just disliked the fact that she was fat and ugly.

"I know that this is short notice for you. It's also short notice for me, but like I explained to you earlier, we can always come back to get the rest of your things," Bertha explained. "Are your brothers packed and ready to go?"

"Why don't you go see for yourself?" Rain answered. "It's not like you have a problem roaming through other people's houses."

Bertha was trying her best to be patient with Rain. She understood the pain of her loss.

"Listen to me, Rain. I apologize if you're bothered by me coming up here to get you and your brothers, and I realize that this sudden situation is not easy for you. However, I will not have you speak to me any ol' kind of way. Do you understand me?"

Rain rolled her eyes, turned away from Big Bertha, and then yelled, "Jody! Jerome! Come on. We gotta go!"

Bertha turned to walk away, satisfied. "I'll be downstairs waiting."

"And I'll find a way to let that pissed man out of your body so that you can finally talk like a real woman," Rain said under her breath.

When Rain and her brothers reached their new foster home, Bertha informed them that the placement was only temporary. Since theirs was an emergency situation, she had to place them somewhere immediately. She assured them that within a week, she would have a permanent home for them. Rain barely listened as she eyeballed the beat-up looking house with disgust. She was instantly unimpressed by the graffiti paint job, the filthy yard, and the peeling, worn-out flaps that acted as a roof. Rain was repulsed that anyone lived inside a house where the grass was as tall as the trees.

I hope we don't drown in weeds.

The house looked as if it was condemned or abandoned, except for the fact that there were teenage kids hanging out the windows like untaught orphans.

They don't look disabled, so why can't one of them cut the damn lawn? Rain thought.

It was pitiful that Ms. Bertha had moved them from the projects to the ghetto. This was not a major step up in life. Rain was afraid to go inside, because she didn't know what to expect. Judging by the day she was having, she expected the worst.

Jody touched Rain's shoulder. "Are you all right, big sis?"

"I don't know yet," she answered. Rain took her sweet time unloading her bags from the trunk.

Bertha didn't lift a finger to help. She would probably pass out from the simple labor, Rain figured.

Rain feared for her life as they dodged cuts and scrapes just to get to the door. Bertha rang the doorbell and realized that it didn't work after numerous attempts. Rain didn't understand why no one met them at the door in the first place. She was certain that the group of kids hanging out the window saw them coming, or at least heard the crackling of dry, dead grass as they approached.

Bertha began to bang on the door impatiently. That caught someone's attention. A boy around sixteen years old slowly pulled the door open. A strange smell instantly smacked Rain in the face. The aroma was a combination of old urine, old cigarettes, and old vomit. Rain felt the sudden urge to add to the stink with her own vomit.

Rain began to feel sorry for herself and for her brothers. She stood still in the doorway, trying to figure out what they had done to deserve this.

The teenage boy who had answered the door took off running in another direction of the house without a word. He left them standing there feeling lost and stupid.

"Hello!" Bertha yelled out. After a couple minutes, a black woman resembling Aunt Jemima appeared. She looked to be in her late forties and had sweat pouring down her face. She wore a red-and-white checkered do-rag, yellow cleaning gloves, and a white apron.

"Please forgive me," the woman said. "I didn't hear you come in. I was in the back trying to do some spring cleaning."

That could take all spring, Rain thought.

The lady removed her gloves.

"Are you Ms. Darby?" Bertha asked.

"Yes, I am," the woman answered, extending her hand to greet Bertha.

"If you don't mind me asking you, Ms. Darby, how many children do you have residing here with you?"

Ms. Darby understood what Bertha was getting at. "I don't mind you asking me. I know it looks like there are about a hundred kids hanging around," she said, laughing, "but actually, I only have two boys and two girls. It's a five-bedroom house, so I can fit up to eight children if I put two in each room."

Bertha nodded her head, pleased with her answer.

Introductions were made. When it was Rain's turn to shake Ms. Darby's hand, she refused. She didn't even acknowledge the woman. In an effort to defend Rain's inappropriate behavior, Bertha felt obligated to tell Ms. Darby about their father's passing from a drug overdose. Ms. Darby listened intently but seemed untouched by the news, as if she heard it every day.

"I'll be coming by in a couple of days to take the kids to get the rest of their clothes," Ms. Lee explained. "I'll call you first to make the arrangements."

"That will be fine," Ms. Darby said.

"You have my office numbers if you should need to speak to me before then." Bertha turned around to look at Rain, Jody, and Jerome. "You kids try to be good, and I'll see you soon."

Surprisingly enough, Rain didn't want Bertha to go. She didn't want to be left behind in the disgusting house. Rain looked over at Jody and saw the same disoriented expression, with his mouth up to his nose, trying to duck the fumes.

"Let me show you to your rooms." Ms. Darby led the way downstairs and into the basement. She put Jerome and Jody in one room and led Rain farther down the hall to her new bedroom.

She had a room all to herself, just like at home. She didn't mind that at all. What she did mind was that her new bedroom already looked lived in. Dirty clothes covered the floor, and the two twin beds in each corner of the small room were both unmade. One even reeked of urine. Rain wished she had thought to pack her own blankets.

"Excuse the mess, dear. Sometimes the girls come down here to sleep. I tell them time and time again to clean up behind themselves, but when children leave home, they bring their bad habits with them," Ms. Darby said.

"Do the two girls sleep upstairs?" Rain asked.

"Yes, they share a bedroom across from mine. I could show you around if you'd like," Ms. Darby said.

At that moment, Rain didn't need to see any more of the funky house. "No, thank you. Where do the other two boys sleep?" Rain asked.

"Their bedroom is next to your brothers' room," she answered.

"How come I'm the only girl sleeping down here?" Rain asked, confused. "Why can't I be upstairs with the other girls?"

"Oh, well, that's because I keep all my temporary kids down here. Now, let me go get you some clean sheets."

Rain watched with sad amazement as Ms. Darby left the bedroom, and listened as she trudged up the stairs. Rain wanted to sit but was terrified to touch the beat-up mattress for fear she might catch something, so she stood and waited.

She heard someone coming toward the bedroom and assumed it was Jody, but it wasn't. It was the boy who had answered the door for them earlier. He stood before her with a strange, dumb look on his face. Rain was getting irritated.

"Do you speak, or are you slow?" she asked the boy.

"Yeah, I speak," he said and held out his hand. "What's up? My name is Nick."

Rain shook his sweaty hand. "My name is Rain."

"Rain. That's a hot name for a hottie girl like yourself."

Hottie girl . . . where the hell is he from?

The boy seemed awkward to Rain, almost as if he didn't know what he was going to do next.

"Listen, Rain, my room is right down there." He pointed down the hall in the direction of Jerome and Jody's room. "You can come and sleep with me if you get scared in here all by yourself." The look he gave Rain made her skin crawl.

"Thank you, but no thank you," she replied. "If I get scared in here by myself, I'll just go get my brother Jody, who sleeps in the room right beside yours, and have him beat the mess out of the ghost for me."

Read between the lines, weirdo.

Nick sized Rain up one last time before leaving the room. She hoped he had gotten her silent message loud and clear. Nick gave Rain the creeps, and now she definitely didn't feel comfortable being the only girl in the basement.

After waiting for Ms. Darby for nearly twenty minutes, Rain concluded that she was never coming back down. So, she walked down the hall to check on Jody and Jerome. Their bedroom didn't look as bad as her room did. In fact, it looked almost livable.

Jody spoke first. "What do you think about this place?"

"Yeah, right. Do you really have to ask?" Rain responded. "I mean, look around you. Besides your bedroom, this house is a shithole."

Jody laughed.

"Have you talked to the boy Nick yet?" Rain asked.

"No. Who's that?" Jody asked.

"He's the scrawny boy who answered the door for us earlier. His room is right next to yours."

"What about him?" Jody asked.

Rain didn't want to tell Jody what Nick said to her earlier, because she knew it would upset him. "Nothing much," she said. "He just creeped me out, that's all."

Rain walked over to where Jerome sat on one of the twin beds. She plopped down beside him and started rubbing his head.

"You're awfully quiet, Rome. Are you all right?"

"Of course he's not all right," Jody answered for him. "He doesn't understand this any more than you or me."

Jerome sat there, still silent. Rain could feel his pain. She reached out to him and held him like a baby as she slowly rocked him to sleep. Jerome had the closest relationship to their father, so the loss hurt him deeply.

After laying Jerome down gently on his bed, Rain decided to find some blankets herself. Watching Jerome sleep so peacefully put her at ease. She stood up to leave the room.

"Where are you going?" Jody asked.

"I'm going upstairs to get a clean comforter for my dingy bed."

Jody was bored with the Smack Down vs. Raw portable video game he was playing and needed something else to do. "I'll go with you," he said. Jody placed the handheld game on his bed.

"You need to hide that thing," Rain suggested. "I personally wouldn't trust anybody in here, especially your next door neighbor."

Jody picked up the game and stuck it deep into his pillowcase. This was something he had watched Rain do with her diary back at home on many occasions.

"I've got to find me a new hiding place," Rain joked.

They headed upstairs, tripping over heaps of clothes and trash along the way. When they got upstairs, they saw the two girls Ms. Darby had mentioned earlier.

The first girl was tall, dark, and lanky, like an old, stringy mop. Her clothes were so loose and raggedy that they looked like they were trying to run away from her to find a body they could fit.

The other girl looked a little more decent—a thick, pretty redbone with silky locks falling down her shoulders. Rain wouldn't mind getting at her. She wondered if the redbone was into girls.

Both girls sat on the stairwell kicking their feet back and forth while spitting sunflower seeds on the floor.

So much for that idea. Baby girl don't have no home training.

Rain didn't like the mean, nasty looks the girls gave her. "What is wrong with everybody in here?" she asked Jody rhetorically. "I feel like I'm in the Twilight Zone."

The girls whispered something to each other and erupted into hysterical laughter. Rain didn't feel threatened by them at all. She knew that she could knock the smiles right off their faces if they provoked her.

"Come on, Jody." Rain walked right up to the girls. "Excuse me, but can you tell me where the clean blankets are?" Rain hoped that she had disappointed the girls by not letting them intimidate her.

The tall, lanky girl spoke first. "It's in the hall closet."

Very funny, Rain thought.

"Okay, where's the hall closet at?" she asked.

The redbone spoke now. "It's down that hall to the right," she said, pointing.

"Thank you," Rain said, walking in the direction of the closet with Jody right behind her.

"Hey!" one of the girls yelled loudly. Rain and Jody stopped in their tracks.

"We're sorry for being so rude. We didn't even introduce ourselves," the redbone said.

Rain figured that they had finally gained some sense. The girls walked over to where Rain and Jody stood.

"My name is Sleet, and this is Hail. You must be Snow. Ms. Darby told us all about you," the redbone said.

Oh, they are trying to be funny, Rain thought.

Jody stepped back. He knew what was about to happen next. Rain didn't allow anyone to make fun of her name. She took pride in the birth name that her mother had given her. When she was alive, Evelyn would always tell the story behind Rain's name. Rain was a special name, because she was conceived on a rainy night and born into the world on a rainy day.

Rain balled up two tight fists, turning her knuckles red. She'd had enough of these bitches. She swung the first blow at the red bitch who had called her Snow. It came so fast that the bitch didn't know what hit her. Jody watched in amusement as the girl dropped to the floor.

I can't believe I was feeling your dusty ass.

The second blow came instantly, hitting tall wonder with a solid shot to her scrawny little nose. Blood oozed out and dripped down into the girl's mouth as she fell to the floor.

"Don't you bitches ever disrespect me again! You dig?"

Rain and Jody walked off, Rain slapping imaginary dust off her hands. Jody grabbed what they had come upstairs for in the first place from the top shelf in the closet.

When they reached the top of the stairs to head back down into their dungeon, they froze at the wicked sound of Ms. Darby's voice.

"Excuse me, young lady! I don't know what gang you come from, but there will be absolutely no fighting in my house! Consider yourself punished for the rest of the night!" she yelled.

Punished? Rain had never even been punished by her own mother or father. She didn't pay Ms. Darby any mind. It was punishment enough just living in her house, whether Ms. Darby knew it or not. Rain proceeded down the steps, ignoring whatever else Ms. Darby had to say, with her faithful little brother right by her side.

"I'm going to my room to unpack," Rain told Jody. "I'll come and check on you and Rome in a little while."

When Rain got back to her room, she noticed that her bags had been moved. Who had come into her room? Jerome was still asleep, so she knew it couldn't have been him. Rain searched her bags to see if anything was missing. After going through all her things, she noticed that her diary was gone. Had she even packed it? She was almost sure she had, but since everything else was still in its place, she could've been wrong. She would have to remember to get her diary when Ms. Bertha took them back past the apartment.

Rain took a pair of socks out of one of her bags and put them on her hands as gloves. She didn't know which one of the girls had slept in which bed, but she didn't want to touch their nasty germs. She chose the least smelly bed and discarded the sheets from the pissy bed and put clean ones on to help get rid of the odor.

Rain opened the two windows to allow some fresh air in and finally felt comfortable enough to take a nap. Unfortunately, loud noises from upstairs kept her from falling asleep. Instead, she tried to rest her eyes, hoping exhaustion would win and let her sleep. Vivid images of her father entered her mind, forcing out all other thoughts that floated around.

Rain's mind took her back to when she was

seven years old, when her father first taught her how to hold her guards up to fight. Her mother sat on the sofa in front of them observing, but she was less than thrilled about their only daughter learning how to throw punches. Rain could hear her mother's voice like it was yesterday.

"Jim, a beautiful girl like Rain should be taught how to sing and dance, not how to assault people."

Jim had laughed and pulled little Rain in front of her mother, holding her balled fists into the air and said, "Tell Mommy to put 'em up."

"Put 'em up, Mommy," Rain had said, imitating her father.

Evelyn had laughed and said, "Oh, for real? You don't want it." Then she threw a fake jab at Jim, and he fell over, pretending to be hurt. They both had tickled Rain silly.

Tears rolled down Rain's face while she reminisced about those long lost days. Eventually, she cried herself to sleep, forgetting all about the noises above her head.

When she awoke several hours later, she was disoriented and unaware of the time. She assumed that it was well past midnight, because the house seemed peaceful and quiet. The only sound she could hear was the evening song of crickets that sang into the late night and into

Rain's open window.

Rain wasn't sure what had awakened her so suddenly, until she saw a shadow tiptoeing toward her bed. A body stood right in front of her.

"Jody?" she whispered, praying that it was her little brother.

"No, hottie. It's not Jody. It's Nick."

Rain's heart began to pound hard inside her chest while the butterflies spread their wings in the pit of her stomach.

What the hell is he doing in here this time of night?

As if he could read her mind, Nick answered, "I came to see if you wanted some company."

Rain sat up in her bed, trying to focus her vision to get a better look at him. She had to strain her eyes to see him in the dark bedroom. The street light beaming from outside finally helped her focus in on him.

Oh my God, he's naked! Rain watched as he perversely rubbed his exposed manhood. She watched it rise and graduate to its rock-hard erection.

"Get out, you horny bastard!" she said in an angry whisper, only loud enough for him to hear. She didn't want to wake Jody and Jerome. She would try to handle this situation herself.

"You don't mean that, sweet lips," Nick said.

Rain sat up to get out of the bed so that she could protect herself, but when she looked down at herself, she noticed that she was naked too. Horror and fear overtook her entire body. She felt herself tremble with rage. Did he do this to her?

"Where are my clothes?" she asked, louder than before.

"Shhh! Be quiet. You don't want to wake the whole house and let them catch us like this, do you?" Nick reached out his hand and gripped the back of Rain's head, forcing her to put her mouth to his erection.

"Suck it, sweet lips. Suck it like you sucked Terrance's."

Rain was humiliated. So she had brought her diary after all, and Nick had stolen it.

He pushed her head back onto the bed using all of his strength. "Just let me put it in, baby. It's big, but it won't hurt. I promise." He forced his body on top of Rain's. For someone who looked so scrawny, he felt like he had the strength of ten men.

She could feel his cold sweat drip down her breasts and run down her stomach. Rain didn't know what to do. She felt panicked and helpless. She began to kick, punch, and scream at the top of her lungs.

"Get off me, you freak! Jody, help me! Get off

me, you nasty freak! *Jo-dee!*"

Nick covered Rain's mouth with one hand to stifle her screams. Rain tried to bite the meat off his hand with all of her might. He struggled to free his hand from the tight grip of her teeth.

When Rain finally released after she tasted his bitter blood, he slapped her hard in the face. Rain continued to spit, kick, and scream, but Nick refused to move. The fight made him want her even more. He began to rub his nature against her breasts, stroking her hair and ignoring her cries.

"Oh, baby, just let me put it in for a minute. Please, baby." Just as he was about to put his cock inside her and take away her sacred virginity, Jody stormed into the dark bedroom. He flicked on the light switch to see what was going on.

"Thank God! Help me, Jody!" Rain cried.

Without hesitation, Jody reached into his pants and pulled out a loaded nine millimeter. Rain couldn't process the surreal moments that followed. Neither Rain nor Nick saw it coming.

Pap! Pap! Pap! The sound of three shots pierced the air, followed by a deafening silence. With three shots in his back, Nick slumped over Rain's body. She could feel his erection getting softer as the seconds passed by.

Jody pushed the dead body off of Rain and let it drop to the ground. "Put your clothes on," Jody said to Rain.

Rain was in a traumatized state of shock, but she tried to dress herself as much as she could.

"Don't get used to this," Jody joked as he pulled her shirt over her head. "Twice in twenty-four hours is your limit."

Rain tried to force a chuckle. "Where did you get a gun?" Rain asked.

Jody never got the chance to answer. Just as Rain finished buttoning her pants, the whole house appeared at her bedroom door. Dreadlocks and Mop & Glo wore the same stupid smirks on their faces as they looked down at Rain. Ms. Darby couldn't believe her eyes.

"What have you children done?" She ran over to Nick's dead body and rolled it over onto his back. She took her two first fingers and placed them on his neck to take his pulse.

"He's dead," she said in a barely audible whisper.

The three bullet holes in his back covered in blood could have told her that, Rain thought.

"Tammy, go upstairs and call the police," Ms. Darby instructed the redbone who Rain had punched in the nose.

What happened next added terror to Rain's worst nightmare. Jody was immediately arrested and taken to an all-boys detention center. Ms. Darby ordered the officers to take Rain away as well.

"That girl is the devil," Rain heard Ms. Darby tell them.

"What about Jerome?" Rain asked the officer as he escorted Rain out to his car.

"Who is Jerome?" the officer asked.

"He is my youngest brother," Rain explained. "Can I at least say good-bye to him? He must be so confused right now."

The officer saw the sincerity in Rain's face.

"Make it quick. I don't have all night."

Rain quickly ran back into the house right past Ms. Darby, who she wanted to stop and spit on, but continued into Jerome's room.

Jerome sat up in his bed, crying and trembling. Rain broke down and cried too. This was too much for even her to handle. She ran over to comfort Jerome, who looked weak and helpless.

"They took Jody to jail," Jerome told her through his silent cries. "They took him to jail for killing that boy." Jerome continued, "He used Daddy's gun."

Rain was confused. "What are you talking about, Rome?" Rain asked.

"He took it out of Daddy's dresser while we were packing. He showed it to me, but he made me promise not to touch it."

Rain wiped away his tears before she spoke. "Jerome, Jody's not in jail. He's going to be sent to a home for boys who have done bad things. He's not in jail, Rome, and he will be fine." Rain took Jerome's face into the palms of her hands and held it there.

"Rome, look at me. I need you to be a strong baby brother. I know you are hurting, and it hurts me to see you cry, but everything is going to get better. I promise you, Rome. I have to leave now. They're moving me to a different home because there's way too much drama up in here, but I will be back to see you. I'm going to leave you with my friend's cell phone number, and I want you to call this number if anybody does anything to you in this muthafucka, do you hear me?" Rain was serious now. She would kill for her baby brother, just as Jody had killed for her.

"His name is Terrance," Rain continued. "I'll let him know that you'll be calling." Rain wrote down the phone number on a scrap of paper she found in the hallway.

"Don't lose this, Jerome. This is our only way of talking to each other for right now."

Jerome stuck the number in his shoes.

"Don't get no nasty feet germs on it, or it might smear," Rain joked. She had to lighten the air somehow; it was too thick.

"Well, shorty, I have to go, but I won't be gone for long."

Jerome hugged Rain so tight she nearly had to peel him off of her.

"I love you, Rome."

"I love you too, Rain."

THREE

Sunshine had been adjusting well since the death of her mother, which was nearly a year ago. She eagerly anticipated her senior year of high school, and although she hadn't gained any new friends, her relationship with Cathy was so tight that someone could have assumed they were related. Only the difference in their skin revealed the truth. Although no one could take the place of Sunshine's biological mother, Cathy was able to pick up where Ayanna had left off.

Sunshine didn't yearn for anything. Cathy made sure that Sunshine had counseling to help her cope with her loss. Before summer vacation, Cathy drove Sunshine to school every morning and picked her up on time every afternoon. Sunshine spent her summer days by Cathy's side.

There was no limit to the things she would do for Sunshine. In fact, Cathy made sure Sunshine looked fresh in all the latest gear. She owned an

entire walk-in closet full of Prada, Donna Karan,
Christian Dior, and Baby Phat tags that kept her
looking fly. As her body began to take its true
form of a sexy, young woman, Sunshine fit her
clothes in an exotic way. Her shoe racks were
filled with Gucci, Louis Vuitton, and Kenneth
Cole. She had more than twenty pairs of Jordans
and some tennis shoes she hadn't even worn
yet. Cathy even bought her a pair of three-hun-
dred-dollar Dolce & Gabbana sandals with a
matching two-hundred-dollar purse. She had
a jewelry box filled with all kinds of jazzy accessories to coordinate with her outfits.

Sunshine was not materialistic; she was content with or without all the glamour, but she
had to admit that it felt nice having nice things.
Sunshine even had her own cell phone, so Cathy
could get in touch with her should they ever
separate.

Sunshine had no clue how Cathy afforded
such a life of luxury. She felt that it wasn't her
place to ask about Cathy's financial status. She
never saw Cathy go to work, not even during the
summer, and she naturally assumed that the
only money Cathy received was the money she
got from the state every month to help support
her. It seemed outrageous, and she wondered
why everyone didn't get into the foster care

business. The state must've sent her a lot of money, because Cathy was paid!

Cathy entered Sunshine's bedroom while Sunshine sat at her desk writing a new poem in her scrapbook.

"Hey, pretty. I've got some good news for you," Cathy said.

Sunshine smiled. She loved when Cathy called her by cute little pet names. It made her feel like a little girl.

"Hey, Cee," Sunshine said, putting down her pen and turning her chair around to face Cathy. "So what's the good news?" Sunshine asked.

"We have a new girl coming today. She is your age, and she's on her way here right now."

Sunshine turned her smile upside down.

"Awww! What's wrong, pooh?" Cathy asked, noticing the quick change in Sunshine's expression.

Sunshine didn't bite her tongue. "I don't want anybody to move in yet. I like having you to myself."

Cathy felt her insides churn like butter. It meant a lot to her to hear Sunshine say that. "I know how you feel, honey," Cathy empathized. "Change is difficult, especially when you don't know what to expect. But I hope you know that I'm not gonna switch up on you. I told you before, I don't show favoritism, and I mean that. And just to let you know, I look at you as my real daughter, cutie pie, and nothing or no one can ever change that."

Sunshine's smile came back to life. "What's the girl's name?" Sunshine asked, suddenly getting curious about her competitor.

"Can you believe that her name is the opposite of yours, and just as unique as yours?" Cathy asked.

Sunshine took a guess. "What is it, Sunset?"

Cathy laughed. "Not the exact opposite. Her name is Rain."

"Rain." Sunshine repeated it out loud, as if it were a foreign word. "That is different."

"Well, she should be here any minute, so I'm going to get her room ready," Cathy said.

"Would you like some help?" Sunshine offered.

"No, honey. I got this," Cathy answered.

She left Rain with her thoughts while she continued her poem:

Forever I will remember you; Not ever will I forget you.

Together we made dreams come true; We never ran out of things to do.

Not one day would pass that we did not pursue; Not one secret hidden that you never knew.

I will cherish my memories of just us two;
I will cherish the day when I'm in heaven
with you.

Sunshine read her work and was pleased. She put her scrapbook away for the moment and decided to go downstairs to watch TV until Rain arrived. She was eager to see what Rain looked like and if she was any real competition.

Sunshine didn't usually make it a habit of being nosey, but she would make an exception this one time. If curiosity was a shark, she would have been eaten alive.

Sunshine walked down the hallway to peek in on Cathy. She must have already finished straightening up Rain's bedroom, because she wasn't in there. Sunshine looked around the small bedroom. It was nice and fit for a princess. It shared the same feeling as Sunshine's room, only this room had different colors. The walls were painted in a soft baby pink with shiny sparkles like miniature diamonds. The deep burgundy-colored carpet brought life to the bedroom. A small cherry wood entertainment center sat in the corner by the window. It held a large 25-inch television with a Sony DVD player and a Sony CD player, just like Sunshine's. Books and picture frames accented the decor. The burgundy comforter perfectly matched the carpet, and deep red, floral print curtains covered the oversized windows. Sunshine did not know Rain, but she was sure that she would be more than satisfied with her bedroom.

Sunshine could hear Cathy downstairs and went to see what she was doing. When she reached the bottom of the stairs, she realized that Cathy was in the living room, talking to someone on her cell phone. Sunshine didn't want to disturb her, so she sat quietly on the bottom step, looking outside at the street through the screen door, which led to the front porch. She wondered for a second if she looked too anxious, and decided she was okay.

Sunshine didn't intend to eavesdrop on Cathy's conversation, but bits and pieces were loud enough that she couldn't help but overhear. From what she heard, Cathy was talking to somebody named Caesar, and it sounded like a very important conversation.

"Caesar, I don't think that it's official for you to be doing business with that youngin' from around Potomac Heights. His boasting and bragging on himself could get all of us in some deep shit. We're not talking no chump change here, Caesar. This is twenty-five Gs."

Twenty-five thousand dollars! That's a lot of flow, Sunshine thought. *Who has that kind of money? And who is Caesar?*

She had never heard that name mentioned before. Suddenly, Sunshine didn't feel comfortable sitting where she was able to hear Cathy's business. She might hear something else she wasn't supposed to hear, and she certainly didn't want to upset Cathy.

Sunshine stood up and walked to the front porch. It was a beautiful Friday afternoon, a perfect day for Sunshine to oil up her body real nice, sit out in the sun, and bake herself until she turned a golden brown. Cathy was always telling her that it wasn't a good idea for her to sit in the sun for hours; she claimed it could cause skin cancer. Nevertheless, Sunshine found sunbathing relaxing, so she held onto her bad habit. Besides, that was more likely to happen to Cathy than to her.

Sunshine wondered if she should go out back into the pool, swim a few laps and then sit out and enjoy the sun. She quickly scanned her current cocoa tan and knew she would be overdoing it. Her caramel skin was sexy enough, and turning it into midnight blue would be a sin.

Sunshine watched as a white car pulled into the driveway. Two people stepped out carrying four small grocery bags.

What's with all the food? Sunshine wondered why they had all of those bags. As they neared the porch, Sunshine realized the bags contained the girl's clothes. Sunshine stood up from the lawn chair to introduce herself.

"Hello, you must be Rain." Sunshine held her hand out for greeting. "My name is Sunshine," she said with a smile.

Rain rolled her eyes in fury and turned away from Sunshine.

I don't have time for nobody's jokes, Rain thought. *My name is Sunshine,* Rain mocked silently. *If Miss Prissy thinks that she is going to make fun of my name like those chicken heads at Ms. Darby's, she better think again. She could get it too, a vicious ass-whooping like Mama used to do it.*

Sunshine ignored the attitude Rain was giving and opened the door to let the rude guest inside. "I'll go get Ms. Stone. You can wait right here." Sunshine spoke more to the social worker than to Rain. The girl seemed to have a temperamental vibe before she even stepped foot in the door. Sunshine didn't have to take that from anyone. After all, she was only trying to be polite.

She walked into the living room just as Cathy was ending her phone call. She could tell that Cathy was frustrated.

"Are you okay, Cathy?"

Cathy's face was turning a pinkish color. "Yes, precious, I'm okay. Just trying to take care of some business." Truth was, Cathy was beyond frustrated, but she couldn't let her darling little Sunshine know what was going on. What she didn't know wouldn't hurt her.

Cathy was still caught up in the unsettling conversation she'd just had with Caesar. She barely heard Sunshine continue talking.

"Earth to Cathy!" Sunshine said, adding an extra bass note as she spoke. "Something *is* wrong with you. You're not even listening to me."

"I'm sorry, princess. Maybe I do have something on my mind, but it's all good. What were you saying anyway?"

Sunshine shook her head at Cathy for not paying attention. *"Hello.* I said there is someone waiting at the door for you."

"Oh, snap! I almost forgot about the new girl." Cathy quickly walked past Sunshine and into the hallway to greet her visitors.

"Hello," Cathy began. "I hope I didn't keep you two waiting too long."

Long enough, Rain thought.

"No, we're fine," the social worker said, speaking for herself and Rain. The two women shook hands.

"How have you been, Cathy?" the worker asked.

"I can't complain. How are my boys doing?" Cathy asked.

"Well, since they left you and went back home to their mother, they seem to be maintaining. I've done a few follow-ups on the case, and they have been asking about you."

"That's good to know," Cathy said. "I've talked to them a couple times, but I haven't seen them since the day you took them home."

"Is that so?" Ms. Watkins asked. She impatiently turned her wrist around so that she could check the time on her watch. Time was racing, and she would have to leave soon.

"Ms. Stone, this is Rain Concise. She experienced some unfortunate trouble at her previous home over at Ms. Darby's, so we had to do an emergency transfer."

Cathy bent her face up at the mention of Ms. Darby. Everybody in the business was fully aware that she was only in it for the money. The old hag couldn't care less about the kids.

"Ms. Darby? They still allow that woman to keep kids . . . and they pay her for it? She's getting easy money," Cathy stated.

Rain agreed with Cathy one hundred percent. She was beginning to like this lady already. For a white woman, she definitely possessed a lot of soul.

Rain admired the way that Cathy carried herself. Ms. Cathy was fly as hell, and her house was the shit.

"Because this is a spontaneous transfer," Ms. Watkins began, "I haven't had a chance to organize the paperwork for you to sign. If you can stop by my office on Monday morning, I'll have it all ready and prepared for you."

"I'm sure I can squeeze that into my schedule," Cathy said.

"Well, Rain, good luck. And Ms. Stone, I'll see you Monday."

Cathy and Rain stood face-to-face for a silent moment, feeling each other out. Cathy broke the silence.

"So, Rain, have you met Sunshine yet?"

Rain looked at Cathy, surprised. "You mean Sunshine is her *real* name?" Rain asked, feeling a little bit guilty.

"Is *Rain* your real name?" Sunshine asked, arriving to meet the two ladies in the hallway.

"Yes, Ms. Stone, we met earlier," Rain answered Cathy's original question.

"If that's what you want to call it," Sunshine added.

Cathy noticed some slight hating in the air, but she chose not to get involved unless it became serious. Just like cats, Cathy understood that it took time for two women to bond. As long as there were no cat fights, everything would be just fine.

"Sunshine, if you don't mind helping Rain with her bags and showing her to her room, I would really appreciate it. I have some really important phone calls to make."

Sunshine conceded to help Rain get settled in, but only because Cathy needed her to. "No problem," Sunshine spit out along with a small laugh. "Messing around with you and that cell phone of yours, Sprint is going to get paid some mega bucks," Sunshine said.

Cathy laughed along with her. "Very funny, but they're not getting paid no mega bucks from me today. My cell is free after nine and on the weekends, doll baby." Cathy headed to her bedroom where she could talk in private.

Rain could already tell that Sunshine and Cathy had a special kind of relationship. The way they interacted with each other was something Rain longed to share with someone. Suddenly, she missed her mother.

Once Cathy was gone, Rain turned to Sunshine. "I'm sorry for ignoring you earlier when you spoke to me. I thought you were making jokes about my name."

Sunshine looked confused. She didn't understand. "Why would I do something like that?" Sunshine asked curiously. "I don't even know you to make fun of you. Besides, that's not my style to make fun of anyone. Come on. Let me show you to your new room."

When they arrived at Rain's bedroom, Rain couldn't believe her eyes. She had to touch the wall to make sure that it was real and that she was really in such a fly room. Rain was completely and totally speechless. The room looked more like a small paradise that belonged to a superstar's child, like something you might see on *MTV Cribs*.

Damn! Ms. Cathy must be paid! Rain thought.

Everything looked brand new. The only thing Rain had to complain about was the pink walls. It was a little too girly for her taste, but the burgundy flourishes that highlighted the vast room would help her tolerate it.

"Is there a phone somewhere in this room?" Rain asked. She needed to contact Terrance as soon as possible.

"Yes, it's right there." Sunshine pointed toward the cherry wood nightstand to the cordless phone. "Thank you. I have to make an important phone call if you don't mind."

"No, that's fine. Just pick it up to make sure that it's working. I'm not sure if she had it installed yet," Sunshine insisted.

Rain walked over to the nightstand and picked up the receiver praying for a dial tone.

"Yeah, it's all good," she said.

"All right, well, if you need me for anything, my room is straight down the other end of the hallway," Sunshine said.

"Okay, I won't be long," Rain said.

Once Sunshine left the room, Rain took a deep breath and prepared herself for this conversation with Terrance. Rain wasn't sure what she would say, but one thing was certain. If that heifer answered his phone today, Rain would make it her business to reach her hand into the phone and wring that wench by the neck until she choked to death.

Surprisingly, when his cell phone was answered, it was Terrance's deep, seductive voice Rain heard, and not the tramp's. Just hearing him say *hello* sent orgasmic signals downtown. Rain teasingly wet her lips with her tongue, picturing the day she'd allow him to make love to her for the first time. She had to stay focused, though, because she didn't call to get all mushy with him. She called for a reason.

"Hey, Terrance, baby. What's up with you?" Rain spoke in her softest, sweet-like-candy voice.

"I'm chillin," Terrance answered nonchalantly.

"Have you missed me?" Rain wanted to know.

"Umm . . . it depends." Terrance hesitated.

She could hear him sucking in the smoke from his blunt while he puffed.

"What does it depend on?" Rain asked.

"It depends on who this is," Terrance said slowly while exhaling his hydro. Rain didn't let his lack of knowledge upset her.

"Who do you want it to be?" Rain asked him in a teasing way.

"It would be nice if this was a booty call from some good booty," Terrace teased back.

Rain was getting jealous now, and she began yelling into the phone. "Don't play with me, Terrance!" Rain's frustration started to show.

"Don't play with *me*," Terrance responded casually. "Who is this for real though?"

Rain paused for a moment and then answered, "I evaporate from the ground, into the sky, and fall back down. They call me . . ."

"Rain. Oh, what's up, sexy?" Terrance asked.

"What's up? That's all you have to say to me after all the head action I gave you?" Rain asked.

"Hmmph." Terrance let a short, cool breath escape from his chest. "No, sexy, that's not all I have to say. Can the rain fall back down and help my cum evaporate?"

"You are so nasty, Terrance."

"Yeah, I ain't said nothing wrong, and you know that's what you love about me."

"Yeah, a'ight, whatever," Rain said, not denying the truth. "What I don't love, though, is you letting stank-ass bitches answer your cell."

"Come on now, Rain, you know better than that. I don't let nobody answer my phone," Terrance said calmly.

"Well, who was it then?" Rain asked with a small hint of obsession in her voice.

"That must have been my little sister playing with you and shit," Terrance answered.

"Well, tell your little sister that she was about to get her little ass smacked." Rain spoke in a playful way. She didn't want to upset him, but it was obvious to Rain that Terrance was faking.

Rain didn't want to live in the conversation about the broad anymore. She could feel the air being torched, and she might get mad and say the wrong thing. Since he was her only link to Jerome right now, she decided to chill out and let it ride.

"How's about I smack that phat ass?" Terrance shot back.

"This ass is for admiring, not for harassing," Rain joked.

"A'ight, well, how about I admire it, and then I harass it?" Terrance asked seductively.

"Damn, I can't win for losing with you." Rain laughed. "No, for real, though, I called you on a serious note."

"That ass is serious," Terrance continued, laughing and choking simultaneously from the weed.

"Listen to me, Terrance." Rain interrupted. "My little brother might call you looking for me. If he does, I want you to call me ASAP. I know you heard by now about what happened to my father."

Terrance now spoke with some sincerity. "Yeah, that's messed up that big J went out like that. Are you okay?" Terrance asked softly.

Rain could feel her tears about to betray her again. "Well, it's like they say: When it rains, it pours, and right now it's pouring down real heavy," Rain answered. "Jody got locked up, I've been to two foster homes within twenty-four hours, and now the fuckin' state done split me and Rome up. I don't know what to expect next. It's some foul shit going down right now," Rain continued. It felt good to vent and get some of her troubles off her chest.

"Damn, baby, I'm sorry to hear all that," Terrance said. "You are too sexy to be going through this shit. If your little youngin' calls me, I'll be sure and get at you. Do you want me to call you at the number that came up on my caller ID?" Terrance asked.

"Yes, this is where I'm laying my head for right now," Rain answered.

"Can I come and lay my head beside you?" Terrance asked, back to his old tricks.

"It depends on which head you're talking about," Rain retorted. She was back on joke time, too, stepping up her game with him.

"I see that you've made yourself at home," Cathy said, startling Rain.

"I have to go now." Rain hung up the phone with a quickness and gave her undivided attention to Cathy, hoping that she wasn't in any kind of trouble just for making a call. If she was in trouble, she would just lie and say she was calling to find out when her father's funeral service was going to be held. She wasn't sure how much of her conversation with Terrance Cathy had overheard.

Rain automatically started pleading her case. "I had an important call to make. I asked Sunshine and she said that it was okay for me to use the phone."

Cathy started smiling, amused by Rain's bewilderment. "Of course it's okay for you to use the phone. That's why I had it installed, not just for decoration. I'm not some uppity old witch who smiles easily by making young girls' lives like yours miserable," Cathy added. "Believe it or not, I was a young girl once, and I know how vital a telephone is. I don't have a problem with you using the phone, as long as your male friends don't call past eleven and your girlfriends don't call disrespecting."

Rain was relieved and could now allow the tension in her shoulder muscles to loosen up. "That's what's up," Rain said, smiling too.

Rain sensed that Cathy was exceptional. She had all the divine assets of a classy woman from the hood. For one, the fresh Louis Vuitton halter-top with the belt and sandals to match set her style off to a higher level. Secondly, her personality was smooth and easygoing, almost like a dude. She wasn't sassy or uptight like most of the women Rain had bumped heads with. And finally, who could overlook her exquisite house, with all of the Italian leather and imported statues? Life-sized portraits adorned the walls and emphasized wealth and style. She even had an oversized framed photograph of herself with Snoop Dog and Tupac. Now that was some real gangsta shit.

"I came up here to tell you and Sunshine that I made dinner reservations for us at Royals. It's an all-American cuisine restaurant. I figured that since this is your first night here, it would be a great way for all of us to get to know one another."

Rain nodded her head in agreement. "Do I have to dress up?" Rain wanted to know. She mentally assessed the few articles of her wardrobe she'd brought and knew she definitely didn't have anything worth wearing somewhere nice.

"No, it's a nice place to dine, but it's not too high-class. You don't have to throw on no suits or gowns. You'll be fine wearing some slacks and a nice blouse to match." Rain didn't think she even owned a pair of slacks or any pair of nice pants, for that matter. Usually, she would wear skintight jeans with different colored tank tops.

Cathy could read the uneasy look on Rain's face. "If you don't have anything casual to wear, don't stress. We can stop at a shop in Georgetown to pick you up something fierce. Royals isn't that far from the shops anyway."

Rain liked that idea a helluva lot.

"We'll be leaving in about an hour, so that should be enough time for you to shower and freshen up," Cathy said. "There's a bathroom down the hall to your left. You'll find everything you need to beautify yourself, not that you need much help in that department."

Rain was psyched. She loved when people openly admired her beauty. She knew that she was sexy down to the very thin layer of her bone, and compliments only confirmed the truth.

"If you don't see something that you need in the bathroom, just let Sunshine know. I will be downstairs getting myself together. I am very excited about tonight. I'm looking forward to getting to know each other better," Cathy added as she turned to leave.

Rain jumped up from her bed and ran down the hall to get ready like a child on her way to Chuck E. Cheese.

The bathroom was enormous and filled with full-length mirrors for Rain to admire her brick house. There were even mirrors on the ceiling.

Damn, this joint is sexy, Rain thought.

Rain searched to see if she could find a small radio to listen to while she bathed. She couldn't find one, but that didn't matter. She would just grab the clock radio from the nightstand in her room. She raced back to get it. She had to have her music playing while she got ready.

Behind the brown, genuine leather shower curtain covered with thin plastic, Rain found a tub that you could live in.

"The hell with a shower. I'm taking a bubble bath," Rain said to no one. She noticed an assortment of bubble baths lined up along the vanity that stood next to the tub. There were so many that it was hard for Rain to decide which one to use. Finally, she decided on a soft Hawaiian silk fragrance.

She ran warm bath water and let the delicate scent fill the air. She plugged in the little radio and tuned it to her favorite hip hop station. Rain began to finally relax from all the past days' tensions. For the moment, she could exhale and not dwell on the death of her father, not worry about how her brothers were, not trip about Terrance, and not stress about what would become of her in this life.

While the enormous tub took its time filling up, Beyonce's powerful voice squeaked out of the teeny tiny radio. Rain wished she could get more volume out of the infant radio, but that didn't stop her from moving and twisting her naked body all around to the beat. She watched herself in the tall mirrors while she bounced her ass up and down like she had seen Beyonce do so proudly in so many of her videos.

"Beyonce, you are one vicious woman, but you ain't got nothing on me." Rain smacked her apple bottom with a loud *SMACK!* as she continued moving seductively to the music. Gradually, she grinded her way to the ground, while slowly winding her hips in a tick-tock motion, grooving her way back up.

"Let me stop fucking around and act like I have somewhere to go," Rain told herself. As she soaked herself clean in her foam bath, the thought crossed her mind that she'd much rather stay in the house and just order some shrimp and rice. She wasn't sure if this nice neighborhood had a Chinese carry-out restaurant, but she would've bet money that it did. Why wouldn't it? Her old hood had a carry-out on every other corner. Most carry-outs sat next to the liquor store, which was usually right next to a beauty supply, which was generally accompanied by a mini-mart. Rain would surely miss her old hood. On the other hand, she was definitely not unhappy about her new hood.

Rain wondered how Cathy could afford such a luxurious house with such fancy trimmings. *Clearly, she's not getting no fat check from the cheap-ass government, that's for sure,* she thought. *Maybe she got herself a nice, paid boyfriend who's pushing bricks, 'cause it ain't that much foster caring in the world.*

"Do what you do," Rain said out loud. Rain had seen enough drug dealing in her life to be in her right mind to start her own business. Of course, she would never do that, because she also saw what happened to most drug dealers. One of four things: jail, shot, killed, or they became rappers selling hate records to young thugs.

Knock! Knock! Knock!

"Rain, it's Sunshine. Cathy thought I should let you know that we'll be leaving in fifteen minutes."

Rain quickly sat up in the tub, splashing bubbles everywhere. "Oh, shit!" Rain had gotten so relaxed in her bath that she had lost track of time. "I'll be right out," she yelled.

Rain hurried out of the bath and into her room. She attacked the bags with all of her belongings inside, searching for a decent outfit to wear.

"All this gear is played out," she mumbled while tossing wrinkled clothes all about.

"This might work." She held a long summer dress up against her frame and observed herself in the full-length mirror.

Yeah, if I was going to a cookout, she thought. Rain threw the dress on the floor. *Cathy did say that she would buy me an outfit if I didn't have one, so it really doesn't matter what I put on for now,* she told herself. Finally, she decided on her green tank top and green Capri pants to match. *It's not dinner-wear, but it's what I'm wearing.*

When Rain got downstairs, Cathy and Sunshine were at the door waiting for her, and dressed to kill. A man could actually get hurt if he tried to look too hard. Rain was mesmerized for a moment, trying to figure out which fashion magazine they had just come out of. They were so dolled up that it looked as if someone had cloned two top models from *Essence*.

Cathy's body was serious about her outfit. The black satin mini-dress she wore clung to her skin for dear life. She set it off with a tall pair of black stilettos.

Sunshine was on the scene with a tight Baby Phat wraparound skirt with a matching blouse that purposely fit too small. Her sandals were decorated with diamond Baby Phat emblems all over them. She was too much.

Rain felt a little out of her league but still knew that a compliment was mandatory. She would be hating if she didn't recognize their jazzy attire.

"Y'all are going to get somebody's man in trouble," Rain said. "They're gonna be mad 'cause their man supposed to be cutting their steak, but instead they'll be cutting their eyes at you," Rain added.

"Thank you. I'll take that as a compliment," Sunshine said.

"Yes, thank you, Rain. You're looking cute yourself, but I would still like to get you something fresh to wear," Cathy said. "Because when we step up in Royals, all three of us are going to make everybody do a double take. We gonna make them cry and beg when we step up in there like we're Destiny's Child or something. You feel me?" Cathy asked.

'Well, I'm Beyonce," Rain said while rolling her eyes wild to every direction in the room.

"Okay, well, then I'm Kelly," Sunshine said, smiling. She twirled her whole body around in an exotic circle while holding up an imaginary microphone to her mouth."

"Well, then I guess I'm Michelle," Cathy said. She put on her best dumbfounded look, trying to duplicate the confused and lost look Michelle always seemed to have when she was on stage. Rain and Sunshine broke out into tears from laughing so hard, as they continued to watch Cathy tripping over her own two feet. She looked more like a retard than a songstress.

"Oh, that's messed up, Cathy. So what are you trying to imply?" Sunshine asked, still laughing.

"Let's keep it real, girls. We all know that Michelle is a little off-balance sometimes with that threesome. She's better off doing gospel music. That's what she's good at," Cathy stated.

"But don't get me wrong. The girl can *sang*. Not sing, but *sang*, you dig? I just feel like her presence is not as strong and sexy as Beyonce and Kelly. Michelle should be a solo act, *sanging* some wholesome church music." Cathy had to laugh at her own self.

"Come on, Kelly and Beyonce, let's go turn some heads."

Rain was beaming with happiness. For the first time since the death of her father, she actually felt good about herself and her life. Rain realized that she and Sunshine almost got off to a bad start because of her foolish assumptions, but now she felt as if she may have made two new friends.

FOUR

The Georgetown scene was filled with energy. People from all walks of life roamed about casually, lighting up the sidewalks and streets. Rain looked around the city streets as if she were a tourist.

She didn't tell Cathy or Sunshine, but this was her first time ever being in Georgetown. She had never seen so many different cultures in one place at one time. All the hustlers in her hood always bragged about G-Town, always remaining fresh and geared up from the flyest stores like Solbiato, Coogie, and LaCoste. Rain felt official just by walking past the high-fashion, overpriced stores. It was exciting. Jewelry stores, foreign restaurants, antique shops, and designer clothing shops stood side-by-side, babysitting each other. Rain even observed one store with skimpy lingerie, silver handcuffs, and feathers displayed in the outside window.

Is that legal?

"What kind of place is that?" Rain asked curiously, dangling her first finger toward the adult toy store.

Sunshine noticed the store and was just as clueless as Rain, so she shrugged her shoulders as if to say, *If you don't know, I don't know either.*

"That, my inquisitive young ladies, is a special store that I will take you both to when you're grown up and married," Cathy said. "Until then, don't worry your teenage heads about it."

"Oh, so that's what a freaky-deak store looks like?" Rain said teasingly.

Cathy turned the volume down on the radio because she wanted to hear Rain clearly before she answered her next question.

"And what do you know about a *freaky-deak* store, Ms. Thang?" Cathy was trying to figure out what kind of young girl she was dealing with—a roller, or just an inquiring one.

Rain could feel an unwanted speech coming on, so she gave a simple answer. "Not much, only that they sell cool nightgowns for men and women."

"Uh-huh, just checkin'," Cathy said, satisfied with her response.

She's a smart one, Cathy thought.

Cathy turned into a residential neighborhood just around the corner from the shops. The streets were so congested that there was no room left for parking. Cathy turned off the ignition to her top-of-the-line Lincoln Navigator.

"Let's go, girls. We gotta be quick because I'm parked on private property, and I can't afford no parking tickets. I've got two teenage girls to support," Cathy said.

Cathy began to walk the busy streets with stride, knowing exactly where to go as if it were her second home. She led Sunshine and Rain into a small urban store with all the latest fashions.

Rain was surprised that such a tiny store could have such enormous style, with prices to match. Within the first three minutes of strolling through the small aisle, Rain spotted three outfits that she would die for. She didn't bother to tell Cathy. Since it was Cathy's money, Rain would wait to see what Cathy had in mind.

Rain thought about stealing the shit but decided against it. The store was so closed in, she was sure that the owner could see her just thinking about it. Instead, she just placed the clothes to the side, in case Cathy decided to splurge on more than just one outfit.

Rain watched as Cathy quickly scanned through the items like a professional fashion consultant. Rain beamed as Cathy held different garments up to her to see what was appropriate.

Sunshine stepped off to the other end of the store to look around. She wanted to give Cathy and Rain an opportunity to interact alone. However, she didn't want to leave them alone for too long. She wasn't going to let Rain get greedy with her Cathy.

Sunshine thought she liked Rain but wasn't ready to commit to that opinion yet. She had to spend some more time getting to know her before deciding whether she was official. As far as she was concerned, Rain was still competition. She looked around the clearance racks as if she was interested, but nothing inside the store impressed her that day. Cathy had just brought her to this same store not even a week ago, so the merchandise was already familiar to her.

Sunshine stole subtle glances at Cathy and Rain. She watched them as they walked side-by-side to the cash register, looking like an all-too-familiar mother and daughter. That's when she realized that their quality time was just about up. Sunshine couldn't fake it any longer. She hurried back over to them like a green-eyed tiger cub abandoned by her mother.

Cathy noticed Sunshine standing behind them and gave her a gentle love tap on her cheek. Sunshine exhaled her envy; no one could come between them.

"Do you see anything in here that you want to get, Sunshine?" Cathy asked. Sunshine shook her head no. Cathy paid for the three outfits that Rain had her eyes on earlier, plus a silver alligator purse and a sky blue stretch Versace dress that she would wear to dinner.

The only thing left to purchase was a pair of shoes that would match the authentic dress. Cathy had the perfect place in mind for that.

"After the cashier scans this stuff, I want you to go into the dressing room and put this one on," Cathy said. She pointed to the Versace dress. "Be careful when you take the tags off. You don't want to accidentally rip the dress."

The cashier handed the dress to Rain. "You're going to look real fly in this," she said. "This is one of our hottest sellers this summer."

Rain already knew she would look good in the shit. She didn't need a cashier making pennies to tell her.

She walked into the dressing room and did as she was told. The mirror inside the dressing room showed her that the dress was a perfect fit. *Just like I thought.* Rain didn't know what she liked better: the way the dress perfectly fit her curves, or the fact that she was wearing designer couture for once in her life.

Rain could remember numerous times begging her father for all the latest names. He would always cry and complain about how there was never any money left over after paying all the bills. It was funny to her, because he still managed to find a way to buy an eight-ball after paying *all* the bills.

The broads would hate on her if she walked down the street in her old hood with this bad muthafucka on. Nevertheless, she didn't have time to think about the old hood. She was moving up in the world, and this Versace dress proved it. Rain walked out of the dressing room strutting as if she were walking a Baby Phat runway.

Cathy put one hand on her hip and gave three zigzag snaps with the other one. "Now that's what I'm talking about!" she affirmed.

Even Sunshine admired Rain's new look She had to admit, the competition looked *good!*

Cathy glanced at her watch and realized that they had spent more time inside this one little store than she had intended, and they still had to buy some shoes. That could take the rest of the day.

"Come on, Beyonce and Kelly, we've got one more spot to hit." She pointed at Rain's worn sneakers that didn't complement her new dress at all. The sight was breaking one of Cathy's major fashion commandments.

"It's crime number four in my book to look first-class from your head to your knees and get down to your feet and look like you forgot that you were on high status. No disrespect."

Rain and Sunshine shared a laugh.

Cathy rushed the girls along the busy streets of motorists and pedestrians to their final destination. She didn't want to be late for their dinner reservation, or the meeting that she was going to have with some of her boys.

Cathy figured that Royals would be a great way to take care of business dealing with home *and* work. She had called both Caesar and Irvin personally the night before and asked them to meet her at the restaurant to discuss some important business with them and the rest of the crew. Given that Royals had two lounge areas, she made a reservation for one table on each level. That way, Sunshine and Rain wouldn't bump heads with her entourage.

Siheed, the owner of Royals, was one of Cathy's major customers. The New Yorker had balls of steel. He owned a big part of many cities, while pushing that 'caine throughout its zones like thunder, all thanks to Cathy. Shit, if Cathy wanted to shut the whole bitch down for the night, Royals would be all hers, and she wouldn't have to pay a dollar. Siheed was her man, and they looked out for each other.

After running a couple more blocks, they arrived at The Shops, a fancy mini-mall with giant prices. The mall was damn near exquisite with all of its exotic statues that stood tall and proud from within, as soft waterfalls flowed throughout each one. The names were all classy and unfamiliar, unlike other malls they were used to in Iverson or Forestville. The patrons were mostly upper-class families and out-of-town tourists who busied themselves by splurging the restless wealth that sat in their fat pockets.

The food corner left a teasing aroma in the pit of their bellies as Cathy whisked them away in a hurry. Rain was disappointed that they couldn't indulge in the flavors for a minute.

The Shops had a variety of interesting stores that Rain wanted to check out, but there was no time for that, because Cathy had a one-track mind. Once they reached their target, they shot in and out of the store so fast that Rain wondered for a moment if they had even purchased anything. Once she told Cathy her shoe size, the rest was history.

Rain didn't bother to ask any questions until they were safely back inside the truck. "Do I even get to see the shoes that I'll be wearing now, or are we still on that high-speed chase?" she finally asked. She was excited to see the final hook-up that Cathy had for her.

"Oh my gosh! I'm sorry, Rain. Here you go." Cathy handed Rain the bag with her new shoes inside.

Judging from Cathy's own unique style, Rain already knew that her shoes were the bomb. When she slipped on the sky blue, open-toed leather pumps, Rain felt like an urban Cinderella. She couldn't wait to get out of the truck so she could get the full effect of her brand new attire.

Royals was loaded with paid niggas and females to match. The mood was instantly set to chill mode, once you walked into the candlelit background. Deep red leather seating surrounded the scene, accompanied by cherry wood tables decorated with lamps. The scent inside the restaurant reeked of hard-earned money, with a hint of the root of all evil: cold cash.

Rain was beside herself with enthusiasm. She didn't know how to act. She had never been around so many ballers before, and she was trying to figure out what somebody like Cathy would know about a place like this.

Her previous theory about Cathy was coming to life as she looked around at all the paid hustlers and hustlettes in her presence. Rain tried to remain cool, as if she wasn't fazed by this new world of treasures that Cathy had introduced her to, while Sunshine took it all in naturally, like it was nothing.

The wait for a table would have been forever, judging by the over-crowded lobby, but Cathy and her guests were immediately escorted into a cozy booth right next to the stage where a live jazz band performed.

"Will anyone else be joining you, Ms. Stone?" the hostess asked politely.

"No, Serena. It's just me and my two girls tonight."

Damn, Cathy even knows the staff by name, Rain observed. She also noticed that none of the staff wore those big ol' billboard signs they call name tags, with their full name blasting across them like in the fast food diners she was used to. Even the dress attire of the servers was professional and elegant. You could mistake them for customers if you didn't pay close attention to the big, black loafers they all wore, which was a sure sign that they were employed.

Serena placed three menus on the table and said she'd be back shortly to take their orders.

Cathy stood up immediately after the server left. "I'll be right back, ladies. Sunshine, order me my regular." Cathy stepped off so quick that Rain didn't even see which way she went.

"What was that all about?" she asked, looking at Sunshine for answers.

"Your guess is as good as mine," Sunshine answered and immediately changed the subject, not caring to get into Cathy's personal business with a newcomer.

"The band sounds real nice, right?" Sunshine asked.

"Yeah, I guess if you like to listen to music with no words in it."

Rain was a little disturbed with how Sunshine blew her inquiries off with no interest, but she didn't let up. Rain smiled and playfully tapped elbows with Sunshine. She leaned in close to Sunshine's ear so that she could be heard over the music.

"So, do you think Cathy has a hot date that she's secretly dining with on the second level?"

Sunshine glared at Rain for a moment, wondering why she was so curious about Cathy anyway. Rain stared back into Sunshine's eyes mischievously, wearing a world-size smile that could con Jesus. Assuming that Rain's curiosity was harmless, Sunshine decided to fill her in.

Sunshine scooted closer to Rain. She rested her face on her shoulder just above her ear. She whispered like a best friend who was about to expose her deepest, darkest secret.

"Well," Sunshine began, "every time we come here for dinner, which is usually once a month, Cathy creeps off to the second level. I believe she does have somebody hiding up there."

Rain began rubbing her hands together naughtily while Sunshine spoke. "Now we're getting somewhere," Rain said with satisfaction after Sunshine was done. "Come on. Let's go find her and see what kind of baller she's into!" Rain shouted with enthusiasm.

Sunshine looked at Rain with interest. "Are you serious?" she asked.

Before Rain could answer her, Serena returned with her pen and pad, ready to take their orders. Rain realized that she hadn't even bothered to look over the menu yet.

"You go ahead and order first," she told Sunshine.

Sunshine hadn't peeked inside the menu either; however, she was already familiar, and she knew exactly what she wanted.

"I'll have two sweet iced teas to drink. For an appetizer, we will have your jumbo shrimp cocktail with warm butter and lemon. For our entrees, we'll have two grilled salmon Caesar salads," Sunshine said.

"Make that three salads, and a Coke with a little bit of ice," Rain added.

Serena wrote with the same speed that Sunshine and Rain spoke. It was apparent to Rain that Serena had been in the business for probably her whole life.

"Oh, and don't forget to bring some—"

"Extra dinner rolls." Serena finished Sunshine's sentence for her.

How cute, Rain thought.

Once Serena the wonderful hostess was gone, Rain grabbed Sunshine by the arm. "Come on. Are you with me or not? I know you're just as anxious as I am to see the type of dude a classy chick like Cathy would be sporting—or should I say concealing?"

Sunshine giggled at Rain's spunky determination. "Are you serious, Rain?" she asked.

Rain thought for a moment. "No, not really, but it will give us a chance to check out some of these dudes up in here."

Sunshine shook her head like an old lady in dismay. "You're on your own. I'll stay here and watch our purses," Sunshine said.

Rain stood up. "You mean your purse. I'm going to need something to put my phone numbers in."

On her way to the ladies' room to fix herself up, Rain bumped into Terrance.

"Damn, shorty! Watch where you—Rain, is that you?" Terrance asked in bewilderment.

Rain lifted her head up after picking her new bag up off the floor. Rain could feel her blood blowing bubbles in her heart. She always got like that around Terrance.

"Terrance, what's up, boo?" She gave him a sexy hug, making sure her big ol' titties were all over him. She even slid her hand gently across his enlarged print to arouse him and make him hunger for her.

"I see you're doing fine," she answered for him as she squeezed his pool stick and juggled his balls.

"Yo, you look good as hell! You bangin' the shit out of that dress," Terrance said. He reached for her nipples that were doing a terrible job of hiding underneath her dress.

"You're probably up here with some bogus-ass nickel-and-dime-pushing nigga," Terrance said.

Rain sucked her teeth. "Oh, don't fake like you big timing. And why you worried about who I'm with anyway? You jealous?"

"Damn right I'm jealous if you sucked his dick better than you sucked mine," Terrance answered.

Rain put her finger up to her mouth and teasingly licked the tip of it, just like she did his dick in his car on their last date.

She placed her wet fingers on his lips and said, "I don't think that no man's penis can taste as good as yours, and I don't even want to find out."

Terrance was tempted to slip Rain into the men's room, but he looked at his watch and realized that he was late for his engagement.

Terrance squeezed Rain on her ass. "Keep that tongue wet, baby girl." He walked off without another word.

Rain was left standing there, being watched by a snooping waiter. The underpaid maitre d' must have heard everything that she said to Terrance. He was licking his own lips and staring at Rain so hard that she just knew he could see the tampon she was wearing.

"In your dreams, waiter boy." Rain walked away and into the ladies' room, not giving the waiter a second thought.

What's up with everybody in this joint? she wondered. *Everybody keeps rolling out on me like they got same top-secret shit going on. First Ms. Cathy rolls out without an explanation, and now Terrance done got ghost on me.*

As she squatted over the toilet to let out her golden shower, she wondered if Terrance was meeting a girl. Maybe he was there to see Cathy.

Nah, Ms. Cathy ain't going like that. Terrance ain't even on her level. He must be here to meet that dirty bitch Simone.

"I know he ain't disrespecting me like that," she said out loud. At that moment, while she was in the bathroom stall, wiping her pussy and talking to herself out loud, she realized that she was in love. Rain swiftly changed her soaked tampon, washed her hands, and hurried out of the restroom so she could find out what was going on up in that place.

During the short amount of time that Rain spent in the bathroom, Royals had accumulated even more consumers. Desperate men posted up near the restroom, just so they could watch the honeys swarm out. Rain couldn't even get out the door good before one guy aggressively grabbed her arm and turned on his weak-ass game.

"Hey, cutie. Heaven must be awfully lonely up there, losing such a lovely angel."

Rain was not impressed. *Is he trying to tell me I'm sexy, or that I should be dead and gone?*

Rain responded to the pest sarcastically, "And the hustlers must feel awfully broke without their favorite pipehead straggling down the street geekin'." Rain threw his puny hand off hers with disgust and walked away. The biggest bamas always had the biggest hearts. What in the hell would make his pathetic ass think that he could get with a phat to def, gorgeous, fine, sexy ass like herself? Rain shook her head at the nonsense and went in search of Terrance and Simone.

Cathy was irritated. She had made it clear that everyone was to be on time for this month's meeting. The only person allowed to get away with being late was her, 'cause she ran the shit. Even still, not even she would allow herself to show up late for this particular meeting. Important business needed to be discussed because a major move was about to be made, and she needed all her soldiers to be on point. It was critical that everyone involved showed preciseness so that nothing would fuck up or nobody would get fucked up. Even the little things mattered, like being on time for discussion.

Cathy was furious when Tee came pimping to the table twenty minutes late, as if this were his show. She didn't know this new cat, Tee, all that well, and she didn't like him already. Her time was precious, and she would be sure to let him know, along with everyone else, that if he couldn't be prompt about his shit, then she didn't need his ass.

Drinks and appetizers had already been served when Tee finally arrived. Cathy decided to take the opportunity to make an example of him so everyone would not forget who was in charge of their cash flow.

Tee pulled up the only available chair surrounding the large round table. Cathy had to be smooth about this one. She didn't want to humiliate the youngin' too much, because he might get petty and retaliate in some vicious way that could harm her. She knew a lot of ganstas from D.C. who reacted without thinking. They would put a bullet in their own man if they thought he was trying to front on them. Instead of simply approaching his comrade like a real man would, they'd shoot him in the back like a cold killer, with no remorse toward their friendship or their family. Sad. Cathy had certainly seen some foul shit in the city.

Cathy figured she had two options. She could send his last-minute ass on his merry way before he even got the chance to get comfortable in the leather seat, or she could flunk him for a little while, keep him close to her, but far from her business; that is, until he could build a better rep with her. Either way she looked at it, his pockets would be fucked up while he earned her trust. Of course, he had the option of going to work for somebody else, but everybody at this table knew that everybody in these streets was getting their shit from Cathy. She had the golden butter that made them heads steal from their own family, so regardless of how he got it, he would still be selling her shit and still secretly working for her.

Cathy waited patiently while Tee pulled up his too-big Azzure jeans that were hanging way past his butt cheeks, so that he could sit down properly. Why a simpleton would pay over a hundred dollars for a pair of jeans and let them sag off his butt was beyond Cathy.

Once he was finally situated and had eventually pulled his body closer to the table, the first thing he did was reach for one of the chilled bottles of Moet that had already been popped.

Caesar cut his eyes over at Cathy. Cathy could read his mind loud and clear: *What's up with this muthafucker? He's late and disrespectful.*

At first Cathy was willing to let this cat be down, but on second thought, she decided that she couldn't even take this scrub anymore. She would have to throw his ass back to the mean streets, which would only allow him to hustle nickels and dimes. Evidently, he was not ready for the big time.

Tee took a sip of his Mo, then finally decided to speak. "What's up, homies?"

By this time, Gucci, Caesar, and Irvin were looking from Cathy to Tee, and from Tee back to Cathy. Everyone seemed to be aware of Tee's behavior except for Tee, but nobody said a thing to him. Not even Irvin, who was the reason why Cathy had let Tee come on board in the first place.

Cathy looked deep into Tee's eyes for any sign of awareness. He didn't have a clue.

"Is that Nectar Imperial any good?" Cathy asked.

He looked confused. "The what?" Terrance asked, unaware of what he was drinking.

"The Moet you're sipping on. Is it good?" Cathy repeated.

Tee was hip now. "Oh, yeah. This shit here is what's up."

"Good. I'm glad you like it," Cathy said sarcastically. "Now take it with you."

Tee looked a little bit mystified, so Cathy broke it down for him. "Listen, small time, I don't need you, so you can pull your pants back down, take your drink, and get up from my table, you dig?"

Now Tee was feeling her. "Oh, it's like that?" He looked over at Irvin for some assistance.

Irvin finally spoke. "I'll holla at you later, dog."

Tee grabbed his drink and bounced without another word. He never looked back as he disappeared into the crowd.

Cathy looked over at Irvin and asked, "Where did you get him from?"

"That's my cousin, Cee," he answered nonchalantly.

"Oh, well, that explains everything," Cathy joked. Everyone around the table busted out laughing, including Irvin, and the air felt light again.

"Talk some sense into that boy, and then tell him to holla at me. Until then, my niggas, let's get down to business."

FIVE

Sunshine looked at her watch. Cathy and Rain had abandoned her for over twenty minutes. *What is this, a conspiracy?* Sunshine was left sitting at the table looking Destiny's Childless. Fortunately, their entrees hadn't been served yet. Unfortunately, she had managed to eat all of the jumbo shrimp out of boredom, so now there was none left for Cathy or Rain. She also had to re-order all their drinks twice, because they kept getting watered down from all the crushed ice. She was enjoying listening to the band play various smooth jams, until they stopped to take a break.

Sunshine wondered if she should go search for Cathy and Rain. Maybe they got stuck in a toilet or something. Sunshine laughed at the thought of itsy-bitsy little Cathy swimming around in the restroom like a mermaid. She could probably even fit down the toilet; she was so small.

Sunshine was still caught up in the silly image when a tall, slim, simply gorgeous guy walked up to her and interrupted her thoughts. He didn't waste any time introducing himself.

"Hello, sunshine, my name is Diego. Do you mind if I sit down?"

Sunshine was stunned for a moment by his sexy bodily features and his smooth baritone.

"I don't mind if you do," Sunshine answered. She was excited that she had someone to talk to until Cathy and Rain got back.

Diego looked familiar to Sunshine. Seconds after staring into his pretty face, she realized where she recognized him from.

"You play for that band, right?" Sunshine asked.

"Yes, I do. How did you know? Were you checking me out?" he said, flashing such a beautiful white smile that Sunshine swore she saw his front tooth sparkle like a diamond.

Sunshine blushed. She was beginning to feel a little shy, as she usually did whenever a fine man tried to talk to her.

Relax, Sunshine, this is just general conversation. It's not as if he's asking you out for a date.

"Yeah, I noticed you playing the bongos, and you sounded tight. But I'm sure you already know that," Sunshine said.

Diego let out a brief laugh. "Of course I know, baby girl, but it reassures me when I hear it coming out your pretty lips."

Sunshine couldn't help but lick her lips at his compliment.

"So do you have a name to go with that sweet face?" Diego asked.

Sunshine realized then that Diego was just using "sunshine" earlier as a pet name. He had no idea that he had actually called her by her first name. She extended her hand out to meet his.

"My name is Sunshine."

Diego seemed surprised when she told him her name. "Well, sweetheart, let me be the first to tell you that your name fits you without a doubt, because your beauty shines like a hot, sunny day in July, beaming down to the sea, causing the waves and ripples to gleam."

Diego reminded Sunshine of Cathy, the way he called her by a different pet name every time he spoke. Speaking of Cathy, she would have to go look for her soon.

"Would you like to dance with me, Sunshine? I've got ten more minutes before my break is up."

Sunshine listened to the intermission music that played through the piercing speakers. She

didn't care too much for the song that was playing, but she had never danced with a man before,
and decided, *What the heck.*

On the dance floor, Diego was as smooth with
his moves as he was playing the bongos. Sunshine
did her best to follow his lead. He was so gentle
with her; he made dancing with him come naturally. Diego wrapped his arm around her waist
and pulled her closer to him. Sunshine was now
so close to him that she could smell his aftershave,
deodorant, and cologne. If they were any closer,
they would be one.

He began to grind her softly with his body. She
could feel his nature rising against her and had
to pry herself away from him. She was starting to
tingle in places she didn't know existed.

"I have to go sit down," she said, barely above a
whisper. I'm starting to feel a little lightheaded,"
she lied.

Diego looked concerned. "Are you okay? Can
I get you some Tylenol or something?" he asked.

"No, thank you. I have some inside my purse."
Sunshine took off without another word, leaving
Diego to dance alone to his own beat.

When Sunshine reached the end of the stage,
she saw Rain approaching, and it looked as if she
had found herself a dance partner too. Sunshine
gestured her hand, pointing toward their table to

let Rain know where she was going. Rain nodded her head to show she understood her.

When she got to the booth, dinner was waiting, but there was still no Cathy. She decided to call her on her cell phone, instead of walking the entire restaurant. She might miss her due to the dim lights and all the people.

Cathy answered her phone on the first ring. Her caller ID must have informed her that it was Sunshine. She didn't even say hello. She simply said, "I'll be right there, baby doll."

"Well, you better hurry, because our food is here," Sunshine informed her.

Within minutes, Cathy was at the table, apologizing nonstop for her long departure. She was saying something about bumping into an old friend, when she stopped dead in the middle of her lie. Her eyes popped out like bubbles and her jaw dropped to the floor like a cartoon character.

Sunshine followed the direction to the distracting scene that had caused Cathy to stop so abruptly.

Cathy was almost delusional as she watched Rain and her new date bump and grind all over the dance floor like a pair of wild animals. The lights were so mellow that Cathy wasn't sure if she was seeing correctly. She was almost certain that the boy who Rain was bouncing her ass all over as if they were in a bedroom, and not on stage, was Tee.

The interlude ended, and Diego and the rest of his crew began to replay their swift beats.

"Who is that guy Rain is dancing with?" Cathy asked Sunshine.

Sunshine shrugged her shoulders. "I don't know. I think it's someone she just met."

Cathy and Sunshine sat in silence for a moment while Rain and her dude walked closer to the table. As the couple came closer to view, Cathy gasped. She locked eyes with the wanna-be, jeans-hanging-off-his-ass-wearing bama who she had just kicked out of her world upstairs on the second level.

Terrance glared right back into Cathy's big green eyes. He wore a sly grin on his face, making Cathy feel uneasy. He never said a word.

He gently placed Rain into her seat like the perfect gentleman, giving her an innocent kiss on her cheek. With his every move, his eyes never left Cathy's face. Sunshine stared at them both, trying to figure out what was going on. Rain wasn't paying the intense scene any mind.

Rain was just about to introduce Terrance to Cathy and Sunshine, and even offer him a seat, but he had stepped off with a swiftness. Cathy watched as he left, thinking about the stupid grin he had spread across his face while he tucked Rain in her seat. She didn't like it. And where the hell did he get manners from all of a sudden?

He must have picked up some charm on his way back down to the first level.

All three ladies watched as Terrance slipped out the door of Royals.

Cathy played the situation cool, even though she didn't like it one bit. She had a bunch of questions running wild in her head.

How does Rain know Tee? Did she just meet him? Not the way they were dancing. What kind of ghetto girl did the agency send to me? Is she involved with the streets too?

This was no good. If Rain found out that she was selling them thangs, some shit could go down. Or, did she already know? None of her kids knew her hustle, not even Sunshine, and she liked it that way.

Rain interrupted Cathy's thoughts. "I am worn out. Did you check my moves out on the floor? Terrance couldn't even keep up with me."

Sunshine let out a small laugh.

Rain continued, "We would still be out there grooving, but they had to let that weak-ass band back on the mic. The tape they had going sounded much better than them. I personally think that music with no words is meaningless."

Sunshine felt the need to comment on that ignorant statement. "Rain, when you hear music with no words, that's when you add your own words or thoughts. It's serene. But you wouldn't know nothing about that," Sunshine added wisely.

"You might be right about that, but I do know one thing: We need to bless this food before it gets ice-cold," Rain said.

They all held hands while Cathy led the prayer. "Father, thank you for this special opportunity for us to come out and enjoy some good music, good company, and good food. Please bless this food in our bodies, and put it in all the right places."

"Amen!" all three ladies shouted.

"I liked that prayer," Rain added.

Cathy didn't waste any more time before she started showering Rain with questions. She had to find out how serious this thing was between Rain and Tee.

"So, Rain, who was your male friend?" Cathy asked while stuffing her mouth full of romaine lettuce and salmon.

Cathy noticed how Rain's eyes melted when she asked about Tee. Rain sat up proudly, ready to share with the world about her love for Terrance.

"That is my boyfriend, Terrance. He lives around my old way." Rain knew she was lying. Terrance never officially said that he was her man, but she was working on that.

Cathy became more engrossed as she listened to Rain. "How long have you been dating him?" Cathy asked.

"On and off for about three months," Rain stated egotistically.

Cathy plastered a fake smile on her face. "Awww, that's cute," Cathy said, trying to sound sincere. She continued with her interrogation. "So what does Terrance *do* for a living?"

Rain almost choked on her lettuce. She hadn't expected Cathy to go there. She didn't want to lie to Cathy, but the entire truth wasn't called for, either.

"He doesn't have a living," Rain said, chewing her food like it was trying to escape her lips, just like the lie she told. Rain didn't exactly tell a bald-faced lie, though. Terrance didn't work for a living. But that wasn't the question. The question was what did he do for a living? Rain hoped that Cathy didn't notice the way she had to flip the script on her.

Sunshine could tell that Cathy had something deep on her mind, and it was obviously about Terrance, because she was doing a lot of inquiring about him. But for what, she didn't know. Sunshine was just thankful when Cathy stopped with the twenty questions, because Rain was beginning to get nervous. It showed in the way that she was fidgeting with her food and didn't take her eyes away from her salad bowl.

Cathy was also aware of the change in Rain's attitude, and that's why she eased up with her questions. She also didn't want to appear paranoid or suspicious. It was not like she had anything to worry about anyway. If Tee knew what was good for him, he wouldn't fuck with her. But, to be on the safe side, she'd have to remember to call Irvin tomorrow, so he wouldn't forget to give Tee that pep talk.

Cathy was exhausted by the time they got home. Her day had progressed non-stop from the time she had gotten out of bed that morning. She was too sleepy to even take off her clothes, so she went straight to her room and plopped her head down on her pile of pillows. Within seconds, she was in a deep sleep.

After showering and changing into her pajamas, Sunshine went downstairs to go check on Cathy. She could hear Rain taking her own shower as she passed by her bathroom. When she reached Cathy's room and saw her sprawled lifelessly across the bed, she felt a daughter's instinct hit her. She walked over to Cathy's bed and slid off her shoes and clothes. Cathy was unconscious and unaware as Sunshine rolled her body over back and forth. Finally, after a minor struggle, she was able to remove Cathy's mini-dress. It was like peeling off a second skin.

Rain appeared in the doorway, dressed in her nightgown. "You need some help?" she asked.

"I'm done now. All I have left to do is cover her up with these blankets."

"Is she all right?" Rain wanted to know.

"Yeah, she's fine, but if I didn't know for certain that she doesn't get drunk, I would assume that she was feeling it," Sunshine said.

After covering Cathy with the blanket, Sunshine turned on her TV and changed it to Lifetime, Cathy's favorite channel. She slept like a baby when she had her TV on. Sunshine lit the two scented candles that sat on her nightstand, just like she liked it. Quietly, Sunshine and Rain crept back up the stairs.

Sunshine went into her own bedroom but felt far from sleepy. She decided to read a book to relax herself until her eyelids got heavy and she could eventually fall asleep. Rain was right behind her when she walked into her room.

Evidently, she wasn't sleepy either, but she wasn't in the mood to read books.

Rain made herself comfortable on Sunshine's bed. She began bouncing her body up and down like Tigger, making the whole bed bounce back in sync with her flow. Sunshine felt as if she were on a see-saw. It was clear that Rain still had a lot of energy left to burn.

"So, who was that guy I saw you slobbing down in the middle of dance floor?" Rain asked teasingly.

Sunshine grabbed one of her throw pillows and threw it at Rain jokingly. "Don't play with me. You didn't see me kissing on no one," Sunshine said. "What you saw me doing is what they call dancing where I come from."

"Yeah, well, who was he?" Rain asked again. "He looked kind of fly from what I could see of him, but I was looking from a distance. He might have looked like an ulcer if I got close up on him," Rain teased.

Sunshine had to laugh. "And what does an ulcer look like?" she asked.

"You should know," Rain continued. "An ulcer looks like the dude you was slobbing down on center stage, so don't fake. And don't skip the question either. Who is the dude?" Rain and Sunshine were both laughing now.

"His name is Diego, and he doesn't look anything like a nasty boil," Sunshine corrected her.

"Is that your boyfriend?" Rain asked.

"No!" Sunshine screamed loudly as if boyfriends were contagious.

"What does he do for a living?" Rain asked. Both girls rolled over in a ball of laughter at the way Rain harmlessly imitated Cathy. Sunshine took it a step further and began imitating Rain. She used her finger as an imaginary fork, put it in her mouth, and then started to pretend as if she were gagging, similar to when Rain had almost choked on her salad when Cathy began her twenty questions. Tears ran down Rain's cheeks from laughing so hard.

"I couldn't help it. I was stuck when she asked me that shit," Rain shouted in her own defense.

"A-duuh! Stevie Wonder could have peeped that," Sunshine said sarcastically.

Rain looked at Sunshine, embarrassed. "Was it that obvious that I was trying to cover for Terrance?"

"You surely didn't fool me. I could tell that you didn't want to let it be known whatever it is that Terrance does. So, what is he, an informant, a gigolo, or a cold-hearted killer?" Sunshine asked.

"Guess again," Rain answered.

Sunshine gave it one last thought. "It's only one thing left," Sunshine decided. Then, as if someone else were in the room listening, she whispered softly, "A drug dealer."

"Bingo!" Rain said, letting Sunshine know that she was on point. "Now you gotta promise me that you won't snitch and tell Cathy."

"If she doesn't ask me, I won't tell her," Sunshine promised. "But I won't lie to her if she does ask."

Rain couldn't do anything but respect that.

Sunshine felt the sudden urge to give Rain some of her own personal friendly advice. "Rain, you are a very attractive girl. That was the first thing that I noticed when you got here. You can do way better than Terrance," she said.

"You sound like somebody's mother," Rain teased. "But on the real, I know that I can get any nigga I want, and Terrance is what I want. I love me a gangster nigga. I can't do nothing with no church boy, and they can't do nothing for me. Besides, it ain't like I'm giving him some pussy. I'm just funning for right now. Maybe when I do settle down and I'm ready to share this sweet pooh-na-na, it will be with the right type of dude. A college muthafucker, a doctor, or hell, I might go all out and fuck with an astronaut. We could do something funky like make love on our way up to the stars. I'll suck his dick dry and make his ass fall from the sky. Picture that."

Sunshine and Rain talked for over two hours, filling each other in on everything from their families to the sexiest rapper on the scene. They both agreed that Method Man won that award. It was well after midnight when Rain finally went off into her own room to fall asleep.

That night she had a pleasant dream. She was at the mall with her mother, father, and little brothers. Somehow she had gotten separated from them. She wandered around, lost and confused. She was afraid at first, until she ran into a young girl her age. The girl stayed by her side and comforted Rain. Together they searched the mall for her family until they found them. The girl's name was Sunshine, and they became best friends.

SIX

As the hot summer weeks progressed, Sunshine and Rain became inseparable. The two spent all their summer moments together, sharing secrets or grooving to all kinds of music. Some days they would spend sunbathing at the spa, going to the most popular nail salons to get manicures and pedicures, or just hanging out at the local park and feeding the ducks. They had come to know each other so well that they could even pick out each other's clothes without the other one being present. Some nights, just for fun, they would kick it downstairs in the basement and watch scary movies while pigging out on all kinds of delicious junk foods.

Cathy was happy for Sunshine and Rain. They both had unfortunately had rough lives, but life had brought them together. Now both of them had someone their own age they could relate to. Although their personalities were different as night and day, they had a special time learning from one another, like seasons changing.

It was one o'clock in the morning, and Rain couldn't sleep. She had tried everything from drowning herself in television to trying to read one of the boring self-help books that sat with dust posted on her shelf. She had even tried taking three tablespoons of cough syrup when she wasn't even sick. Her body must have been immune to the medicine, because she still lay awake and restless in her bed.

Rain took out some blank paper and a pen and began to write Jody a letter. She would put it in the mailbox and send it off to him first thing in the morning, so he could get it by the weekend.

Hey, Hey, Little Brother,
Wuzup with you? I hope you're doing okay. I know it's rough for you right now, but I talked to your attorney on Monday and he assures me that you will be out soon. Everyone knows that it was self-defense. I don't understand why they asses ain't been let you out. You ain't no criminal. You saved my life, shit, and I will always love you for that, li'l brother.

I still haven't talked to Jerome yet. I called over to Ms. Darby's stanking-ass house, but her old ass done gone and got her number changed. I wish I knew how to find where she lives, 'cause I would go snatch Jerome up and roll out with him, and let them charge her with neglect. I try not to worry about him. I suppose if anything went down, they would have to call me and let me know.

Anyway, I'm sending you a money order for $150. I hope it holds you down until the next round.

Oh, yeah. Don't drop the soap!

Luv, Rain

Rain sealed the letter in an envelope and placed a stamp in the right-hand corner. She still felt restless. She tried calling Terrance to see if he was still awake, but all she got was his voice mail. Rain thought about calling Sunshine on her line, but the house was so peacefully quiet that she didn't want the ringing of the phone to scare the shit out of anybody.

Rain got up from her bed and slipped on a long Tweety Bird nightgown that Sunshine had given to her. She tiptoed down the hallway and silently entered Sunshine's room. Instead of turning on the small lamp that provided adequate light, Rain opted for the main overhead light. She plopped her body on the mattress beside Sunshine's resting body.

Sunshine jumped up. "Rain, you scared the mess out of me!" Sunshine cried through sleepy eyes.

"My bad. Were you 'sleep?" Rain wore a devious smile on her face, because she knew damn well that Sunshine had been asleep. Nevertheless, she was bored and she needed something to do. If Sunshine didn't wake up, Rain would go insane.

Sunshine began slipping away, dozing back off into her comfortable, deep sleep.

"Wake up, dammit! I'm bored," Rain whimpered. Rain began shaking Sunshine's stretched-out body until she was awake and irritable.

"Are you some kind of freak vampire or something? Normal people are all sleeping at this hour. I wish that you would stop waking me up out my sleep during the middle of the night like this."

Rain wasn't trying to hear all that. "Get up and get dressed," Rain ordered.

Sunshine looked at Rain like she was certifiably crazy. "Okay, humor me, Rain. Where could we possibly be going this time of morning, and how do you suppose we're getting there?"

Rain took the stolen keys that sat beside her and dangled them in Sunshine's face.

"How did you get the keys to Cathy's truck?" Sunshine asked in amazement.

"Trust, it wasn't hard. So, what's up? It's still early on my block. You trying to go for a ride or what?" Rain was wide awake and obviously on a mission.

"Rain, that wouldn't be right. I mean, Cathy would hurt us if she found out," Sunshine said.

"That's why she's not going to find out. Now stop acting like a goodie-goodie all your life and bring out the gangsta that's dying to get out of you, boo. You know you from the hood just like me, and ain't nobody from the hood that damn innocent."

Sunshine was insulted, but she wasn't going to fall for Rain's elementary reverse psychology. "Okay, you're right. I may have come from the hood, but that doesn't mean that I have to have a hood rat mentality," Sunshine said in defense of herself. "I can't just sneak behind Cathy's back and ride around in her truck without her permission, and you shouldn't either. Cathy's got big love for me and you, and you shouldn't take advantage of her like that. You make me

wonder what you would do behind my back if
you go out like that."

Rain's shoulders began to droop. The exciting
vision of joyriding with Sunshine was slowly
disappearing, while pastor Sunshine's preaching
began to sink in.

"See, I told your ass you were a goodie-goodie.
I'll put the damn keys back, but don't think I'm
soft . . . and I'm still bored."

"Do some jumping jacks, crazy," Sunshine
joked.

Cathy was on her way to check on Sunshine
and Rain before she went to bed for the night. As
she approached Sunshine's door, she could hear
Rain's voice. She was about to open the door to
see why they were still awake, when she heard
Rain asking Sunshine to go out for a ride. Cathy
stopped to make sure she was hearing her correctly. After listening to their entire conversation,
Cathy was pleased with Sunshine for not taking
the bait, and for actually talking some sense into
Rain's knuckle head. Cathy was even happy that
Rain had backed out and took Sunshine's advice.

Cathy tiptoed back downstairs to her bedroom,
remembering the days when she used to steal
her own mother's Buick to go out and visit her

first love. They would ride around all night long until the gas ran out, and they would have to bum some gas money to fill the tank back to where her mother had left it. Cathy smiled as she thought about the many nights they had used the back seat of the Buick to make love until it was time to take him home, usually just before the sun came up.

Those were the days. Cathy laughed to herself.

Cathy climbed into her bed and pretended to be sleeping when Rain safely brought her keys back downstairs and put them on her dresser where she had gotten them.

I have got to remember to find a new spot for my key ring.

The next morning, Sunshine awoke before Rain. She went to her bathroom to wash her face. She applied the apricot cleansing scrub to her face and let it sit while she washed away her morning breath. After rinsing away the mask and dabbing a hand towel over her face to dry, she was ready to face the day.

Still wearing her night clothes, she walked down the hallway to check on Rain. Rain was still knocked out in a heavy-duty sleep. Sunshine was tempted to harass Rain like she had done to her just a few hours ago.

Scratch that. Rain is one evil queen when she first wakes up in the morning.

Sunshine closed Rain's door behind her and went downstairs to bum-rush Cathy. She knew that Cathy would be awake. When she got to Cathy's room, however, she noticed that the door was closed and locked. Cathy hadn't started locking her door until Rain had come to live with them. Since the episode that happened last night, Sunshine could understand why.

Where could she be? Sunshine wondered. *Maybe she's just sleeping. I won't disturb her.*

Sunshine walked into the kitchen to start breakfast and noticed a note lying on the dining room table.

> *Good morning, girls.*
> *I hove some very important business to take care of. I will be gone for most of the day. There's plenty of food for you, so eat up. I wanted to wake you, but you were both sleeping so peacefully I didn't want to disturb you. Sure you guys weren't up all night taking the truck for a spin? Because you were sleeping kind of heavy! Just kidding. Any who, I'll be back this*

evening. Call my cell if you need me. I left fifty dollars for both of you inside the envelope. Don't spend it all in one place.

Hugs & Kisses, Cathy

Cathy worried Sunshine sometimes. She was always doing something on business, or being extremely secretive while on her cell phone talking business.

Sunshine went to the fridge and took out some eggs, cheese, and corned beef hash. She whipped up a quick breakfast for two, as she knew that Rain would be awakening soon.

As soon as the thought crossed her mind, Rain dragged herself into the kitchen.

"Well, hello, Miss One-o'clock-in-the-morning, wanna hang out in the hood and party like a big girl all night but can't even wake up," Sunshine greeted.

"Wuz up," Rain said, barely hearing Sunshine and barely awake. Somehow the smell of breakfast had made her get up from her comfort zone and sleepwalk her way to the kitchen. "What are we eating?" Rain asked.

"Breakfast," Sunshine answered. Sunshine set both plates on the table and poured two glasses of Welch's grape juice.

Sunshine noticed Rain waking up a little more with every bite she took. She slid Cathy's letter to her to read when she felt as though she was coherent enough to comprehend.

Rain read the letter.

"Okay, so where's the money?" she asked once she was done.

Sunshine handed Rain her half of the money.

"My girl is having a cookout today down at Anacostia Park. Everybody under the sun who got it going on in D.C. is going to be there. She throws the gig every year, and every year it gets better and better. You trying to go with me?" Rain asked.

Sunshine was quiet. She did not know how to tell Rain without offending her that no freaking way on this green earth would she go to S.E. without a bulletproof vest and a grenade or some form of protection. Sunshine also knew that she wouldn't be comfortable hanging out with Rain's clique. She enjoyed hanging out with Rain on a solo tip, but to be exposed to a whole slew of Rain's crew in one gathering was way out of her league.

"I know that look, Ms. Sunshine. You had better change it, 'cause yo' ass is going. So you might as well go upstairs, get your stinky butt in the shower, and throw on something fly, 'cause we way up in there. You hear me?"

"Well, then in that case, I'd better carry some mace," Sunshine joked.

"Stop faking, Sunshine. If you scared, say you scared," Rain said.

"I'm scared," Sunshine cried.

After breakfast, Rain put in a Tae Bo DVD. She and Sunshine did a thirty-minute workout, and afterward, they hit the showers.

After her shower, Rain charged into Sunshine's room while she was still wrapped up in her towel, busy oiling down her body.

"Damn, phatty girl, you looking mighty sexy. You need some assistance with that oil?" Rain asked jokingly.

"Yes, you can help me. Can you please hand me my Victoria's Secret right there beside you on the dresser?" Sunshine pointed toward her perfume.

Rain tossed the small bottle over to Sunshine. "It ain't nothing secret about that body," Rain said while walking toward Sunshine's closet.

Rain had seen Sunshine undressed and naked on many occasions, and even Michael Jackson would agree that Sunshine had a lethal body. It didn't get better than Sunshine. However, strangely enough, Rain didn't look at Sunshine like that for real. She played and joked with her every now and then, but actually, she looked at Sunshine more like a sister.

Sunshine was very much aware of Rain's bisexuality. Even though she seemed to have a bigger crush on guys, females were certainly not excluded from the picture. Rain played with her often, but Sunshine was fully secure in her own heterosexuality and understood that it was all in fun, so she didn't get all uptight about it. Most times, she would have fun playing along with her.

Rain loved to borrow Sunshine's clothes, because her selection was unlimited. Her gear was on Trina or Eve's level, nothing but the real McCoy. Rain couldn't wait until her own closet was filled with the finer things.

Sunshine was way ahead of Rain this time. "Ahem." Sunshine cleared her throat and pointed to her never-worn Apple Bottom capri set that she had laid out for Rain to wear.

Rain looked over at the outfit and was completely satisfied with it. "You see why I love you? I'm gonna be the tightest one in the piece." Rain ran off to get dressed.

SEVEN

The yellow cab dropped Rain and Sunshine off at Rain's friend Miami's house. Miami lived two blocks over from where Rain used to live with her family. As the cab rode past her old apartment, Rain wanted to point it out to Sunshine. However, looking at the run-down building now secured by pipeheads and dopefiends brought negative feelings of shame and embarrassment. Sunshine might not be able see past the basics; she might not understand that once upon a time, this building meant everything to Rain.

Tears came to Rain's eyes as she remembered how it used to be. This was where she had lost her mother, her father, and in a way, Jody and Jerome too.

"Hey, are you all right?" Sunshine asked Rain noticing her red, watery eyes.

Rain rubbed her eyes to push back the load of tears that wanted so anxiously to fall, so they wouldn't make her seem childish or weak. She was far from weak and didn't want Sunshine to get the wrong impression.

"Yeah, girl, but what you do, pour the whole damn bottle of Victoria's Secret on? My eyes are burning."

Sunshine sucked her teeth. "Very funny, Rain. I know you not trying to say that my perfume is burning your eyes," Sunshine added.

"Yeah, well, it's either that or you ain't use no kind of soap to wash yo' ass this morning," Rain goofed.

Sunshine landed a playful punch on Rain's shoulder. "Or maybe it's your upper lip," Sunshine said.

"You so played out," Rain said.

Rain hadn't talked to her boo in over a week. She had hoped to see Terrance standing on the corner or at least riding past before Miami answered her door. No such luck. Miami answered the doorbell so quick that Rain thought she had been posted up by the door waiting for a piece of action.

"Damn, hood rat, you pressed for company," Rain teased.

Miami's eyes grew wide with excitement. "Hey, hey, beeyatch. I miss yo' ass so much. Shit ain't been the same around here since you rolled. Everybody out here trying to be the baddest bitch. You know what I'm saying? But we the originals; they just carbon copies. You feel me? Ooh, girl, I've got some shit to tell you." Miami was talking a mile a minute with no break for air. She didn't seem to even notice Sunshine.

"Oh, shit, my bad. Who is this fresh meat you got with you?" Miami asked.

"If you would shut the hell up for five seconds I could have been introduced you, mighty mouth. I see you ain't changed," Rain said.

"Not for nobody," Miami added.

"Miami, this is my cousin, Sunshine. Sunshine, this is my ace, Miami."

Sunshine reached out to shake Miami's hand but was left hanging.

"Wuz up, Sunshine? That name is real cute. What, your folks some hippies or some shit like dat?"

"Not even close," Sunshine answered.

"Well, whatever they is, they sho' know how to pick out a fly name. So anyway, Rain, girl, you betta sit down for shit, 'cause I'm 'bout to blow yo' mind."

Rain and Sunshine both sat down on the love seat next to the couch. Miami had their undivided attention.

"Guess who Terrance is fucking?"

Rain's heart dropped somewhere in the basement. Miami didn't wait for her to go get it.

"He fucking wit' Simone."

Rain thought she heard wrong at first. "Excuse me? Say that again."

"You heard me, bitch. *I said,* he fucking wit' Simone."

Rain shook her head. "That's what I thought you said."

Rain could feel a possessed demon rise within her, like it was time to kill. "Miami, don't be lying. I hope you got your facts straight before you be putting some shit out there like that."

"Whatever, Rain. Like you said before, ain't shit changed about me since your ass left the hood. All my shit is still official, and I can prove it."

"Prove it then," Rain said.

Miami left and came back with her cell phone. She dialed a number and put it on speaker phone.

"Hello." Rain recognized the hideous, screeching voice right away.

"Wuz up, Simone? You coming to my cookout today or what?"

"What's up, Mi Mi? You know I'll be there. It wouldn't be right if I didn't show this adorable face up in the place. You know I'm already there," Simone answered.

"Is your baby coming with you?" Miami asked.

"Who, Terrance? His ass went to New York without me last week to visit his sister. He wont be back in town until tomorrow. But that don't stop the show. I'm still gonna party with you."

"A'ight, I'll see you at the park. It starts at two, and we gonna be posted by the big red, white, and blue playground. You won't miss us, 'cause we gonna be *deep!*" Miami said.

"A'ight. Later."

Rain wasn't satisfied. She didn't hear enough evidence. Only thing that was confirmed to her was the simple fact that Simone *assumed* that Terrance was her baby. That didn't necessarily mean that they were fucking, or that Terrance felt the same way.

"That ain't saying nothing to me," Rain said. "You got to come better than that, Miami."

"Oh, yeah? You want better? Wait till we get to the cookout. I'll show yo' ass better."

Rain and Sunshine rode with Miami to the park to help her set up the grills and food. It was noon when they arrived, and the park had already begun to accumulate its Saturday crowd. As Miami drove through the crowded park headed to her destination, she made sure to ride her STS real slow.

"Good God a'mighty, check out the scenery today." Miami didn't hide the fact that she was impressed by all the Escalades riding on spinners, Navigators on 24's, and Tahoes riding on chrome. The way she squealed with every passing ride she liked, Sunshine thought she was having sexual orgasms.

Rain would usually be going crazy with excitement for all the thugged-out dudes and dolled-up ladies who busied themselves by hanging on the side of their booming vehicles, waiting for someone worth their while to put the brakes on for them. Only today, Rain was no longer in the mood to play the dating game. She needed desperately to get down to the bottom of the issue with Terrance and Simone before she would allow herself any fun.

"Sunshine, let me see your phone, boo."

Sunshine obediently unhooked her cell phone from its clip and handed it up to Rain. Rain dialed Terrance's cell number and pushed SEND.

Your call has been forwarded to an automatic voice message system . . .

Click! Rain flipped the phone shut and gave it back to Sunshine without leaving a message.

Sunshine sat in the back seat with a strange feeling in her heart. Something didn't feel right. She wanted nothing more but for her and Rain to jump back in a cab and go anywhere else except for Anacostia Park. Sunshine didn't like Miami, not even a little bit. She was a trouble-maker and an instigator, and now she had gotten Rain all upset about a no-good player.

As the hours passed, Miami's annual cookout became overdosed with people ready to get their party on, their eat on, and their freak on. Good thing she had it at a huge park like this, Sunshine thought, because nobody's backyard could handle all this action, not even Puffy's.

To Sunshine's surprise, she actually found herself having a nice time. She danced to all the songs and ate the best barbecue chicken ever served. She had to lick her fingers after every bite. For some reason, before she got there, she was expecting nothing but fighting, hating, and bullets, but instead, everyone seemed to be fun-ning, playing cards, eating, or getting drunk on the down low, so the cops wouldn't catch them.

Sunshine noticed that even Rain seemed to be having a good time, as she caught up with all her old friends. Maybe she had gotten that player off her brain.

Rain was engaged in a heavy conversation with her friend Andrea about how the twins from Lincoln Heights had gotten shot by the police, when she noticed a silver Acura with midnight-tinted windows. There were hardly any more spaces left, so the Legend parked right in front of two cars, inconveniently blocking them in. Rain recognized the car as being Tammy's, the bitch-ass ringleader of Simone's clique, and Rain's long time rival. Rain could feel her soft brown skin turn red. Andrea must have noticed it too.

"Are you all right, Rain? You don't look so good. We can change the subject if you'd like."

"Naw, I'm good, thanks, but I do gotta step for a minute. I'll holla at you in a little bit."

Simone, Tammy, China, and Damika all piled out of the car, making their unwanted presence known. Rain wanted to charge after Simone and beat her ass, even if it meant getting jumped by her little posse, but she knew it wouldn't be wise to get at her like that, so she had to calm her nerves, humble herself for a minute, and think logically. If she kicked Simone's ass right there, one of them would die, and it was way too many police cruising and too many people to witness.

Rain pushed her way through the heavy crowd and found herself right in front of Simone. She didn't even make eye contact with Tammy or the other two shadows that stood close behind like a pair of pitiful watchdogs.

"What's up, Simone," Rain said with a sly smirk on her face.

Simone rolled her eyes and crossed her arms as if she didn't have time for her visit. All Rain could think was how it was the perfect opportunity to steal Simone a few good times while she wouldn't be able to block the blows.

Calm down, Rain.

"What's up, Rain? Is there some kind of problem?" Tammy asked.

Now Rain looked into the eyes of Tammy and wished that her body had been provided with a poisonous venom that she could sic on her.

"Listen, Tammy, this beef ain't got nothing to do with you—or you, or you," Rain said, pointing and including the others. "This here is between me, Simone, and *my* baby Terrance."

"Your baby? Don't get it twisted, Rain," Simone said with fire in her eyes. "Terrance told me out his own precious lips that you and him are just friends, and that he don't fuck with you like that. Anyway, he's got me now, so he don't need no little girl who's only gonna trick and tease. He needs a duchess like me who's gonna lick and please."

Rain couldn't remember what happened next. She blacked out. She was no longer in control of the situation like she had tried to be. She had hoped that this was all a mistake and they could talk it out like real young ladies, but Simone had just slanted her character. Rain could not feel herself pounding Simone like raw meat. She didn't see the blood that oozed from her nose down into her busted lips while she sat on top of her, forcing her head in the dirt. Simone tried to get up and fight back, but it was useless.

Tammy, China, and Damika started to throw hardcore punches on Rain's back and kick mightily at her sides, but Rain couldn't feel any of it. She was numbed by rage, and Simone was her victim. Rain didn't feel the saliva she spat into Simone's bleeding wounds as a final insult. All she could remember was being pulled back into life and physically dragged off of Simone by nearly a dozen people. One of those people was Sunshine.

"You dirty, filthy, chicken-head *bitch!* Don't you ever lie on *my* nigga again! I will kill you, *bitch!*"

"Knock out!"

"Rain did it again."

"Them hands should be registered."

Rain could hear her friends congratulating her and giving her big props as if she were Layla Ali. However, her mind was not ready to receive the trophy. She still needed to talk to Terrance. She had to know if he fucked with Simone or not.

"Sunshine, let me see your phone again real quick," Rain said through heavy breaths.

"No, Rain, leave him alone. Evidently that guy is no good for you, or anybody, for that matter. He don't know what he wants. He's got two females fighting over him in broad daylight, in a place filled with families, kids, and undercovers, while he's out of town, probably with some other female. So no, I'm not giving you my phone unless you want to call us a cab so we can get out of here, because I'm ready to go."

"We're not going home yet. Let's have some more fun first. You know, what we came here for, then later I can get my girl Andrea to take us home."

Rain watched as Simone tried to continue on partying with a damaged face. After twenty minutes of faking, she gave it up and left. Rain figured she was finally too embarrassed by everyone commenting on her face like it was an appalling work of art.

Never once did Simone look in Rain's direction again, nor did Tammy.

That will teach the bitch to mess with another lady's man.

EIGHT

Cathy was ending her phone conversation with Irvin, about to make breakfast, when her doorbell rang. Sunshine and Rain were still sleeping, so she went to answer the door herself. She was stunned to see Brian and his father standing in her doorway with suitcases and tote bags surrounding them. Brian reached out to give Cathy a great big hug.

"Hi, Mama. I'm home."

Cathy didn't return Brian's warm greeting. She held an obvious look of disappointment on her face. She wasn't expecting Brian back home for another two weeks. She looked angrily at Brian, Sr. She tried not to let the irritation be heard in her voice when she found the air to speak.

"What's going on? I wasn't anticipating seeing you this soon."

Brian, Sr. reached for his handkerchief from the left top pocket of his overpriced tuxedo. He began to wipe away the sweat that drizzled down his forehead. The dark, bulky suit he wore didn't agree with the ninety-degree humidity.

"I'm sorry, Cathy. I know I said I would keep him longer, but I'm going to be away for three weeks. I have to go to Chicago for a very important business trip. I don't want to leave Junior at my place alone. I know you understand," Cathy's ex-husband said.

"What do you mean *alone?*" Cathy asked. "Brian is old enough to take care of himself."

Brian, Sr. gave Cathy a pathetic look, like he wasn't trying to hear it. He held his hand up to stop her from saying anything further. "Cathy, you need to stop being like this when it comes to our son. This is his home, too, and you act as if you don't want him in it."

Brian, Jr. looked at his parents and knew a serious argument was brewing. He picked up a handful of his luggage and switched his ass up to his bedroom.

Cathy shook her head with pity as Junior walked past her. She was disgusted by the way he sported his tight muscle shirt tied up in the back in a rolled-up bun, and the pink spandex tights he wore defined more ass than she had.

She turned back to her ex-husband. "So, I guess he doesn't just act like a bitch now, but he dresses like one too? What else has changed about our son since he's been with you?" Cathy asked sardonically.

Brian rolled his eyes to the ceiling. "Cathy, you really need to come to terms with the fact that our son is gay. I mean, come on. How do you think I feel about this? My only son is walking around like he's my only daughter. But the way I see it is like this: Things could be much worse."

"It doesn't get any worse!" Cathy interrupted. "If it was meant for me to have a daughter, I would have given birth to one with a real pussy!" Cathy was getting very upset and didn't realize that she was screaming.

"Speaking on that, Junior is taking hormone pills. He wants to enhance his body," Brian, Sr. said casually.

Cathy was too through. "And who in the hell paid for that shit, Brian? I suppose you, right? Is that what you work so hard for? To turn our son into a real live girl?" Cathy was now fully aware that she was screaming at the top of her lungs, but she didn't give a fuck.

Brian, Sr. turned away from Cathy and headed for the door. Before he walked out, he looked back at Cathy sympathetically and said, "No matter what, that's our son. He came out of your body, and you have to love him regardless. Let that boy be who he is."

"Now you talking gay, nigga!" Cathy yelled, but she was screaming to his back.

Suddenly Cathy wasn't in the mood to make breakfast anymore. She grabbed the keys to her truck, and with only her housecoat and slippers on, she stormed out of the house, slamming the door to go for a refreshing morning drive, something she loved to do when things were heavy on her mind.

Rain awoke from her asleep from all the loud yelling that was coming from downstairs. She could now feel the pain from the punches that were dealt to her during the fight yesterday. It took her a minute before she realized where she was, as she still felt drowsy. However, when she looked around at her laid-out domain, it all came back to her. She was at home.

Rain was still half sleep and couldn't make out everything that was being said. She could hear the strong voice of a man, along with Cathy's, but she didn't know who it could be. She knew that Cathy didn't have a man living up in there, so she naturally assumed that it must've been Cathy's mystery date from last night. Rain jumped out of bed and headed downstairs to get a peek.

Everything downstairs was quiet and empty. *Maybe I was just dreaming,* Rain thought. She walked to the refrigerator to see if there was something cold to drink. The fridge was loaded with food, so much so that it was damn near overflowing and hard to keep the fridge door closed.

Rain was tempted to make breakfast the way she used to do back at home for her brothers, but her brothers weren't there with her, so there was no need. A throbbing pain shot through her heart as she thought about Jody and Jerome. Once Cathy got used to her living there and she had charmed her with her winning personality, she would ask her if Jerome could come to stay too. Maybe when Jody came home, he could come to live there, too, and they could all be together again.

Rain took a glass from the cupboard and poured herself some orange juice. When she closed the refrigerator door, she almost spilled her OJ when she saw a tall, shapely *shim* standing directly in front of her.

"Damn! You scared the shit out of me," Rain said to the stranger. Rain immediately noticed the boy's budding breasts and protruding hips. His shape was *almost* as ripped as hers.

He had soft, jet-black hair styled just like Betty Boop's. The ol' boy was gorgeous. If it weren't for his fat dick print that bulged from his colorful spandex, Rain would have been certain that he was a female.

"Who are you?" Rain asked.

Brian extended his long, slim fingers out to Rain. She shook the big, brown hand that felt like it could tight-grip a Mack truck with little effort. He spoke in a soft, delicate voice, like Michael Jackson.

"My name is Brian, but you can call me Brianna." It was official; this dude was a big bowl of sugar.

"What's up, Brian? My name is Rain." Rain observed that Brian had a striking resemblance to Cathy. "Are you related to Cathy?" Rain asked.

"You could say that. I'm her son," Brian said. He spoke proudly, with his hand on his hip and his breasts in the air.

Rain admired his sexy, high-yellow cleavage and wondered where he got it from.

"Where is Cathy?" Rain asked.

"I don't know. She hauled ass out of here when I got here. You must be a new girl," Brian stated.

"Yeah," Rain said.

"Well, you'll like it here, and I know you'll like my mother. She'll love you back and treat you like a princess as long as you're straight. My moms don't play that gay shit. That is why she don't mess with me like that. I don't trip about it, though. I figure if I give her some time to accept the new me, she'll come around just like my pops did."

Rain didn't feel comfortable with getting so down and personal with Cathy's son-slash-daughter, and she was relieved when she saw Sunshine appear in the kitchen.

The room got quiet for a moment while Sunshine and Brian sized each other up. Brian spoke up and broke the spell first.

"Mama surely got some beautiful girls living up in here this time. Where y'all come from, a teen pageant?" He didn't take a breath to let them answer the question. "Y'all lucky I'm into my own kind, 'cause if I wasn't, y'all would be on the top of my hit list." Brian placed one hand on his hip and stood in a sassy position with one hip out. "But I like mines like you like yours'—precious, packing, and paid."

Rain studied Brian real hard and tried to picture him as a boy, but it was pointless. His facial features were so appealing and perfect that even if he didn't dress fem, people would still call him a pretty boy.

Sunshine walked to the fridge to get herself something to drink.

"Rain, was that you I heard arguing earlier?" Sunshine asked while taking a seat at the table next to Rain.

"No, chile," Brian answered. "That was my moms and my pops. Girl, don't trip off them. They get into it all the time. I think they still love each other, but they don't know how to show it anymore."

Sunshine gave Brian a confused look. Rain explained the situation to her.

"Sunshine, this is Brian, Cathy's son," she said.

Brian looked irritated, "The name's *Bri-an-na*. It ain't hard! Maybe I'll go to the mall and buy me some of them big gold hoop earrings with my name engraved on them so y'all can remember."

Sunshine looked at Brian and could see the resemblance to Cathy. The attitude was different, but he definitely wore strong features of his mother.

"Cathy told me that she had a son, but she didn't mention that he was . . ." Sunshine couldn't get the word out her mouth.

"That I'm gay." Brian said it for her. "Don't be scared to talk, girl. I am what I am, and I don't get mad when I hear the 'g' word. I get pissed when I hear faggot, or fag, or Tinkerbell. That's when the acrylic comes off and the boxing gloves go on. Some haters out there get it twisted, but I'll show them that I was a man before I was a woman, and I can still whoop some ass."

Rain was getting a kick out of Brianna, while Sunshine, on the other hand, was getting a little irritated because he wouldn't shut up. She had never been around a bonafide homosexual before, and she wasn't quit feeling it.

Sunshine turned back to Rain. "Are you okay, mighty woman, 'cause you put your work in yesterday?"

"Yeah, boo, I'm straight," Rain answered.

Sunshine was about to go back upstairs to her room when the phone rang. Brian was standing up against the wall right beside it, so he answered it before Sunshine could.

"House of beauty, cutie on duty, talk dirty to me!"

Sunshine and Rain stared at each other in disbelief. Brian handed the phone over to Sunshine seconds later, wearing a look of dismay. Rain knew it must have been Cathy on the other end by the look on Brian's face. Sunshine grabbed the receiver.

Brian looked at Rain and began chatting again, but this time in a loud whisper.

"Girl, you think I got issues, that woman got more issues than me. Now she trippin' about how I answered her phone. I don't see what the big deal is. It's not like it's a business phone or something. I just like to have fun in my life. You feel what I'm saying girl? Girl, we as women gotta live a little, 'cause your boys is out here to dog us out in some shape, form, or fashion. It could be our fake-ass friends, our so-called family, or our unfaithful niggas, so shit, we gotta live for us."

Rain was speechless. In a crazy sort of way, he was making sense.

Sunshine hung up the phone feeling fortunate to have missed the words that fell from Brian's lips. She could understand why he annoyed Cathy.

"Cathy said for us not to worry about making any breakfast. She's at the Waffle and Pancake House ordering some breakfast sandwiches."

"Good, 'cause I'm starving," Brian said.

"Rain, she said she's going to take us to the mall to go shopping, so you can get some more things that you need. She's going to give us some money and drop us off," Sunshine said.

"She's going to let us shop by ourselves?" Rain asked excitedly.

"I'll go with y'all," Brian said with no hesitation.

"She's gonna drop us off in VA. She's got some business to take care of out there, and when she's done, she's gonna come back to get us."

"Sounds like a plan!" Brian shouted eagerly. "I better switch up my gear. I can't book no honeys with this raggedy shit on." Brian marched upstairs with Rain and Sunshine not far behind. Each went into her own room to get dolled up.

By the time Cathy got back with the food, all three had met back up in the kitchen. Brian was back to dominating a conversation when Cathy stepped into the kitchen. Cathy looked at the girls dressed all fly and felt the sudden urge to go and freshen up herself.

Sunshine and Rain looked drop dead gorgeous, both rocking brand new outfits. Brian was unrecognizable, and honestly speaking, looked better than Sunshine and Rain put together, which wasn't an easy task.

Brian had on a hot pink, tight mini-skirt with a sheer hot pink top. His makeup was soft and natural, with a hint of pink eye shadow above his eyelids. His pink lip-gloss out-shined his sparkling diamond earrings. The pink outfit he wore brought out his flawless, high-yellow skin that he had inherited from Cathy herself. He was a beautiful redbone. He had even strapped his dick down, or whatever he did to put it away. Thank God Cathy couldn't see his print.

"Pick your jaw up from off the floor, Mama," Brian said jokingly. "Yes, it's me, your son, *Brianna.*"

Cathy straightened up real quick. "Watch your mouth, dammit! And your name is *Bri-an.* I should know. I carried your ass for nine fuckin' months and named you," Cathy stated.

"So, Mama, which mall we going to out in VA, Landmark or Pentagon City?" Brian spoke as if Cathy didn't just carry the shit out of him.

"Who in the hell said you were going?" Cathy asked.

"Please, Mama, I got my own money, and I'm trying to get these Donna Karan leather heels they got at Nordstrom's for half-price," Brian begged.

Cathy ignored Brian. She walked away from him, embarrassed and disgusted. She couldn't believe that her son wanted her to take him to the mall to buy some fucking stilettos. It took all of Cathy's energy not to unleash a can of whoop-ass on Brian and beat all that bitch out of him. Instead, she went into her room before shit got ugly.

Cathy could remember when Brian was nine years old, playing football for the regional recreation center. He was a one-hundred-percent all-natural young thug back then. That following year, when he turned ten, one of his bisexual teammates must have turned him out in the locker room, because that's when Brian started switching up. All of a sudden, he didn't want to play football anymore. He became more interested in going shopping with her, or watching her intently as she put on her makeup.

At first, Cathy had to admit, she thought it was cute, until one day he came to her dressed up in a pair of her boots and a dress and asked her if he could play in her lipstick. After that incident, Cathy immediately took him off the team and basically kept him isolated. He stayed in the house with no TV or company for a whole month.

Realizing that wouldn't get him anywhere, she sought help from counselors and psychiatrists. He would meet with doctors twice a week. Her intentions led to nothing but a waste of time and a waste of money. After constant evaluation, it was told to her that he was just going through a phase. So far, that phase had lasted for more than eight years.

Cathy slammed her door and tried to clear the vision of her son wearing hot pink and focus on getting dressed. She had a major deal she was working on, and if all went well, she would be the first female millionaire playing the game on her side of town. This deal meant more to Cathy than just money; it meant an early retirement. She would get out of the business for good and invest a decent portion of her earnings on stocks and bonds for Sunshine to cash in later in her life. Some of the money would go to charity and church, and she would buy and build a phat-ass estate in Barbados, a place where she liked to vacation regularly. Cathy had major plans, and she didn't need added stress. She was a businesswoman above all else, and she needed to focus on her business.

Sunshine and Rain were fully aware of the fact that Cathy didn't have much love for Brian a.k.a. Brianna. Neither Sunshine nor Rain knew who to comfort first: poor Cathy who wanted her son to be a man, or poor Brian, who wanted Cathy to understand him.

Brian dug into the large bag of fast food and pulled out three steak, egg, and cheese bagels.

Watching Brian move about, seemingly unfazed by his own mother's behavior, made Rain feel even sorrier for him. He acted as if he was used to Cathy's mental torture.

Brian took a giant-sized bite out of his sandwich and noticed that Rain and Sunshine weren't eating. They sat at the dining room table staring into space like they were smacked.

"Y'all girls gonna have some of this good food? 'Cause I will demolish all this." Brian spoke with a mouth full of food.

Rain and Sunshine reluctantly reached into the huge bag of food and slowly took out their bagels as if someone had forced them to eat. Although they were both hungry, their minds weren't on the food.

Brian playfully snatched both sandwiches from each girl's hand. "Hmmph, y'all faking like somebody got a gun to y'all head, making y'all eat this shit. Shiiit . . . give it to me then, 'cause if y'all didn't know, I still eat like a man."

Sunshine launched out of her chair first, laughing and trying to snatch her bagel from his clutches at the same time.

Brian held the food way up to the ceiling with his stretched arm, singing, "Nanny, nanny, boo, boo."

Rain watched for a minute as Sunshine struggled to free her meal from the palms of Brian. No longer able to resist the tussle, she stood up to help. Rain climbed on the kitchen chair and tried to pull his lengthy arms down, using all her strength. She was no match for him. Brian whisked her away from the chair, dangling her in midair.

Rain screamed with laughter. "Put me down right now!" She would have let go; however, she was afraid that she might break one of the heels on her shoes when she landed.

Sunshine began to tickle him to see if he'd give up.

"Oh, puh-leez, girl. What's that gonna do, excite me?" Brian said mockingly.

Finally, Brian put Rain down and handed his opponents their food. He was pleased to see smiles on their faces.

"Now we're speaking the same language. Let's eat," Brian ordered.

Rain was out of breath from all her squealing and kicking. "Damn, this dude is strong as shit," she said.

Brian looked offended. "Who are you calling a dude?" He put his food down, reached over, and pretended as if he was going to put Rain back up in the air. Rain went back to her kicking and screaming.

"Nooo!" she yelled. "Okay, I'm sorry. I'm sorry! What I meant to say was this *bitch* is strong as shit."

"That's more like it," Brian said, satisfied.

Cathy came out fully dressed and with a new attitude to match. "You all sound like you're killing each other in here."

Of course, Brian had to speak up and give an explanation first. "Everything is cool now, Mama. I just had to show your new girls who's boss around here."

"Yeah, whatever," Rain said, sucking her teeth.

"Well, all of you look very lovely today. Try not to hurt 'em too bad," Cathy said.

The girls looked around at each other in amazement. No one could believe that the mega-beast, Cathy, had just fed her son a girly compliment.

Brian urgently ran over to his mother's rescue. He began to fan her with his napkins. "Sit down, Mama. It's gonna be all right. Take deep breaths." He rushed Cathy over to sit at the dining room table.

"Sunshine, you get her some cold water. Rain, you dial 911!"

"Boy, get off of me," Cathy said while she picked herself up from the chair. She couldn't help but laugh at Brian's crazy ass. "Is everybody ready to leave? Because I got to go," Cathy said.

"Yes, master, we's ret' to go, master. Can we's sit in the seats today, master, instead of in the trunk, master?" Brian kidded.

Everyone shared a laugh at Brian, who was so full of life and so full of jokes.

NINE

The warm summer breeze felt as if it were seducing Cathy's skin. It was so refreshing that she chose not to turn the A.C. on, and rode with the windows down. Brian, who sat in the back where the wind came blowing in full effect, had a hissy fit. Regrettably for Rain, she had to sit in the back with him, and so she got to hear all his bitching.

"Damn, Mama got all the windows down like we joy-riding in the country," Brian whined. "By the time we get all the way to V.A., my Betty Boop 'do gonna look like a Betty Blip don't." Brian tossed and turned in the leather seat to try to save his hair. Rain was relieved when he finally settled in a fetal position, because it kept him quiet for the moment.

Rain looked up front and noticed that Cathy and Sunshine were holding hands. A slight twinge of jealousy stung her right in the heart, but she realized how ridiculous she was being and let the bruise heal. She had to talk some sense into her head.

Look, Rain, you can't be hating on these folks you only been kicking it with for a few weeks, she told herself.

She began to bob her head to old school jams that played on the radio. As promised, Cathy dropped the girls off at Pentagon City. She gave Sunshine eight hundred dollars to spend. Rain got fifteen hundred, and she even gave Brian a grand. Rain totaled the full amount up in her head and got a sum of $3,300. She couldn't believe that Cathy had just dished out so much cash as if it was nothing. Rain didn't care anymore how Cathy was able to afford to give out that much money. She was just happy that she was sharing the wealth. Rain had never been in possession of this much money in her life. The most she ever held was the twenty-dollar bill that her father had given her to go to the store for groceries.

Cathy rushed them out of the truck, saying she had to hurry up so she could get to her appointment.

Rain couldn't wait to see what Bebe and Victoria's Secret had on their racks that would soon bless her closet. She was even anxious to see what the Gap had. Hell, she wasn't too good to shop for a good bargain just because she had a hefty bankroll.

Sunshine was also excited to have some extra spending money, but she had already accumulated enough attire to last her the rest of the year. She would pick up only a few items just for the heck of it.

Brian was eager to go to Nordstrom to get his new shoes.

They had three hours to shop before Cathy would be back to pick them up at the same entrance where she had dropped them off. When they got inside the mall, it was hard for any of them to focus on shopping right away. The shopping center was filled with top-flight niggas of all flavors. There were chocolate niggas, raspberry niggas, vanilla niggas, and even butter pecan niggas. . . . *Mmm, delicious.*

"Damn, I am in stiff-dick heaven. God help me!" Brian blurted out.

"Calm down, Brianna. You wouldn't want to arouse anything," Sunshine teased while pointing toward his manhood.

"Oh, girl, you real funny, but I got that thang tucked away and sealed so tight, it's gonna take me two whole days to peel all the duct tape off," Brian shot back

"Ouch!" Rain said. "That is too much info."

"You'll be all right," Brian consoled.

Brian led the way to the first stop, his long-awaited destination. All the men were feigning predators as Sunshine, Rain, and Brianna strolled past them, although Brian was getting the most play. Three fine-ass dudes walked past, sweating them, and turned back around to get a glance at Brian's ass. It was as if Sunshine and Rain were invisible walking beside Brian.

"If only these fellas knew what we know," Rain whispered to Sunshine.

"Damn, red!" one loud-mouth screamed out at Brian. "Yo, shorty in the pink, can I holla at you for a minute?'"

Sunshine turned around first to see the nuisance who was doing all the yelling. She was surprised to see that the pest was actually very handsome. She tapped Brian on the shoulder.

"Hey, Brianna, he's actually somewhat cute."

Brian looked back to see the truth for himself. Big-mouth got excited when he noticed Brian checking him out, and walked over to him.

"Damn, all three of y'all fine as hell. It's almost hard to choose, but I got to say that Big Red, you got it going on. So what's up? Can I take you out later?"

Brian stared at lover boy for a moment, checking him out. His instincts told him that this man was as straight as a hard-on. "You don't want it," Brian said, trying to warn the brother.

The man grabbed Brian by the hands. "Listen to me, baby girl. I know what I want and when I want it, and right now, I want you."

"You listen to me, boo. You fine as wine, and I would love to make you mine, but right now is not the time, 'cause you got my game messed up," Brian said.

Sunshine looked at Brian and wondered if he was getting ready to share with this guy that she was really a he.

"Step over here to the side with me, Mr. Biggs. I want to explain something to you," Brian said. "If you down with it, then we cool, but if you not, then I ain't got nothing but love for you," he added.

The boy had a smile as big as Texas. He must have thought his game was wrapped so tight that he was about to get those digits.

Brian and his new friend left Rain and Sunshine standing side by side with his two homies left behind. The bamas didn't even attempt to make the slightest conversation with Rain or Sunshine.

Faking like they all that, Rain thought.

"I guess we just chopped liver. Look at them two jokers. They just standing there waiting like two flunkies," Rain whispered.

"You're just mad because they're not trying to get at us," Sunshine replied.

All of a sudden, they heard a loud gagging sound as if someone were severely choking. Rain and Sunshine both focused their attention back over to Brian and his new friend. His new friend was bent over, vomiting right there in the middle of the mall, all over the floor. Customers walking past pinched their noses shut in an effort to avoid the hideous smell.

Brian casually strutted his stuff back over to Rain and Sunshine. He wiped some imaginary dust off his hands and said, "Well, my work here is done."

Sunshine asked first, "What happened, Brianna? Did you tell him?"

Sunshine and Rain were both anxious to hear the scoop. Brian was straightforward as he filled them in. "Yeah, I told slim that I'm a transsexual, and like I said, he couldn't handle it."

Within an hour of their shopping spree, the girls had collected dozens of shopping bags from all the hottest stores. It became difficult for them to walk around comfortably with all the bags.

Sunshine was beginning to feel ridiculous walking around like a bag lady. They couldn't even get into a store good without a sales rep demanding for them to check in their bags for security reasons. Since Cathy wasn't due back for another two hours, Sunshine suggested that they each take turns watching the bags at the food court, while the other two continued on shopping. She knew how much more important it was for Rain to get her shopping done, and how crucial it was for Brian to get his ho stroll on, so Sunshine opted to go first. They helped Sunshine to the bottom level to the food court with all the bags, and then rushed off to go commit some more diva damage.

Sunshine situated the bags so that they wouldn't look so sloppy and thrown around everywhere. She placed them all underneath the table so they wouldn't be in anyone's way walking past. She kept one bag out that she had purchased from a small bookstand, and took out her new book by Nikki Turner. She was about to begin reading when she felt someone tap her gently on her shoulder. Sunshine knew that it couldn't be Rain or Brian, as she would have heard them coming a mile away. Besides, only ten minutes had passed since they left.

Sunshine turned around to find out who her mystery guest was, but the person quickly covered her eyes and said in a disguised voice, "Guess who?"

Sunshine couldn't make out the voice. All her possibilities were either on the top level shopping, or out at an appointment taking care of important business. Sunshine found herself getting excited by this elementary game.

"Give me a hint," she said.

"I am tall, fine, and plan to make Sunshine all mine."

"Wow," Sunshine said. "You're a poet, too, but I'm totally clueless."

The soft pair of hands released themselves from embracing Sunshine's eyes, and the mystery man exposed himself. Sunshine was thrilled to see her dance partner from Royals.

"That's a shame you don't know who your future man is," Diego said, smiling.

Sunshine was smiling too. "I see you're way ahead of the game," she replied.

"If I play the game right, I might win," Diego said.

Sunshine felt herself being eaten alive by Diego's boyish charm.

"I'm going to order some bourbon chicken with rice. Would you like to have lunch with me?" Diego asked.

Sunshine hadn't eaten anything besides that breakfast bagel earlier, and she was feeling famished.

'I'll have what you're having, with an ice tea," she said, accepting his offer. Sunshine reached into her MCM bag and pulled a ten-dollar bill out.

Diego held up his hand in protest. "Please don't insult me. Put your money away, I got this."

She gladly put her little money back inside her purse.

Sunshine watched Diego as he walked to the small Chinese cafe. There was nothing thuggish about his style, not in the way he talked or the way he walked, not even the way he dressed. Sunshine adored him. The beige linen shorts and button-up shirt showed him off to be the gentleman that he was. He left Sunshine sitting there dazed, with just the evidence of his presence and the arousing scent of his cologne. While his fragrance lingered on, Sunshine watched him get in the line to pay for their cuisine. He nibbled on a small piece of bourbon chicken sample handed out by a little Chinese woman.

Sunshine was busy trying to take in all the scented air around her when her cell began to vibrate on her hip. She knew without even looking that it was Cathy. With the exception of Ms. Waters, Cathy was the only person with her number. Sunshine rushed to answer, wondering if Cathy was calling to say she'd be back to get them sooner.

"Hi, princess. What are you doing?" Cathy asked.

Sunshine was trying to consider if this was the best time to tell Cathy about Diego. "I'm sitting here, getting ready to have lunch with a friend," Sunshine answered.

"Who? Rain and Brian?" Cathy asked.

Sunshine was getting ready to spill the beans, but the beans came walking back with two trays of food and drinks in his hands. Sunshine would have to tell Cathy about him later on, but for now, she would have to get her off the phone before she started asking too many questions.

"Cathy, what's up? Are you outside waiting?"

"No, pumpkin, I was just calling to check on you and Rain." Cathy had to think for a minute, "Oh, and Brian, but evidently your *friend* must be more important than little ol' me, because you're literally throwing me off the phone. It's all good, though. I'll just pick myself up out the dirt, and I'll be there to pick y'all up in an hour and a half. And we can talk all about your little *friend* then," Cathy added.

"All right, I'll see you then," Sunshine said. "Did you need me to pick something up for you while I'm here?" Sunshine asked.

"Matter of fact, see if you can find me an off white silk blouse. If you see a fly one, buy it and I'll reimburse you when I see you. That will save me a trip to the store," Cathy said.

"I'll see if they have it inside Macy's," Sunshine said.

Sunshine almost felt guilty for the feeling of relief she got when she hung up with Cathy. She was pleased to have Diego all to herself again. But Diego didn't look so happy anymore. His whole demeanor had changed. Sunshine wondered what could have happened that fast to upset him. He wasn't even trying to eat his food that he had just stood in line for an eternity to get.

"Are you all right, Diego?" Sunshine asked.

"I'm cool, baby girl. I just need to ask you something before I even play myself," Diego answered.

"Sunshine, I'm sure you already know that I'm feeling you. I was feeling you that night when you gave me the sexiest slow drag I've ever had. I didn't want it to end, but you weren't feeling well, so I had to let you go. And to keep it real with you, I was feeling you way before that night. I've seen you plenty of times before then, when you came to the restaurant with your mother.

That was just the first time that I worked up the nerve to say something to you. And you were as precious as I dreamed you were."

Diego looked deep into Sunshine's eyes. "Sunshine, I like your style. You seem way different than the other girls I come across. You seem soft and gentle, like an angel. Now, I know you don't know me all that well yet, but you can get to know me. I'll take you out wherever you want to go. We can talk and learn each other until there is nothing left to tell. Then when you're feeling me like I'm feeling you, we can make it happen."

Sunshine felt like warm, gooey honey inside.

Diego continued to speak. "But first, I have to know one thing. Do you already have a man?"

Sunshine was at a loss for words. Diego had just fed her quite a bit of game, and she wasn't sure if she could digest it all.

Diego took Sunshine's hesitation as an answer to his question. "You do have a man, don't you? I should have known that. You're too beautiful not to. Was that him you were just talking to on the phone?" Diego asked.

Now Sunshine understood where all this was coming from. When he walked back over to the table, he must have thought she was hanging up with a boyfriend.

Diego searched Sunshine's face like a lost puppy while he waited for her to say something.

"No, that wasn't my man on my cell phone. That was my mom. And to answer your original question, no, I don't have a man. I don't even have any male friends at all," Sunshine said.

"Except for me," Diego said. He sat up taller in his seat, clearly satisfied with Sunshine's response.

They both began to eat their lunch and held light conversation. Twenty minutes passed, and Diego explained that he had to leave to go and prepare for a show he was performing at Tacoma Station. Sunshine didn't want him to leave. She was enjoying his company so much she felt as though they were the only two in the mall. She could have sat there and just watched him chew his food for the rest of the day. He was so chilled and laid back that Sunshine felt herself falling for him.

He pulled out two tickets to his show and placed them on the table, along with his number. He slid all three items in front of Sunshine and told her that he hoped to see her there.

Rain and Brian finally arrived back at the table with over a dozen more bags. Sunshine only had forty minutes to do the rest of her shopping. Brian sat down in the chair next to Sunshine.

"Girls, I can't take no more. These shoes are killing my pinky toe." He slid off his pumps and let out a loud sigh of relief. "Whew! Y'all go ahead, 'cause this bitch is through."

Sunshine wasn't the least bit disappointed. She'd rather tell Rain about Diego without Brian there anyway. But first, she would have to wait for Rain to finish her own ranting and raving about all the gear she had bought.

They headed up the escalator to the upper level to find Macy's.

"Sunshine, I wiped this muthafuckin' mall out! I can't wait to rock my new dress I got from Bebe. You got to see it, Sunshine. It's silver and it's got rhinestones all over it. Shit, I might even go around the way and flex for all those haters who thought they was better than me. Now I got something to show their ass.

"I also bought this bangin'-ass outfit that would look hittin' on you, too. It's a Donna Karan spandex dress. I got the black one. I want you to get the brown one," Rain said with excitement.

"But where are we going to wear a tight, hoochie mama dress like that?" Sunshine asked.

"I don't know. We'll figure that part out later, but believe me, that dress was meant to be a part of this body."

All of a sudden, Sunshine's instincts automatically went into overdrive. "I do know this one spot we could wear the dresses to."

"What you holding back for? Let a sister know what's up," Rain said.

Sunshine pulled out the two tickets that Diego had given her and flashed them in Rain's face. Rain snatched the tickets out of her hands with excitement. She anxiously read over the tickets to see who was playing. Rain's expression became sour as she recognized the band's name.

"That's weak, Sunshine. I thought you had something good for us like Method Man, or Red Man. Shit, I'd even settle for Juwanna Mann, but Swift Beats? No, thank you," Rain said. "That's the band that played at Royals, the one your boy play for? No disrespect, but guess what? They suck." Rain was only keeping it real with Sunshine.

Sunshine was still determined to go, and Rain was the only person she knew that she could go with, and she would only go if Rain went. Cathy was too old to party with her, so that was out of the question, and Brian might start his own show with his boisterous ways and nonstop talking about everything. There was only one thing left for Sunshine to do: Size it up.

"Well, I guess I have to go and show off my new Donna Karan dress for all those ballers all by my lonesome," Sunshine said in the best pitiful voice she could find.

"Ballers? Did I hear somebody say ballers?" Rain said, feeding into Sunshine's playful deceit. "You are real slick, Sunshine, but I like your style. That's what's up. We way up in Tacoma Station tonight. You hear me?"

Sunshine followed as Rain led the way to the infamous Donna Karan dress that Rain couldn't stop singing about. Sunshine almost reconsidered when the cashier gave her the total amount of two hundred dollars, but Rain wouldn't let her leave the store without buying the dress. Rain even put up forty dollars of her own stash so that Sunshine would get the dress.

Afterward, they went to Macy's to purchase a silk blouse for Cathy. The shirt totaled up to be eighty-nine dollars. Sunshine was now left with a little over two hundred dollars. So much for her idea of light shopping. She bought a pair of gold hoop earrings that she got on sale, and a gold anklet with dangling stars. She also bought a pair of brown leather stilettos, with fishnet stockings that went perfectly with her new dress. She was going to make sure that she looked her absolute best for Diego tonight.

Sunshine and Rain were having so much fun shopping, that they had almost lost track of the time.

"Oh, shit. We gotta get back before Cathy mess around and leave our asses," Rain said with urgency.

When they got down to the food court, Brian had his long, yellow legs spread even in one chair, sleeping with his head leaned back in another chair. Sunshine and Rain looked at the emptiness that surrounded him and couldn't believe their eyes. All their bags were gone; not a single one left. Even the book that Sunshine had left on the table was missing. Rain got hysterical.

"Brianna, wake up! Wake up!" Rain was shaking the life out of Brian.

Brian finally woke up, about to go hysterical himself. "Oh my God, girl. What? What's wrong? Why are you shaking me so hard? You trying to traumatize the ol' girl?" Brian put his hand up over his heart as if he were trying to stop it from beating out of his chest. "Why y'all looking all crazy and deranged like that? What's up? Y'all ready to go?"

"Ready to go? Look around you, dammit! All our bags are gone, Brianna, and you're lying here sleeping like a Gerber baby while somebody done stole all our shit!" Rain yelled.

Brian looked around him and saw nothing but a bunch of suspicious-looking customers eating their food. Everybody looked iffy.

"Oh my God! I can't believe this shit!" Brian yelled. "Which one of y'all muthafuckers stole my shit? Y'all broke muthafuckin' hoes couldn't afford to buy your own shit, so y'all come around taking other people's shit!" Brian was yelling at any and all customers within his shouting range. "All y'all some broke-down bitches! If I catch one of y'all stupid bitches wearing my shit, I'm going to kick all y'all bitch asses just like y'all stole somethin'!" Brian was yelling so loud that he was scaring the innocent babies sitting in their strollers. Some patrons left with a quickness, afraid Brian might pull out a gun on them during his outrageous temper tantrum.

Security eventually had to come and escort Brian out of the mall. Unfortunately, that didn't stop Brian from going off on them too.

"And look at these RoboCops. Who in the fuck do you think you are? I know one damn thing: You better not put your fucking hands on me. I don't need no help walking my ass out your stankin' mall! And where the hell was your rent-a-cop ass at while they were stealing all my shit, huh?" Brian was on a rampage. Rain tried to calm him down, but he wouldn't even hear her.

All he heard was himself, yelling and blaming the security guards when it was really his fault.

Once they got to the exit, Sunshine noticed them first—the Virginia County Police, standing right outside the exit. They looked serious, as if they were ready to lock anybody up who decided to act a fool or even looked like one. Sunshine knew from watching the news that Virginia didn't take no mess. The predominantly Caucasian native state was filled with wealthy, high-society people, and they would go out of control if the law didn't handle their business. Even the smallest issues became a major deal.

Sunshine tapped Brian on his shoulder and pointed in the direction of the law enforcement. Brian paused in mid-sentence for a moment, looked at the police, then back at Sunshine with little interest.

"And! So what? RoboCop called his pappy and folks. They can't do shit to this ol' girl, 'cause I ain't do shit. If anything, they owe me an explanation. I come all the way the fuck out here to Crackerville to spend my money and make their community richer, and all I got to show for it is this fake-ass security all up my ass! They got the game messed up. I wish they would come at me wrong. I'll sue the hell out of this whole state and own Pentagon City. You hear me?"

Sunshine gave up. There was nothing that could calm Brian down right now.

Sunshine was pleased when they got outside and she saw Cathy's truck parked alongside the police. Cathy ran over to the chaotic scene with a quickness when she noticed her girls and Brian being escorted out by security.

"What's going on here? What's wrong? Where are the rest of your bags? I left you here for three hours. I know you bought more than that," Cathy said.

"Mama, can you believe that somebody got us for all our shit?" Brian screamed.

"Watch your mouth!" Cathy screamed back.

"I'm sorry, Mama, but I'm blow right now. A lady can't close her eyes for one second without getting jacked for her brand new gear in broad daylight."

Officer Friendly interrupted Brian before he went into yet another frenzy. "Excuse me, ma'am. Are these young ladies your daughters?"

Cathy looked at Brain with curiosity for a moment, and then answered. "Yes, officer, these are my two and a half daughters."

The officer didn't catch the hint of sarcasm that Cathy threw when she answered, but Rain and Sunshine did.

"Well, ma'am, unless they want to file a complaint about their missing items, I'm going to have to ask them to leave. They are causing a disturbance and scaring all the shoppers," the officer said.

"The shoppers are scaring me," Brian said, obviously not afraid to speak up, even in front of the police.

Cathy was getting nervous. She thought about what was in the back of her trunk. She was dirty, riding around with a half kilo and over fifty thousand dollars in cash. Brian was running his mouth like a bitch and making her shit hot. She had to get away from this side of town real quick, before Brian caused any more trouble.

Cathy turned on her charm, speaking with her most soft, sensual voice and staring seductively into the officer's eyes. "No, thank you, officer. We won't be filling out any reports. All that stuff is materialistic. I'm more than sure that we will be blessed with more material things," Cathy said and turned to leave. "Now, come on, Sunshine, Rain, and Brian. Let's go."

The officer looked confused when Cathy used Brian's real name. Besides his partners, he didn't see any other males present.

Oh, well, he thought. He wouldn't worry about that. He was just pleased to be sending those troublemaking black folk back to the ghetto that they came from. If the tall, light-skinned girl with the big ass and the big mouth continued running her trap, he would have locked all their asses up, and who felt like going through all that paperwork?

Sayonara, you black bitches. The officer waved a fake army salute to Cathy as she backed her SUV away from the scene and back onto the highway. If he hadn't been so lazy, he could have had the biggest bust of his career.

Cathy was relieved to be back on I-495 and on the way home. Her whole operation and all she had worked for was about to be put on the line because of Brian. But there was no need in getting in his shit now. It was all over, thank God.

Cathy looked at Sunshine, who looked to be a little upset herself about the whole thing. "So I suppose you don't have my shirt?" Cathy asked, being funny.

"Actually, I do have your shirt. I bought it just before we found out all our stuff was gone." Sunshine pulled Cathy's blouse out of its bag, to get her approval.

"That is perfect, sweetheart, and it will go just right with the black leather slacks I'm going to wear. I've got a very important dinner date tonight, and I've got to look the part," Cathy said.

"You've been very busy lately," Sunshine said.

"I know, sugar, but in about a week, I'm going to take some time off. I just have a few more moves I have to make. After I'm finished taking care of my business, we're gonna take care of some of your business. Since you've got your license and your birthday is coming up, I was thinking we should start shopping for your new car. What do you think about that, sugar?" Cathy asked.

"Can you spell BMW?" Sunshine asked with excitement.

Rain sat in the back seat, listening to every word they said. Although her mind was still preoccupied with her loss, she was focused. She heard Cathy loud and clear when she said she had moves to make. Rain was also very much aware that she was talking in a hustler's language. Rain was all too familiar with gangster talk from dealing with Terrance.

The brief thought of Terrance gave Rain chill bumps. *Maybe I'll call him to see if he wants to go to Tacoma Station tonight,* Rain thought. Then she wondered if and when Sunshine was going to mention their plans to Cathy.

Brian sat next to Rain just like before, but this time he was knocked out. After hours of nonstop talking, he had talked a hole in his own head and put himself to sleep. Rain watched how peaceful he looked while he slept. Who would have thought, watching him sleep, that he was filled with so much energy and fire? Rain decided to do what Brian was doing, lay her head back and get some rest for the remainder of the ride home. Even though she was still angry, she wasn't going to allow her mind to trip about her stolen clothes or shoes anymore.

TEN

The first thing that Rain did when they got home was run up to her bedroom to call Terrance. She didn't care what Simone thought. Terrance was Rain's man, and now she would just have to work harder to prove it, that's all.

When she went to reach for the phone, she noticed that the voice mail light was blinking. She played with the phone until she was able to figure out how to retrieve the message. She listened as the automated system informed her that she had one new message. She pushed play and listened with anticipation to see who had called her.

Rain couldn't believe her ears. She screamed out loud as if the message were from Puffy or some other big-timer. She was beyond excited as she squealed like a lovesick puppy at the sound of Terrance talking to her. She began to fan away the sweat beads that had already started to form. No matter how many asses she had to kick, she would always love Terrance.

Terrance must really be feeling me, Rain thought. *He even took the time to leave a message.* Most dudes she knew thought they were too cool to leave a message. They figured that their number showing up on the caller ID was informative enough.

Sunshine barged into Rain's room, curious to see what all the excitement was about. "What's going on? Are you okay?" Sunshine asked. "I heard you screaming from all the way in my room," Sunshine added.

"I'm sorry, boo. I didn't mean to scare you, but my baby's daddy called me," Rain said with enthusiasm.

"Your baby's daddy? Rain, you didn't tell me you had kids," Sunshine said, clueless.

Rain shook her head in pity. "No, silly, that's just a figure of speech. Oh, I forgot you from the suburbs and shit. I got to talk to you like I got some sense," Rain kidded. "Let me put it to you in your terms," Rain continued. "I was flabbergasted to hear from a dear old friend of mine, and so I screamed like so. I hope I didn't frighten you." Rain spoke, impersonating an old English woman.

Sunshine gave Rain a dirty look and said, "Don't patronize me just because I don't speak hood language." However, she still didn't understand why Rain referred to Terrance as her baby's father if they didn't have any kids together, and if other females were claiming him as well. "Anyway, so what did he say?" Sunshine asked.

"I don't know yet. The way you ran up in here, I thought it was a raid and I threw the phone out the window," Rain said, trying to be funny.

This time Sunshine had to shake her head at Rain. "It wasn't even that serious, boo," she said, stealing Rain's words. "But anyway, I asked Cathy if we could go out tonight, and she said we could go, but our curfew is midnight," Sunshine said.

"Midnight?" Rain repeated.

"That's what I said; however, I explained to her that we're going to a cozy little jazz spot, and things don't even kick off until around midnight. When I told her that, she agreed to let us stay longer. She even said she would pick us up at two. She said she doesn't want us to ride home that time of night with just anybody.

"The only dilemma is, we have to find our own way there, because Cathy is leaving to go on a business date. We could catch the subway, but we gonna be all sticky and sweaty by the time we reach the place."

Rain looked at Sunshine in amazement. "How in the hell do you know so much about partying and shit?"

"Don't sleep," Sunshine said, shaking her ass like a natural-born go-go dancer. She laughed at herself, and then said, "No, seriously, I know so much because my mom used to party every Thursday through Sunday when she was alive. She would come home at dawn and tell me everything about her entire night. That's how I know all about the club scene and I've never been to one."

"Damn, your moms was cool," Rain said with respect.

Sunshine suddenly drifted into a slight hypnosis while she reminisced about Ayanna and how she used to share all her wild adventures with her. Rain broke that spell real quick, dramatically snapping her fingers in front of her face.

"Shake it off. Earth to Sunshine . . . Earth to Sunshine," Rain chanted.

Sunshine jiggled her head to bring herself back to reality.

"Are you back? 'Cause I lost you there for a minute," Rain said. "It sounds like you and your moms were more like sisters. It's all good," Rain said, hugging Sunshine, who looked as if she wanted to break down and cry. "We are gonna party for your mother and my mother tonight," Rain said, stroking Sunshine's hair while she held her like a baby. Tears had already begun to fall from her eyes.

Cathy walked into Rain's bedroom right into the emotional scene. She walked over to the two girls. At first she couldn't tell who was comforting who, and then she saw the sweet teardrops escaping from Sunshine's eyes.

"Oh, no. What happened, baby?" Cathy asked, concerned.

Rain answered for her, so she wouldn't have to speak. "She's thinking about her family," she said.

Cathy understood now. "Well, I've got something that will cheer you up, Sunshine, and you, too, Rain."

Sunshine slowly lifted her head off Rain's shoulders, and she wiped away her tears with her shirt. "What is it?" Sunshine asked, feeling better already.

Cathy went into her pockets and pulled out an enormous bankroll wrapped in a rubber band.

True baller, Rain thought.

She must have hit the lottery, Sunshine thought.

Cathy unraveled ten hundred-dollar bills and handed them over to Sunshine. Sunshine's face lit up at the sight of the all the money. It temporarily eased her pain. Then, Cathy counted fifteen more hundred-dollar bills and handed them to Rain. Rain was in la-la land. Both girls were thrilled to have some more money in their hands. Cathy had replaced their funds from earlier as if it were nothing.

"This money is so you can both shop for some new clothes to get back what was taken from you. I told y'all earlier at the mall not to worry, because those material things could be replaced, and I meant what I said. Only this time I need you to be more responsible, because I'm not going to keep putting out all this money."

"Thank you, Cathy," Sunshine said. "But how come you keep giving me the least amount of money?" Sunshine whined playfully, like an ungrateful three-year-old. "That's not fair," she added, acting like it really bothered her to get less money than Rain.

Cathy could tell Sunshine was only kidding, and she was pleased to see her smiling and joking again. Then she said, "You don't even need that much money. You've already got clothes out the ass. Matter of fact, take half of your stash and give it to Rain," Cathy said. "She needs it more than you do."

Sunshine put a tight grip on her stack and held it close to her heart and said, "You gotta kill me first."

Rain leaped on Sunshine first and hit her with her best Chyna Doll move. Then Cathy jumped in the tussle. She dived in the middle of Sunshine and Rain and started tickling them. Rain and Sunshine filled the house with laughter.

"Just like a mother to play the tickle game," Rain giggled.

Rain was alone again, after Sunshine went back to her room to get ready for her new friend Diego. She promised Rain that she wouldn't wear her Donna Karan dress until Rain was able to replace hers, so she had to go through her whole closet to find something just as sexy to wear.

Cathy had gotten dressed and left to go meet with her mystery date. Rain heard her as she pulled out of the driveway alone, and assumed that Cathy was going to meet her date somewhere. Brian was asleep in his room with the door closed, like he was in a serious coma. Rain took the opportunity to listen to her message from Terrance.

"What's up, sexy? I've been thinking about your fine ass ever since I saw you looking all fly at Royals. What's up with you? I see you can't even hit a nigga. It's all good, though. I'm still trying to see you. I miss you. I even got a nice little surprise for you, something I think you'll look tight in. Call me back, ASAP!" Terrance said.

Rain replayed the message again and again, taking in the deep, hypnotic sound of Terrance's voice. She picked up the receiver and dialed Terrance's cell phone.

"Who dis?" Terrance yelled from the other end of his phone.

Damn, he even answers the phone sexy, Rain thought.

"Don't fake, nigga. You see my number on your caller ID," she said.

"Oh, what's up, Drizzle?" Terrance asked humorously.

Rain excused Terrance's playful insult. She didn't mind when he teased her about her name, because he sounded cute doing it. Anybody else could get it.

'I'm chillin' right now, but I'm trying to hook up with you tonight. Are you down or what?" Rain got straight to the point.

"What you trying to get into, shorty?" Terrance asked.

"Me and my girl trying to go to Tacoma Station," Rain answered.

"Is your girl trying to get with one of my boys? 'Cause I got my nigga Ron right here wit' me, and he been trying to find some ass to get into all day."

"It ain't even that type of party, Terrance. She's already got somebody she's meeting there," Rain informed him.

"I see. Well, I'll bring my man anyway, just in case shit don't work out with her and her dude," Terrance said.

"That's cool and all, but she might not feel comfortable riding with some nigga she don't even know," Rain said. She felt as if she knew Sunshine well enough already to speak for her.

"My man got his own ride. He can follow us." Terrance had the final say. "Where you at?"

Rain thought it was best not to bring Terrance to Cathy's house until Cathy told her that it was okay for her to have visitors. She wasn't going to do anything to disrespect Cathy, because she fucked with her like that. Rain thought for a moment about a good place to meet, and then she gave him the address to the house three houses up from theirs. That way they wouldn't have a long walk, and she could always give him the right address later, after she discussed it with Cathy first.

"I'll be there at eleven thirty, so be ready."

"Perfect. By the way, I got a bone to pick with you," Rain said.

"I'm already hip. I heard about how you whooped Simone 'cause you *thought* we was messing around. But Simone ain't my girl and neither are you, Rain. No disrespect, but we just kicking it, baby." Terrance summed it all up for Rain.

"I know we never put a title on us, boo, but you know and I know that we are more than friends. If you want to go all the way, then we can, but you can't be messing with those scalawags."

"Rain, Simone is nothing to me. I never fucked her, I never kissed her, and I don't even think she's sexy, so you definitely don't have to worry about her. But if you still trying to go all the way, I can come get you right now," Terrace said half jokingly.

"Boy, you crazy. I'll see you at eleven thirty." Rain hung up the phone and ran to inform Sunshine, who was almost already dressed and coming along quite nicely. Rain took a speedy wash up to freshen up before she left. She had one hour to get ready.

Forty-five minutes later, Sunshine and Rain were dressed to kill. Sunshine's cherry-red Baby Phat body suit was so vicious and skin tight that she could stop a man's heartbeat. She hooked it up adequately with a pair of sizzling red leather stilettos, showing off her freshly pedicured toes. The silver chain belt that hung from her tiny waist couldn't do anything but emphasize her perfectly round, curvy hips that protruded from each side. Her small, sexy cleavage was just enough to make a grown man whimper. She hooked it up with a dangly pair of Baby Phat earrings to go with the Baby Phat necklace that hung from her neck. The outfit lived up to its name as she wore it well, showing off all of her baby phat. Her soft lips were in flames from the red-hot M·A·C lipstick she had on, and topped with a thin layer of lip-gloss, they looked almost edible. She replaced her everyday ponytail with a long ,stylish Cher look.

Rain was on the same level as Sunshine, the high-class diva level that many chicks attempted but could never achieve. She didn't have much to choose from, and so she decided on one of the outfits that Cathy had bought her from Georgetown. Under ordinary circumstances, she wouldn't have worn such an everyday outfit to a club, but after the way she hooked it up, one would have thought it was made just for the club. She damn sure looked pretty, hot, and tempting wearing an off-white halter top with a hefty pair of double Ds pouring out from the top. She wore a tight pair of denim booty shorts that left almost nothing to the imagination. The white thigh-high boots that Sunshine let her borrow set it off. She kept her makeup light and simple, applying just a layer of clear lip-gloss to her mouth. Her hair was swept up in a casual bun. Rain knew that buns were played out, so she sized it up with a few spiral curls falling down her face. Perfect!

ELEVEN

They were headed out the door to meet Terrance when Brian appeared at the top of the stairs. He was rubbing his sleepy eyes, trying to get a better focus. That didn't help, so he flipped on the hallway light. He had to do a double take before he realized who the two babes were standing at the front door.

"You better go and get that duct tape. You look like you on the rise," Rain yelled up the stairwell to Brian.

Brian flew down the steps and said, "Y'all can't do nothing for me." Then he looked both of them up and down and said, "Uh-huh, y'all dead wrong. How y'all gonna just roll out on me like that? Y'all ain't right. Rain, you could've woke me up and said something. And Sunshine, you could have slipped a note up under my door or something. Where are we going?" Brian asked as if he were going too.

"*We* are going to hang out with some friends," Rain said, specifying Sunshine and herself only. She didn't want to be invisible tonight, and if Brian went, he would hog all the attention with his pretty self.

"Maybe you can go with us next time," Sunshine added, eager to leave. "Come on, Rain, we have to go before our ride leaves us," she said, pulling at Rain's arm. She didn't want to keep Diego waiting at the club any longer than she had to.

"Y'all hookers really gonna leave me, though? A'ight, I see how y'all is. I ain't even gonna trip. I got some more beauty rest to catch up on anyway. Y'all don't have too much fun without me, though," Brian said.

"We'll try not to," Rain said, laughing. "Lock the door behind us," she told Brian.

As they approached the designated house, they could hear Terrance honking his horn. Rain grabbed Sunshine's hand, and they took a detour around the back of the residence. Rain was laughing; Sunshine wasn't.

"Rain, this is silly. Why didn't you just have them meet us at our house? These people are going to kill us if they catch us in their lawn this time of night."

"Stop crying and come on," Rain said, pulling her harder.

Rain was glad when Terrance finally saw them walking from the side of the house, because he could release the pressure from his loud-ass horn.

Terrance was frustrated. He had been waiting outside of the dark house for over fifteen minutes, and he didn't understand what could be taking them so long. He saw somebody peeking out the window a few times, so he knew that someone was inside.

Rain got in the front seat and was gone off the familiar sweet scent of blunts and Newports. She felt like she was back home again.

When Sunshine climbed in the back seat, she was afraid that she might insult the trifling mess with her presence. He had everything under the sun right there in his back seat: CDs, tennis shoes, old cigarette wrappings, old cigarettes, empty soda bottles, condoms, and more.

While Terrance pulled off, he blazed his blunt, filling the car with the sweet aroma of purple haze. After a couple of pulls, he handed the blunt over to Rain.

Rain felt Sunshine hit her on her shoulder with her fist, and she told Terrance, "Nah, go ahead. You straight." Rain wasn't going to hit it anyway; not with Sunshine right there.

Terrance couldn't care less whether she hit it or not. That meant more for him.

"Where's your friend Ron at?" Rain asked.

"He said he might meet us up at that joint," Terrance answered.

Rain and Terrance continued to hold light conversation. Sunshine could sense that Rain wasn't going to make any introductions, so during a brief interval, she introduced herself.

"Hello, Terrance, my name is Sunshine. We kind of sort of met at Royals."

Terrance was so smacked from the green he was smoking on, and with Tupac blasting from his booming speakers, he could barely hear the shorty in the back seat. "What you say?" he asked while exhaling a mouthful of smoke.

Rain turned Tupac down and apologized for their rudeness. "My bad. Terrance, this is my girl, Sunshine. Sunshine, this is my . . . this is Terrance."

Sunshine sat up in her seat and whispered to Rain, "You forgot the baby's father part."

Rain reached her hand back and pinched Sunshine on her knee.

Terrance turned Tupac back up. He never even turned to acknowledge Sunshine. Sunshine wondered what Rain even saw in him. His braids were long, but they weren't even done. His talk was cheap, and his style seemed weak. Sunshine would make a mental note to work on finding Rain a more polite, less junky, smoke-free, non-hustling boyfriend with manners. Maybe Diego would have a friend for her. She would be sure to find out.

Tacoma Station was small and relaxed, just as Sunshine's mother had said. She felt uneasy at first, being in a place where her mother had partied on many a night. Uneasiness turned into eagerness once she spotted Diego on the stage playing.

She walked past the bar and found a table directly in front of the stage, where she could give Diego plenty of eye action while he played. The seating area was a little small, and the entire club was even smaller than she had imagined. Cathy's house was bigger. Fortunately, it wasn't too crowded, and she had plenty of legroom to stretch her long legs.

Rain and Terrance went straight to the bar.

Not only does Rain have herself a pothead, but he's a drinker too. How sexy, Sunshine thought.

Diego noticed Sunshine immediately. She stood out amongst the "first of the month" females who were strolling up in the place. They would spend their entire first-of-the-month check, which was supposed to be used for taking care of their babies, trying to put themselves together. Sunshine was already well put together, and she didn't need no check. He winked his chinky eyes at Sunshine to let her know that he saw her sitting there. Out of reflex, Sunshine winked her big baby browns back at him.

A tall guy who shined like the midnight sky came and sat in the seat right beside Sunshine. She was confused at first. He held two glasses in his hand and placed one in front of Sunshine. She wondered for a second if he was a friend of Diego's.

"I saw you when you first walked in, and all I could think was *damn!*" the gentleman said. "You are a beast, and I mean that in a positive way. You're the type of woman I could flex on my arm every day for the rest of my life and never get tired of you." When Sunshine didn't respond, the man continued. "My name is Daryl," he said, and then he pointed to the drink that sat in front of Sunshine. "This is for you. I took it upon myself to buy you a drink. I hope you don't mind."

Sunshine finally spoke. "I do mind, and I don't drink alcohol."

"I could tell from a distance that a pretty thang like you don't drink liquor. That's why I ordered you a ginger ale and cranberry juice. It's a good combination. I don't drink liquor either, and I'm drinking the same thing."

Sunshine couldn't help but think about the young girl she saw on the news whose heart busted wide open because her date had put seven ecstasy pills in her drink. She died before they could even get her to the hospital. Without further hesitation, Sunshine pushed her possible death trap back to its owner and politely asked him to leave.

It wasn't that easy to get rid of him. He acted as if he didn't hear her. "You don't have to drink it if you don't want it. I could go and get you something else, anything else, like a virgin Daiquiri or something, or a Shirley Temple. Whatever you want. I just want to get a chance to know you," Daryl pleaded.

Sunshine was becoming annoyed. To be such a fine, tall glass of chocolate milk, he sure was pushy, and that made him more like a half cup of sour milk. If he wouldn't leave, then she would.

Sunshine stood up to go and look for the ladies' room. She walked away, leaving Daryl to sit there alone and looking stupid.

Sunshine stopped at the bar to let Rain know she was going to the restroom. Men from every end of the bar screamed, whistled, and howled when they noticed Sunshine coming near. Suddenly Sunshine was nervous, and she wanted Rain to be with her, but Rain was too busy being mesmerized by all the Heineken Terrance was downing. If Sunshine didn't know any better, she would have sworn she saw Rain drinking one too.

Sunshine stepped off without bothering to ask Rain to accompany her. When she got to the end of the bar, she could feel somebody following her, all up on her ass. He was standing so close that she could feel his hot breath on her neck. She turned around swiftly, on the verge of cussing the stalker out. She was sure it was Daryl.

When Sunshine turned around, she was face to face with Diego. Her long, skinny heels made her almost as tall as Diego, which brought their lips close enough to kiss. She was rushed by the strong scent of him.

What fragrance is that? Oh, it smells so good.

She thought Diego was going to kiss her when he slowly opened his mouth to speak. "So, who was that guy? One of your boyfriends that you say you don't have?" Diego asked. Now she could smell his mouthwash.

Damn! Can I just taste it?

"No, that was somebody acting like he was trying to be my boyfriend, but I gave him the brush-off," Sunshine answered.

Diego looked satisfied, but to Sunshine's disappointment, he still didn't kiss her.

Rain had finally managed to get Terrance off the damn barstool that he had a grip on since they got in the place. She was beginning to think that his ass was glued to it for life.

"Damn, shorty, a brotha is fucked up, and you wanna dance and shit. Why can't we just chill for a minute? I got you later on, I swear," Terrance said.

"Hell no. You got me right now!" Rain shot back. "I didn't come here to watch you post up at the damn bar all night, Terrance. I'm trying to get my freak on," Rain said impatiently.

"Well, go and freak somebody. Ain't nobody over here stopping you. This place is filled with your kind of niggas. Take your pick," Terrance said.

"Oh, for real, it's like that? Well, fuck you then, Terrance!" Rain stormed off. She managed to get about two feet away before Terrance snatched her by the arm and spun her around to face him. He could barely stand up straight.

"Don't play with me, Rain. You better not take all that ass over there and be shaking it for those bamas." Terrance started bouncing around Rain playfully, swaying to the beats. "Ain't this what you wanted?" He bobbed his head in and out of her face while he danced and managed to stay standing all by himself. Then he kissed her on the tip of her nose as a gesture of forgiveness.

Rain allowed a slight grin to form on her face. "You play too much," she said.

They took their moves out to the dance floor and ended up side by side with Sunshine and Diego. Suddenly the band felt the need to play a slow jam. Marvin Gaye's "Let's Get It On" blared through the speakers.

"Oh, shit. This is my joint," Terrance said, grinding his body up against Rain.

"You don't know nothing about this," Rain said. She liked funning with Terrance. She knew that he was older than she was and she had seen his CD collection, and it was stacked like whoa!

Terrance proved Rain wrong and began to sing with the music in a loud, terrible voice that would make Marvin turn over in his grave. *"I've been really trying, baby; trying to hold back this feeling, for so long . . ."*

He stopped to let Marvin sing the rest, then he whispered in Rain's ear, "Grab my dick, baby."

Rain had no problem with that request. She could feel it growing into its full potential as she rubbed and bounced her ass all up against it, and she couldn't wait to caress it with her bare hands. She would just have to be discreet about it so that Sunshine wouldn't see her freakin' him.

She moved up closer to him, unzipped his pants, and continued grinding him while stroking his raw meat at the same time.

Terrance moaned his pleasure in Rain's ear, and she could feel her pussy causing waterfalls as her juices had her soaking wet in her thong. She rested her head on his shoulder while the song played, never releasing his dick.

Terrance had his eyes closed. He wanted to cum all over her grip and all in his jeans, but he figured he'd save that for later. He opened his eyes to focus on something else so that he wouldn't bust prematurely. It had been two days since he'd had some booty, and he was feeling backed up.

As Terrance moved his body in tune with Rain's body, he couldn't help but notice Rain's girl dancing right in front of him. He thought the girl had said that her name was Sabrina, but he wasn't sure. But one thing he was sure of once he got a better look at her: The girl was *fine!* He could feel his dick getting harder than ever while he watched her twist and turn, like he had taken some Viagra or something.

Rain felt his dick rise even more too. "Damn baby, do I make you feel that good?" she whispered in his ear.

"Hell yeah, baby. I can't wait to get you in the car so I can get the full effect," he whispered back. Terrance couldn't say what was really on his mind.

Watching your friend in the red is making my shit so hard. I'd rather take her in my back seat. Hell, on second thought, shorty is hotel material. That's somebody you lay down to fuck.

For a split second, Terrance locked eyes with Sunshine. He must have been wearing a look of desire in his eyes, because she turned her body around so fast that Terrance could only see her backside.

Even better, Terrance thought. *She phat as shit from the back too. Where did Rain ever find a dime like Sabrina? I ain't never seen no broad around the way who look that damn good.*

Terrance subtly continued to watch as Sunshine's curves moved perfectly to each song. No disrespect, but he had to have her.

TWELVE

The band ended a series of slow jams and went back to the upbeat R&B flow. Rain had finally released Terrance. "Boo, you said that you had a surprise for me. What is it?" Rain asked with excitement.

"I'll show it to you when we leave," Terrance said. He thought about the gift and couldn't help but imagine Sabrina with it instead.

"No, boo, I want to see it now. I've been waiting all night, and I can't wait no more," Rain begged. She began to place soft kisses all over his neck, seducing him wisely in the middle of the tiny dance floor.

More out of irritation than anything else, Terrance gave in. "Come on, let's go. You all whining and shit. Didn't your mama ever tell you you not s'pose to beg for shit? A gift is a gift; you get it when you get it. But since you pressing me and shit, come on," Terrance said.

Rain couldn't care less about Terrance's attitude. He could take that shit with him on the way out to the car to get her present.

"Hold on, baby. I gotta tell Sunshine that we'll be right back."

Sunshine. That's her name, Terrance thought.

"Her date had to go back to the band and play, and she didn't want us to leave her in here by herself," Rain explained to Terrance.

I would never leave her by herself, Terrance thought.

"I'll meet you at the car. I'm going to guzzle the rest of my bottle," Terrance said. He walked over to the bar and turned back just in time to see the pair of phat asses wiggle out of the club side by side. Thoughts of himself, Rain, and Sunshine, ass-naked in a warm Jacuzzi, ran wild in his mind. He wondered if Rain would be down for some threesome-type shit like that.

When Terrance got outside, he noticed two dudes standing by his car, trying to kick it with *his* girls. The drinks and the hydro were now kicking in full effect.

"Oh, hell no. These bamas trippin," he said to himself out loud. Terrance checked his waist to make sure he was still strapped, just in case them cats wanted to act stupid. He casually walked over to the group, and to his surprise, reacted calmer than he expected.

He slid right in between Rain and Sunshine, showing an essence of ownership. He gently wrapped his arms around their waists.

"Is everything okay, ladies?"

"Yes," Rain said first. "They were just leaving. Right, boys?"

The two guys rolled out without another word.

Terrance wasn't ready to let go of Sunshine, but he didn't want to make Rain suspicious, so he forced himself to let loose and turned to Rain. "So, I can't leave you alone for five minutes without you cheating on me. What's up with that?"

Rain looked at him like he was crazy. "Nigga, please! Me and Sunshine was thanking Jesus when we saw you come out the club." Rain winked at Sunshine, informing her to play along. "Those dudes ain't have nothing on you, and that's for real," Rain said. "Them niggas looked like they came right out the Rice Krispies box. I couldn't wait for them to crackle and pop their asses right on back where they came from. They so dingy I thought they were coming to ask us if we had some spare change." Rain was on a roll. She couldn't stop joking on the boys.

"Crackle looked like he went to the candy shop and bought a whole bunch of cavities. And what was up with Pop? With them fat-ass doodoo turds hanging from his scalp. I hope he ain't think he was fooling nobody, faking like they s'pose to be dread locks, because they look more like shit locks," Rain joked. "If they smell anything like they look, that nigga some straight shit. You hear me?"

Sunshine was crying, laughing, while stomping her foot to the ground. Rain must have had a contact high from Terrance's weed, because Sunshine hadn't heard her jones on nobody.

Sunshine's laughter became contagious, because soon Terrance was smiling and laughing too. Even Rain had to laugh at her own self, but that didn't make her stop with the jokes. They kept coming.

"I'm saying, did you see their faces before you accused me of cheating, Terrance?' They looked like straight infection, Chlamydia and vaginitis." Rain laughed. "You insulted us thinking we'd get down with those walking, talking venereal diseases. Now, where's my gift at?"

Terrance walked to the trunk. Rain and Sunshine sat on the hood of the car and waited eagerly to see what Terrance had for her. Sunshine was just as excited as Rain, as if she were getting something too.

Terrance walked up with an all-white plastic bag. He hadn't bothered to wrap it, but Rain didn't care. She snatched the bag from his hands, playfully kicking and screaming like a child on Christmas day.

"I can't wait to see it! Oh my God, whatever it is, I know it's tight, just 'cause you picked it out for me, baby!" Rain screamed.

"Just open the bag already, before I open it for you!" Sunshine screamed.

"Okay, okay, hold up. Terrance, give me a hint of what it is before I open it," Rain said. "Psyche! I'm just fuckin' with ya. Look at Sunshine's face. She was about to turn the same color as her pants."

Rain reached into the bag and yanked out her new outfit. As she looked at the dress, she thought she could feel her heart touch her toes. In her hands she held up the exact same Donna Karan dress that she had bought from Pentagon City. The same color, the same style, and the same size.

"Oh, shit, boo." She looked at Sunshine while giving her the elbow. "Sunshine, you see this shit?"

Sunshine's expression was ecstatic. "Yeah, it looks just like—"

"The one we saw in that catalog," Rain finished for her. Rain wasn't certain, but suddenly she had the strangest feeling that Terrance had something to do with their clothes being stolen.

She was holding the evidence in her hands, but she couldn't let him know what she was thinking. She had to figure out a slick way to get the rest of their shit back from this thieving-ass nigga.

Diego walked out of the club and looked around, as if he were searching for a lost child. Sunshine noticed him, and jumped off the hood of Terrance's Crown Vic.

"Are you looking for someone?" Sunshine yelled in his direction.

Diego's face lit up like Las Vegas when he heard Sunshine's voice. Sunshine put her sexy strut into full blast and switched her round hips all the way back to Diego. Her prance didn't go unnoticed by Terrance, who couldn't help but cut his snake eyes in Sunshine's direction as she stepped off. Rain was so busy checking for tags on the dress to see where it came from that she didn't even see Terrance's wandering eye.

Diego scooped Sunshine in his arms and pulled her back into the club for one last dance. Terrance watched Sunshine the entire time, until she stepped back into the club. He would have given up all his loot to be that nigga who was fortunate enough to hold Sunshine in his arms. He imagined himself performing some old freaked-out loving on her like Prince, like fucking her real slow in some purple rain, while doves fly.

Terrance needed some ass ASAP. He focused his attention back to Rain, who was still inspecting the dress.

"So do you like it or what?" he asked.

Rain looked up and put on her best game face. "Boo, I love it! I ain't never seen no Donna Karan dress like this before. Where you get this from? It's fly as shit," Rain asked, testing him.

"Don't worry about all that. Just make sure you put it on the next time I see you, and make sure you forget to wear your panties," Terrance answered. "Come on. Let's get in the car. I want to holler at you for a minute," he said.

Rain wondered if he had heard something from Jerome. She got in the car, preparing herself for whatever he was about to kick to her. If it was bad news, she was ready to deal with it.

When they were both inside the car, Terrance cranked up the ignition and turned on the radio. Rain watched and waited patiently while he flipped through all the stations. Finally, he decided on WHUR. They were playing after-midnight slow jams.

Rain was slowly realizing that Terrance was trying to set the mood. Obviously, they had two totally different agendas. Rain could see that Terrance wasn't planning to converse about her siblings, so she decided to bring it up herself.

While he was undoing his belt, she asked him if he had heard anything from Jerome.

Terrance then began to undo his pants and said, "Yeah, as a matter of fact, little youngin' called me yesterday."

Rain watched intently as he pulled his big, soft dick from the opening of his Nautica boxers.

"Did he leave a number?" she asked, ignoring his boldness.

"Yeah, he gave me a number to give to you," Terrance answered coolly.

"Well, what is it?" Rain asked, getting a little annoyed by his lack of interest in the subject.

Terrance started to jerk his sleeping dick, slowly rubbing it up and down with his rough hand. "Aight, chill, Rain. I got you. I'll give it to you tomorrow. It's at my house."

Rain was disappointed that Terrance hadn't even bothered to tell her this on his own. She practically had to beat it out of him, while watching him beat himself.

"Well, did he say anything important that I need to know? Is he okay?" Rain asked, getting worried about her baby brother.

Terrance began stroking himself stronger and faster, as if her desperate situation was turning him on.

"Yeah, he told me to tell you to give me a hand here," Terrance said.

Rain looked at Terrance in disbelief. She started to cuss his horny, nasty ass out, but then she realized that she needed to be nice to him, not only because of the dress, but because now she had to get Jerome's number from him. She decided it would be best not to press the issue at that moment.

Rain watched Terrance as he jerked his meat off like a pro. "You don't look like you need no help from me," she said.

He stopped stroking his rising meat and reached for Rain's head. He pulled her face to his and stuck his wet tongue deep into her mouth. Terrance pulled Rain's halter top down and urgently caressed each breast with his rough, masculine hands.

Rain could feel her nipples harden like pencil erasers to Terrance's touch, while he twisted and turned them with his fingers. Then, before Rain even knew what he was doing, Terrance tilted his face down and let his lips take the place of his fingers. First he licked her nipples, showering them with his juicy, warm dribble. They must have tasted good to him, because he then began to swallow her breasts whole, taking one titty in at a time and devouring them passionately.

This was something that he had never done before, and Rain wasn't about to stop him. Rain moaned and cried out his name with pleasure and pain as he gently bit down on her nipple. She couldn't resist the touch of his wet, hot tongue and his big, juicy lips. The loud slurping noises he made sounded like he was sucking on a great big ol' lollipop, and he was turning her the fuck on. With every kiss, every suck, and every lick, Terrance shot tingly pains of ecstasy throughout her whole body, until they reached her pussy and then exploded with oceans of her sweet cream. If he would have stuck his finger up inside her pussy right now, it might have drowned.

Rain's body was on fire, and she wanted more. Maybe it was the weed, maybe it was the drinks, or maybe it was just time, but that night, right then and there in Terrance's ride, Rain didn't want to be a virgin anymore. She wanted to see what it would feel like to have Terrance's big, juicy half smoke inside her big, juicy bun.

Terrance raised his head and pulled Rain's head down to his erection. Rain didn't hesitate or fake on it either. She slid her mouth up and down his hard pipe until her jaws locked.

"Oh, Rain. Rain, baby, don't stop. Ooohh . . . don't stop, baby. That feels so good. Baby, oooh yeah. Baby, this is your dick, Rain. Don't stop. Damn, baby," Terrance cried. He used the streetlight to watch the talented head monster give him the best head of his life.

Terrance glanced out the slightly fogged window to make sure that there were no police around. He got excited when he noticed Sunshine exiting the club. He wanted to stop Rain, but he couldn't. The chronic sensations that came from Rain's deep throat and the sight of Sunshine's long, slender body were enough to make all his backed-up nut come shooting out.

As Sunshine sashayed toward the car and Rain's head bobbed up and down his dick like a maniac, he could feel it coming. Ecstasy was working its way from every bone in his body to the tip of his groin. He pushed Rain's head down farther on his dick with intensity, until she swallowed it whole.

"Baby, oooh, Rain. God damn, you feel good!" Terrance began to shake and shiver as he erupted his love potion all down Rain's throat.

Rain, who was damn near gagging from the overdose, lifted her head for air.

Rain was about to ask Terrance if he had a bottle of water or soda in his junky car, so she could wash down his sticky cum, but when she lifted her head from his lap, Rain saw Sunshine peering through the steamy windows. She was staring at them with both her hands on the steamed windows. Rain was devastated.

"Oh my God!" Rain said out loud. "I wonder how long she's been watching us!" Rain was so embarrassed that she wanted to drop her face back into Terrance's sweaty lap and hide from the humiliation.

Rain looked at Terrance. He looked proud. He still had his pants down, revealing all of his maturity, which was still very hard, even after such a vicious relief. If Rain didn't know any better, she would've thought that he was showing off how big and long it was so that Sunshine could witness all his wealth for herself. Little did she know, that was exactly what he was doing.

Rain smacked Terrance upside his head. "Terrance, put that thing away! If you didn't notice, we have company, dammit!" Rain yelled, although she didn't know how he was going to fit all that stiff beef back into them jeans.

She was getting that tingly feeling all over again just watching it. She began to get angry, thinking about how she could have all that good loving up inside her right now. Instead, little innocent Miss Sunshine just had to come strolling out the club wearing that big ol' halo over her head.

Shouldn't she and Diego be somewhere getting down right now? Rain thought. *Why she gotta come out here and bust our groove?*

"Fix your shirt," Terrance said, pointing to Rain's large buttercups, which were hanging all over the place.

Rain looked down at her breasts as if they were a sin. "Y'all get back in there," she said to them while tucking them back inside her top.

Terrance watched Rain, wondering himself how she could fit two humongous, ripe watermelons inside one tiny little shirt. The poor shirt only seemed capable of handling nothing more than two baby peaches. It sure had its work cut out for it.

When Sunshine realized what was going on behind the foggy glass, she stepped back with a quickness. She was sorry she had to witness the porno scene with her new best friend and the vulture she was with. Then again, she had to admit that Rain looked more like the vulture, the way she was eating Terrance alive.

Sunshine looked at her watch. Cathy would be there in less than five minutes. She had to get Rain out of that car before Cathy pulled up and saw her. Cathy didn't condone teenage sexual behavior. She was constantly talking to Sunshine about the importance of saving herself.

Sunshine worried that Cathy might even send Rain back to Social Services, claiming she was a destructive teen or something. She didn't want to see that happen. She liked Rain.

She began to bang on the window with an authoritative force. If Terrance hadn't seen her walk over to the vehicle with his own eyes, he would have sworn she was the police; she was beating so hard.

"Hold up. I'm coming!" Rain yelled.

"Well, hurry up and get yourself together. Our ride will be pulling up in two minutes!" Sunshine yelled back.

"Your ride? I thought I was taking you home," Terrance said.

"Nah, my folks is taking us back," Rain said.

"Who is your folks? The white chick you was rolling with at Royals?" Terrance asked.

"Yeah, that's her," Rain replied. Rain opened the car door and said, "I'll call you tomorrow so I can get my little brother's number from you." She reached for her white bag with her stolen gift inside and shut the door.

Terrance sped off with a quickness. He wasn't trying to bump heads with Cee, especially after what had just happened with Rain. Irvin had hipped him to the scoop on Cee, and basically, she was nothing to be fucked with. Her brother Moses had shit locked down in New York, her Uncle Snoop had shit locked in Baltimore, and Cee was the queen pin in D.C., Maryland, and Virginia. Anybody looking at the pint-sized white woman at first glance wouldn't think that something so small was so powerful, proving the theory that looks can be deceiving.

As Terrance pulled onto the highway in the opposite direction of his house, he thought back to the fucked-up little stunt that Cee had pulled on him the other night. He had wanted to pull his blade out right then and there, slice her pretty little neck, and watch it fall on the table. He didn't give a fuck if she was big time or not; nobody disrespected him in public like that and expected to get away with it. Nobody.

Cathy pulled up five minutes later, just in time to see Terrance pull off. Fortunately, she didn't know the kind of car he drove, so she didn't recognize him. As she parked, she nearly hit the curb with her twenty-twos.

"Damn! I'm not the only one feeling it," Rain said.

Sunshine was busy trying to put Rain's bun back into place when Cathy began pounding on her horn like a mad woman. Sunshine ran over to the driver's side of the truck, wondering what was wrong. She could hear Britney Spears blasting from the speakers.

Cathy hung her head out the window and began shouting the lyrics to the song, showing off all her Caucasian traits.

"Hey, pooh bear, did you have fun tonight?" Cathy yelled out to Sunshine, even though Sunshine stood right in her face. It was obvious that Cathy had had too much to drink, which was surprising to Sunshine.

"Yes, I had a great time, and apparently you did too. Are you all right?" Sunshine asked.

Cathy had a slight slurring effect going when she answered. "No, pooh, I need you to drive. I went to this party at the Marriott after my meeting, and I think one of them ignorant people spiked the punch. I only sipped on one drink, and I am fuuucked up!" Cathy slurred.

Rain was busy getting an Omarion look-alike's digits when she heard Cathy sounding dysfunctional even at a distance. She hated to say good-bye to the dude pushing a fully loaded red Mercedes-Benz S500, but she had to see what was going on with her peoples.

Rain ran up behind Sunshine. "Is everything all right? I could hear Cathy from all the way over there." Rain could tell by Cathy's disposition that she was all right—a little twisted, but all right. However she couldn't believe what she was seeing. She pointed at Cathy, making fun of her and putting her on the spot, while laughing in disbelief.

"Let me find out Ms. Cathy is smacked!" Rain teased.

"Nooo, Ms. Cathy is just a little tipsy, that's all. Now help me get in the back so I can rest my head," Cathy spit out.

Cathy couldn't figure out which shoulder to lean her head on, so she just let it wobble. Rain found the whole scenario humorous and could not stop laughing.

Sunshine shoved Rain on the arm playfully and said, "I know you're not laughing, Ms. Headquarters."

Rain ignored Sunshine's subtle sarcasm. "Come on. Let's get her in the back before she passes out on the steering wheel," Rain said.

It was harder than it looked to get Cathy's dead weight situated comfortably. Looking at Cathy slumped over, Rain decided that it would be best to tell her about Terrance stealing their clothes in the morning, when she got herself together.

After making five wrong turns and missing three exits, Sunshine finally found her way back home. Cathy had passed out by the time they reached the house. Rain had to go and wake up Brian so that he could assist them with dragging her into the house.

"I got this," Brian said when Sunshine and Rain tried to help. He effortlessly lifted Cathy up, cradling her like a baby. He carried her into her bedroom, then dumped her on her bed. Cathy never moved a muscle.

"I could pay you back big time right now, Mama, 'cause you is gone. I could steal a long-lost hug and kiss from you, and you wouldn't even know it. But you'd probably wake up in the morning hollering you got the cooties, so I won't fuck with you." Instead, Brian rubbed her head and stared at his mother, who slept so peacefully.

Sunshine and Rain ran upstairs to their own bedrooms and let Brian have his moment, for whatever it was worth.

THIRTEEN

Sunshine noticed her caller ID flashing and got excited, praying that it was Diego who had called her. She ran to the phone and was satisfied when she saw his seven heavenly digits displayed across the small caller ID screen. He had even left a message, asking her to call him as soon as she got home. He claimed if she didn't call, he would lay awake forever, waiting.

Sunshine was a little more than exhausted from all the partying and the contact from Terrance's weed. All she really wanted to do was lay across her bed and conk out just like Cathy. If it weren't for the sexy urgency in Diego's voice begging her to call, she would have done just that. However, she took off her clothes, not bothering to put on any pajamas, put her head back on her fluffed pillows, and obediently dialed Diego's number.

Sunshine couldn't even recall the phone ringing; he picked up so fast. "Well, it's about time, my little dancing diva. I was getting ready to put an APB out on you," Diego teased.

Sunshine could feel the love jones taking the place of her exhaustion, bringing her whole body to life again when he spoke. Did he possess some sort of magic spell or something? The sincerity in his voice made Sunshine feel as if she were flying with wings to cloud nine.

"If I was lost, I am surely safe now, because you have found me," Sunshine said.

"So do I get to keep you?" Diego asked.

"It all depends. What do you plan on doing with me?" Sunshine wanted to know.

"Mm-hmm." Diego cleared his throat to make way for his oncoming sermon. "Well, first of all, I plan to love you so strong it might make you feel weak. I intend to show you the world you thought you'd never see. And while I'm busy showing you the world, I'm going to share all my private thoughts with you; thoughts I've never shared with any other woman. Afterwards, I'll listen to you tell me yours, until we become best friends with no secrets. Once we become the best of friends, I'm going to touch you and hold you, until you want more, and that's when I'll become your lover. When all is said and done, I want to love not just you but your soul. And when you realize that I'm the one, I will make you permanently mine," Diego preached.

Every cell inside Sunshine's body was now working overtime. "It sounds as though you've thought up a divine master plan for the two of us," Sunshine said.

"Are you with it?" Diego asked.

"As long as you're about it," Sunshine answered.

Sunshine fell asleep with dreams of Diego making sweet love to her for the first time. Her dream seemed so real, like a wet dream, something she had never felt before. She could actually feel herself cumming over and over.

Her orgasm was so real that the next morning her panties were soaking wet with her cream from the passion. She could still feel her nature tingling from her arousing dream as Rain burst into her room moments later.

"Damn! It's about time you woke up. It ain't that much sleeping in the world! I was starting to think your ass had hit some green," Rain said.

"What time is it?" Sunshine asked. She wished she didn't have to get up. She wanted to go back to sleep and feel Diego place more soft kisses all over her. She secretly hoped that Diego felt that good in reality.

"It's time for you to get up,"cause we got some shit to do," Rain screamed.

Sunshine was confused. "What do we have to do? And why are you screaming at me?"

Sunshine looked over at her alarm clock and saw that it was almost noon. She jumped out of bed and reached for her robe. "How could you let me sleep so late?" Sunshine asked, blaming Rain for her laziness.

"Shit, I wasn't messing with you. You was moaning and groaning in your sleep like you was getting some serious dick, and I didn't want to interrupt your flow."

Sunshine rolled her eyes to the sky. "Very funny, Rain."

"While you were busy getting your fuck on in your sleep, I was busy coming up with a way for us to get our shit back from Terrance."

Sunshine stood up to turn on the television, half listening while Rain went on about her game plan. Sunshine grabbed the remote and began to turn the volume up on the television, completely ignoring Rain.

Rain stood up in front of the TV, blocking Sunshine's view like a security officer. "Oh you trying to be funny, ignoring me and whatnot," she said. "For real, Sunshine, I want you to listen to what I came up with. I know you want your clothes back as much as I want mine, so stop playing and listen."

Sunshine held her hand up in the air. "Hold up, Rain. Check this out." Sunshine pointed to the TV.

"I could care less about the TV right now. I'm trying to get—" Rain stopped in the middle of her debate when she saw the news coverage.

An elderly woman had been shot and killed by one of twelve shots that had been sprayed into her house. Her husband, who was asleep beside her at the time of the shooting, was in critical condition and being treated in the ICU. The tragic incident had happened in the wee hours of the morning, and unfortunately, no suspects were arrested at the time. The shocking part about the whole situation was that it had taken place three houses down from Cathy's—the same house where Rain and Sunshine had met up with Terrance the night before.

"Oh my gosh! What a strange coincidence," Sunshine said with amazement.

Rain wasn't as convinced. "I think it's more than just coincidence," Rain said. "Think about it, Sunshine. Why would anyone want to shoot up a couple of old people?"

"What are you trying to say?" Sunshine asked.

"What I'm trying to say is, I don't think those bullets were meant for that couple. I think they were meant for one of us," Rain said with terror trembling in her voice.

"Why would you think something crazy like that?" Sunshine asked.

"Because in case you didn't notice, that's the same house that Terrance picked us up from last night," Rain answered.

"Of course I figured that part out," Sunshine said. "But are you trying to say that Terrance had something to do with it?" Sunshine asked.

"You damn right!"

"But why would your baby daddy do something like that?" Sunshine asked.

"Yeah, why would he do something like that?" Cathy chimed in, appearing in the doorway.

Rain and Sunshine both nearly jumped out of their skin, unaware that Cathy had been listening in. Rain was afraid to say anything else about it. She didn't want Cathy to think that she was some sort of rebel, bringing drama to her house, but when she really thought about it, she realized that she didn't do anything wrong, so she decided to keep it real with Cathy.

Brian walked in while Rain was filling in all the details. He took a seat on the floor and listened in, too, while Rain shared with them her theory about the conniving Terrance. She explained to them in detail why she assumed that Terrance was the one who had taken their shit from the mall. She even fessed up and told them that Terrance was a hustler. After the story was told, Cathy was pleased by Rain's honesty, and Brian was ready to whoop some ass.

"I know one thing: That nigga better come up off my wardrobe before I stick these twelves up his you-know-what. I waited too long to get them damn shoes to have them taken by some thug," Brian said.

"You don't even have to do all that, Brianna. I know the perfect way for us to get all of our stuff back, and it doesn't involve violence. Just a pretty face and a little bit of game, and we've got that nigga."

Everybody was interested to hear all the details, including Cathy, who was also busy making plans of her own.

Rain continued to speak. "All we have to do is set him up."

Sunshine sat up on her bed, trying to keep her half-naked body from being exposed, hoping no one noticed the proof of her orgasm that still wet the bed.

"What do you mean, set him up?" Sunshine asked.

"What I mean is, have somebody call him up like they met him at a club or something, and then set a date with him. Knowing Terrance, he'll probably either take that person to a hotel, or back to his apartment. More than likely it will be his apartment."

"Let's just hope its not in his *car*," Sunshine joked.

"In your dreams," Rain joked back. "Once the person is up in there, they gonna get him twisted to the point where he is too smacked to know what's going on, too smacked to move, and too smacked to notice when she boats outta there with all our bags. I was thinking Brianna could do it, since dudes can't seem to resist her," Rain said.

Cathy shook her head with pity at the suggestion of Brian playing the part.

"Stop hating, Mama. It sounds good, Rain, but I'm sorry, I can't do it," Brian said.

"Why not? I thought this would be right up your alley, Miss Drama Queen," Rain said. "What happened to sticking those twelves up his ass?"

"Oh, don't get me wrong. I can do it; it's just that I can't do it," Brian repeated.

Rain was confused, along with everyone else. "What do you mean, you can do it, but you can't do it? You're not making any sense," Rain said.

"I'm making perfect sense. I can't do it because the bama already saw me while he was jacking me, remember? I was sleeping when it all went down, and I'm sure he didn't overlook all this beauty of mine and just forget. He probably still saw me in his sleep, ya dig?" Brian said.

"She's right," Sunshine said. "I'm certain that Terrance saw her, but I know someone who could do it," Sunshine added.

"And who is that?" Rain asked.

"Me. You should let me do it," Sunshine said eagerly.

"Don't be silly, Sunshine," Cathy said. "You shouldn't get involved in something like this."

"Yeah, don't be silly. He saw you, too, remember? We just went out with him last night, crazy," Rain said.

"That's my point," Sunshine said. "While we was out with him last night, he was all up my behind like hemorrhoids."

"Stop faking, Sunshine. My man wasn't paying you no mind. He was too busy—" Rain had to stop herself before she got herself into some trouble by blurting out her business.

"Listen, Rain, I'm not trying to upset you or anything. All I'm saying is that I noticed Terrance checking me out last night, that's all," Sunshine said innocently.

"I wouldn't put it past the conniving thief," Brian said. "I mean, think about it, Rain. If he is so faithful, what would make you think that he would take the bait with me in the first place?" Brian asked.

"I never said that he was faithful. All I'm saying is that he wasn't checking Sunshine out," Rain said. "He wouldn't disrespect me like that," she added.

Rain was beginning to feel humihated, angry, and foolish, and that wasn't good. She liked Sunshine and all, but she could get it just like any other bitch.

"Listen, Rain, I'm not trying to be funny. All I'm trying to say is that I got a tiny little vibe that he was feeling me, that's all. You know how guys are," Sunshine added.

"Rain can sit and fake if she wants to, but let the truth be told, Terrance is five cent short of a dime. We peep his shorts all the time," Brian said. "Rain, get out your feelings, and Sunshine, let's do the damn thang," Brian said, getting frustrated with the sudden pity party.

Cathy couldn't agree with him more. She was learning to like Brianna's style. Over the summer, he had become a new woman. No more "hiding in the closet cause I'm afraid to come out" Brian. This brand new person was an "open this muthafuckin' closet 'cause I'm coming out!" Brianna.

I always wanted a daughter, Cathy thought, *and they say God works in mysterious ways, but damn!*

"Sunshine, get your cell phone and let's call Mr. Faithful to see what's on his agenda for today," Brian said.

Sunshine grabbed her purse, which sat on her nightstand, reached in, and pulled out her cell. She gave a sideways glance at Rain to make sure that she was cool with all this, but Rain wasn't trippin' anymore. She gave an *I don't give a fuck* look back at Sunshine and called out his number.

"And make sure you put him on speaker phone so we can all hear," Rain ordered.

Sunshine dialed the digits slowly, trying to figure out what she would say with each button she pushed. The room got quiet with anticipation; even Brianna couldn't be heard for a change.

"Who dis?" Terrance asked, yawning from a fresh wakeup.

"Who dis? That's how you talk to your future wifey?" Sunshine asked.

"If you was my wifey, I'd be waking up to some crucial head right now, or at least in some wet pussy. Who dis?" Terrance asked again.

"If you would have brought me home last night, I might be on my knees right now," Sunshine said seductively.

Cathy wore an expression of bafflement as she listened to her baby girl talk dirty.

"I can come and get you right now. Where you at?" Terrance asked, excited. He was waking up now.

"How you gonna come and get me when you don't even know who I am?" Sunshine asked.

"See, now you playing games and shit. I ain't got time for this. It's too early for me. Call me back when you're serious," Terrance said.

"I am serious, Terrance. I went through too much trouble trying to get your number not to be serious," Sunshine said.

"What kind of trouble did you have to go through, baby doll? Tell me so that I can make it up to you."

"Well, first I had to wait until my homegirl fell asleep, which eventually was off the late night, early morning. When she finally dozed off, I had to search high and low for her cell phone, which I finally found inside her pants pocket. Then I had to go searching through about a hundred different names until I came across the right one. And now here we are," Sunshine said.

"Oh, you did all that for me?" Terrance asked.

"You better know it," Sunshine said. "I saw you checking me out at the club last night. I would have asked you for your number personally, but you were too busy kicking it with Rain," Sunshine said, subtly trying to reveal her identity.

"Who the hell is this?" Terrance said, getting a little paranoid.

"This is Sunshine, Terrance, but if you don't want to be bothered right now, I can call you back some other time."

Terrance was blown away. How could this be? He had busted off some serious rounds into Cee's house last night, and there shouldn't have been a living soul left in her house, including the sexy Sunshine. So, unless he was talking to a ghost, it had to be a crank call.

Whoever the caller was, she surely was making his dick rise with her sexy sound and bold conversation. He loved a female that could talk a good game and live up to it, and she sounded like she could live up to any position he put her in.

"Okay, since you like to play games, if this is Sunshine, what CD was I playing last night when I came to pick you and Rain up?" Terrance asked, using a trick he learned way back in the day.

"Oh, that's too easy. You couldn't come up with something better than that?" Sunshine mocked. "But I'll answer your simple question, and I'll even take it take it a step further. You were playing *I Wonder If Heaven Got a Ghetto* by Tupac. You was blazing some crucial green that is still lingering on my clothes today. The back of your car looks like a junkyard, and you drive like an ex-con gone AWOL on a speed chase, dodging the police. Do you believe me now, or do you want more?" Sunshine asked.

"Nah, you got it, baby girl." Terrance was surprised yet relieved at the same time. He didn't want to hurt Sunshine. He almost had second thoughts about the whole thing the night before, but pride was a muthafucker.

"So where's your sidekick Rain at?" Terrance asked.

Maybe she had been spared as well, he thought. After all, the bullets were only intended for that fake-ass gangstress, Cee.

Cathy, Rain, and Brian were all practically breathing into the phone, anxious to hear what would be said next.

"I didn't call you to discuss Rain. I called to see if we could get together today. I told you I saw you checking me out on the down low last night, and I would just like to spend some time with you, 'cause I'm feeling you too."

Terrance understood only too well. She probably wanted to get a taste of his good wood. After seeing the size of it, how could she resist? Only one other problem, though.

"What about the homeboy you was bunned up with last night? He's not going to come trying to hunt you down, is he?" Terrance asked.

"How are we going to enjoy ourselves if we keep worrying about Rain and homeboy?" Sunshine asked. "What they don't know wont hurt them," she added.

That let Terrance know right then and there that Rain was still alive. He was glad to know that. Terrance would find out later if he had managed to reach his target, but for now, he had some Sunshine to tend to.

"You sound good. What are you trying to do today? Lunch, a movie, or would you like to go get wet at that waterpark out in VA?" Terrance asked, getting excited. His dream was about to come true.

"Well, I don't think we should be out in the open all like that. Somebody might see us together and run back to tell Rain. Neither one of us wants that to happen," Sunshine said. "So I was thinking we could rent a DVD, order some carry-out, and chill out at your crib," Sunshine said.

"Damn, now that's what I'm talking about, a girl who knows her way to a man's heart," Terrance said. "Sunshine, I'm glad that you went through all this to get at me. Now I'm going to

show you how I get down. I'm going to treat
you like a woman is supposed to be treated. I
couldn't do that shit with Rain, 'cause she's on
a different level, but you, I can do some real shit
with you," Terrance confessed.

Sunshine felt the pain that shot through
Rain's eyes in her own heart. It was time to end
this conversation before Terrance said something else stupid that would break Rain's heart.

"I'm going to get ready, and I'll call you when
I'm finished so I can get your address," Sunshine
said.

"Bet!" Terrance said. The thought crossed his
mind that it could be a setup, but then he was
one hundred percent certain that Cee wouldn't
be foolish enough to involve an innocent girl in
the mix, knowing what could happen to her. She
wasn't that ruthless. Nah, Sunshine was doing
this from her own free will, 'cause she wanted to
taste his flavor. And he had some tasty flavors
for her ass.

Cathy was the first to speak at the end of the
call. "First of all, Rain, you can dry them tears
right on up, because a nigga is going to be a
nigga every day. Terrance is not God's gift to
this world, so stop crying like he is. You can
do way better than that, sweetie. You've got a
lot more to think about than some ego-trippin'

Terrance, with his brain stuck to the head of his dick instead of the top of his head. 'Cause he's about to get what's coming to him, and you about to get what's coming to you, which is a life consisting of education, dreams, and ambitions, and none of that shit starts with a nigga, okay? So get a grip."

Rain wiped her tears away with Sunshine's comforter and let get-back take the place of sorrow. Cathy's pep talk had given her a second boost of energy.

"I just had to shed a couple of those wet ones to show y'all that I can be sensitive, but now the official Rain is back, and I'm ready to get this thing started. I was born for drama!" Rain yelled.

"And you better know it," Brianna said, slapping hands with Rain.

Everybody was busy putting their plan into action, because everybody had something to gain from it. Some parts of the plan were secretive and unknown to others, while some parts were out in the open and dealt with as another one of life's plans. Charge it to the game.

FOURTEEN

Terrance was busy cleaning his small apartment, emptying all the ashtrays filled with blunt roaches, dumping the overflowing trash can. He even took his empty Remy bottles and built a designer empire underneath his entertainment center. He went into his bedroom and finally changed the filthy blankets that held evidence of all the past week's chicken-head cum stains all over it. He pulled out a fresh satin comforter set for Ms. Sunshine. He also took the time to clean the gruesome ring around his toilet that he thought was there for life and would never go away. With a touch of Ajax and some tough love, the toilet looked almost good enough to shit in.

As Terrance cleaned, he found all sorts of things inside his apartment he didn't even know were there. He found a piece of Tamara's hair weave behind his mattress, and an old condom underneath the couch. He even found a hundred-dollar bill inside his closet. This ordeal was turning out to be more beneficial than he could have imagined.

While Terrance was busy spring-cleaning for Sunshine, Sunshine was busy preparing herself for the swindle, with the help of Rain and Brian.

"If that lowlife nigga lays one single finger on you, you call me ASAP, and I'll be in that mutha-fucka before you can even blink," Brian said.

Rain looked at Brian and rolled her eyes. "Do you even brainstorm before you speak, Brianna? Or do you just like talking shit? 'Cause you let anything come out your mouth," Rain said.

"Girl, I talk first and think later. You better know it," Brian answered while giving his acrylic nails three snaps. Brian watched as Sunshine tried to squeeze herself into the mini dress that Rain had picked out for her.

"Damn, Sunshine! You gonna make Terrance *give* you back *all* our shit in giftwrap with that hootchie outfit on," Brian said. "You make a species like me, myself, want to convert back and try some of that," he said. Both Sunshine and Rain laughed hysterically at Brian's gay sense of humor.

Cathy was downstairs in her bedroom, fully dressed and fully loaded. She was sure to put the silencer on her nine millimeter, so that after the girls had finished playing their little number on

Tee, she would finish him off for good. Tee was dead wrong for shooting up that elderly couple. Cathy knew good and well who he really wanted to hit. When she put it all together, it became very clear to her that Terrance wanted her dead, and all over some petty shit. Too bad he had to take it there, and too bad he didn't do it right when he had the chance.

Cathy couldn't help but wonder what would have happened to her had Rain or Sunshine given him her real address. She might be the one posted up on the TV screen, dead or in critical condition. Now that she knew what Tee had intended for her, she would reverse that shit right back on his dumb ass. Cathy unleashed the safety clip and pulled back the barrel so that the weapon was ready to perform on its victim when the time was right. She gently placed the leather weapon into her Gucci purse until the right time came.

Sunshine pulled up into Terrance's apartment complex, riding in Cathy's burgundy Camry. Cathy only used the Camry for small rip and runs every now and then, so Terrance was surely not going to recognize it if he happened to notice it. Cathy, Rain, and Brian parked three buildings down, so that Terrance wouldn't detect them even if he were to look out his front window.

Sunshine parked the car and called Terrance from her cell phone to let him know that she was downstairs.

"Come on up, sexy, I'm in apartment 203," Terrance said.

Sunshine could hear his excitement through the phone.

When he hung up, Terrance ran to dim the lights and turn on a soft and mellow Earth, Wind & Fire CD. Moments later, when he heard Sunshine's sweet taps at the door, it took all of his body control not to run and swing the door open. Terrance let out a small laugh. He couldn't believe his own self, losing his cool over some female.

When Terrance opened the door, he was reminded of why he was at a loss for control. Sunshine was *all of it,* standing in his doorway looking like a sexy caramel Playboy bunny.

"I must be fucking dreaming, 'cause you look unreal!" Terrance held the door open for Sunshine to come inside. "This has got to be a setup, 'cause shit like this don't happen to me," Terrance said, not caring if he sounded foolish.

"Boy, that must be that weed talking, because you are trippin'," Sunshine teased.

Terrance didn't want to admit to her that he had hit two blunts before she came. But, blunt or no blunt, shorty looked *good,* and that was for real!

Terrance reached for the Blockbuster bag with the rentals that Sunshine carried. "So what are we watching?" he asked while digging into the bag.

Sunshine walked over to the couch and made herself comfortable, trying not to act as nervous as she was.

"I rented two movies: *Love & Basketball* and *Love Jones.* You can pick the first one we watch," Sunshine suggested.

"Damn! Sounds like somebody's in love up in here already," Terrance joked.

"Or somebody's gonna be," Sunshine said half-jokingly. "I'm starving. Can we order some Chinese food now, or do you want to hear my stomach sound louder than the movie?" Sunshine kidded.

Terrance took advantage of the situation and put his ear down to Sunshine's stomach. "I don't hear nothing," he said playfully.

"Oh, you will if you don't feed me soon," Sunshine said.

Terrance then placed a soft kiss on Sunshine's belly before he stood up to get the cordless phone. "What do you want to order?" he asked.

"I want a large chicken and broccoli," Sunshine answered.

While Terrance was ordering the food, Sunshine asked if she could use his bathroom. Terrance pointed her in the direction. Sunshine picked up her purse and went into the bathroom. She locked herself in once she was inside.

She took her cell phone out of her purse and sent a quick text message to Cathy to let them know that the Chinese food was on the way. They would be on point now.

She placed the cell phone back into her purse, then flushed the toilet as if she had really used it. She shook her head in pity.

All this for some damn clothes, she thought.

Sunshine almost felt ridiculous, because for some strange reason, Terrance seemed to be nicer than she had expected. But it was too late to back out now. She checked herself in the mirror, then stepped back out into the living room for take two.

Terrance had already started *Love & Basketball* and was now pouring a bottle of 1738 Accord Royal into two iced glasses.

"I hope that's not for me, because I don't drink nothing that requires an alcohol level printed on the bottle," Sunshine let him know.

"I made it real light, baby. You should barely even taste the alcohol. Just try it. If you don't like it, I'll pour both of our glasses out," Terrance said. "And I'll refill them with a tall glass of ice cold H2O. You feel me?" he asked politely.

"I don't drink water either," Sunshine joked.

Terrance looked at her as if she were crazy. "Not even toilet water?" he asked teasingly.

"Oh, now you're talking. Toilet water, that's my shit," Sunshine said.

They both shared childish giggles at themselves. Sunshine was trying her best not to be herself and to loosen up just like Rain had encouraged her to do. Rain also advised her to throw in a few curse words here and there so that Terrance would feel like she was down. So far, Sunshine was doing just fine.

Sunshine picked up her glass of Remy and sucked the whole thing down in a single gulp. Terrance looked at her in true amazement and laughed at her lightheartedly.

"Whoa, baby girl! Take it easy. You downed that thang like a lush in the making. You got to take cognac real slow, especially if you're not a drinker," Terrance warned. He poured her a second glass, this time being sure to give her even less Remy. He didn't want her to think that he was trying to take advantage of her. "Now be gentle with this one, my lovely lush," Terrance advised.

Sunshine picked up her second glass and began sipping it slowly. "Oh, so now you trying to call me an alcoholic?" she asked.

"Yes," Terrance admitted, "but a very sexy one." Terrance stared deep into Sunshine's eyes as if he were searching for something.

Sunshine could feel the Remy kicking in and was suddenly ashamed to be finding Terrance awfully sexy himself. As she was watching him watch her, she could understand why Rain was all over him. His eyes were dark and seductive, and his long, bushy eyelashes set it off. His lips were edible and seemed to be made just right for kissing—and anything else he wanted to do with them. The long, silky twists in his hair that fell to his shoulders made him look even lovelier. Sunshine was tempted to touch him in places she wasn't supposed to for a second, but then she quickly remembered who he was and why she was there in the first place.

The doorbell rang just in time for Sunshine's blooming hormones to wither.

"I can get it," she offered, needing to stand up so she could feel her legs again. "It's probably the delivery boy," she said before Terrance could protest.

Terrance didn't even think twice about her suggestion. He handed Sunshine a twenty-dollar bill from his pocket and leaned back on the couch. He watched with sweet admiration as he allowed the first female ever to answer his door. He didn't give a fuck if it was another bitch on the other side. He would check that bitch ASAP for disrespecting his precious time with Sunshine.

Sunshine opened the door and paid for the food. When she closed the door, she was sure to leave it unlocked. She turned the top lock so that Terrance could hear it lock, and then quickly turned it back the opposite way, so that Rain and Brian could easily make their way in.

Sunshine was sure that her partners in crime observed the Chinese man come in the building with their food. Now the next move was on them. Sunshine would continue to do her part. She had thirty minutes to get Terrance twisted before her collaborators would be creeping up in there. With any luck, she would have him in the bedroom passed out by then.

She walked back over to the couch and placed the bag of food on the coffee table. "Do you have any more weed?" Sunshine asked as she began to situate the food on the paper plates.

Terrance looked as if he had been smacked upside his head with the Remy bottle. "But I thought you didn't smoke," Terrance said, almost concerned.

"I don't smoke all the time; only when I'm in good hands," Sunshine lied.

Terrance fell for it. He pulled out a Dutch Masters and a brown paper bag half filled with weed, and began rolling it up. Sunshine was beginning to feel sorry for him. He unknowingly made himself easy bait, like he had no backbone. He didn't seem to have any kind of clue that he was being played.

Sunshine played with her food, taking small bites, but truthfully, she really didn't have an appetite. She only ate to convince Terrance that she was really hungry. He didn't eat at all. He seemed content with his liquor and the blunt that he was about to put in the air.

Sunshine looked at the clock that hung on Terrance's wall. She had a little over fifteen minutes left to complete a miracle. Terrance didn't seem to be even halfway where she wanted him. If she had to, Sunshine thought she would go back into the bathroom and text message them to let them know that she needed more time.

Terrance sparked the blunt and hit it several times before passing it over to Sunshine.

Sunshine watched with astonishment as he exhaled the smoke, creating small circles. One even came out like it was in the shape of a heart. When it was Sunshine's turn to hit the blunt, she was surprised at her own self for actually hitting it. She had intended on pulling a Bill Clinton move, but instead she pulled back on it with ease and exhaled her chimney. It was stronger than she had anticipated, because she began to gag uncontrollably.

Terrance took the blunt out of her grip and placed it in the ashtray. He stood over her and began patting her back.

Once Sunshine had finished with her episode, she was totally embarrassed and high.

"Don't feel bad," Terrance said. "That's what you call crucial skunk weed. You probably never had that before."

I never had no kind before, Sunshine thought.

But she had to admit, she did like the way it made her feel. The Remy mixed with the weed made her feel nice and mellow . . . and horny.

Terrance, who was still kneeling over her, bent his head down and kissed her with his tempting pair of lips. Sunshine could feel the print of his hard erection up against her during his gentle kiss. This was not part of the plan, but oddly enough, Sunshine couldn't resist him. His kiss was soft and warm, and when his tongue found its way to hers, a simple kiss turned into a serious slob down. Soon, they were all down each other's throats, searching for the end.

Terrance didn't waste any more time. He scooped Sunshine up in his big, strong arms and brought her into his bedroom. He gently spread her out on his bed, just like he had imagined himself doing in his daydreams.

Sunshine could feel her head spinning. "Wait a minute!" she cried. "We can't do this, Terrance." Somewhere way in the back of her mind she knew that it was supposed to be the other way around. She was supposed to be dragging him in there.

"It's okay, Sunshine. I won't do nothing you don't want me to do. We can take it as slow as you want us to, and I will stop whenever you tell me."

Terrance pulled Sunshine's dress down and was pleased when she didn't resist. He then undid her bra and slid down her panties, exposing a body that was out of this world. She looked better than any broad on any porn he had ever watched. Terrance was so moved by her beauty that he didn't even want to touch her right away. He lay beside her and simply admired her loveliness for a minute before he began taking his own clothes off and allowing his ever-ready body to meet hers.

Sunshine couldn't fight it. There was something alluring about Terrance that permitted him to do whatever he wanted to do to her. When he came out of his boxers, she couldn't believe her eyes were seeing clearly. She had to touch it to make sure that it was real. She placed her hands on his hard flesh. Yes, it was real, every inch of his stiff dick was certainly real.

Terrance's whole body cringed at the tender stroke of Sunshine's hand gliding up and down his erection. He wanted to put it inside her right then and there, but first he had to taste her sweet young breasts.

Terrance sucked on her nipples tenderly and listened to her soft cries of pleasure. He then began to slide his tongue back and forth over each breast, before taking each one and teasingly swallowing it whole. Sunshine was moaning and groaning so softly that he could barely hear her. He wanted to make her sigh louder, so he went down and spread her legs apart and began to suck all over her juicy pink pussy like it was a watermelon. Now he had her screaming his name just like he wanted.

She was scratching his back and begging him to stop, but he couldn't. He had to make her love him, and there was only one way—by making passionate love to her. Terrance lifted his head from his booty heaven and let his throbbing rod gladly take the place of his lips.

Terrance rubbed his penis all over her warm, wet pussy and all over her clitoris, allowing her one sweet orgasm before he gently eased his way inside and gave her multiple. She was so tight, and he didn't want to hurt her, so he worked it in real slow, putting it in inch by inch. Finally, he was all the way inside her, rubbing against her virgin walls and letting his rhythm flow. Now they were both screaming.

Sunshine couldn't believe that this was happening. She couldn't believe that she was making love for the very first time, and with Terrance.

His strokes were becoming longer and stronger, making the whole bed rock to his beat.

FIFTEEN

Sunshine and Terrance were so consumed in their noisy lovemaking that they never heard Rain, Brian, and Cathy enter the apartment.

Rain silently twisted the doorknob and inched the door open. She crept inside with Brian and Cathy right behind her. Rain looked around the apartment and thought she was inside the wrong one for a minute. The place was cleaner than she had ever witnessed it before. She could even see the actual leather of his couch and love seat, without his dirty clothes and underwear thrown all over it. She knew she was inside the right apartment, though, because she could still smell the fresh scent of some crucial skunk in the air.

Cathy was the last one inside the apartment, and she made sure to leave the door slightly ajar, so they could have a clean getaway. She would be the last one in and the last one out, so her girls wouldn't have to witness a ruthless death.

Rain could hear noises coming from the bedroom; however, she couldn't quite make them out. She figured it was probably just the TV or the radio, and maybe Sunshine had turned it on to make sure that Terrance didn't hear when they came in. Rain then noticed the empty bottle of Remy and the two empty glasses on the table, and she knew for sure that Sunshine had done her part to get Terrance fucked up.

Rain quietly guided Brian and Cathy toward the hallway closet, where they searched high and low with no luck for the shopping bags.

"They must be in his bedroom," Rain whispered. "I'll go check. Y'all stay out here and look around," she said.

Rain tiptoed to the back toward Terrance's room. As she got closer, the noises became more apparent. Rain could make out some severe fuck cries.

Terrance must have put in one of his nasty porno flicks, she thought. *Poor Sunshine. She must be bored to death watching that shit.*

When Rain appeared in the doorway and saw the two figures, she was stuck. She could feel her brain lock, and it wouldn't send the necessary message to her body to move. She felt paralyzed in the spot where she stood, while she watched Terrance bounce in and out of Sunshine like a bunny rabbit.

Their clothes were thrown everywhere. Sweat was dripping off Terrance's body onto Sunshine's like raindrops. Sunshine's long legs dangled in the air, while she dug her nails into Terrance's skin.

At first they didn't see her standing there, but just when Terrance was sounding off that he was about to cum, Sunshine opened her eyes and saw Rain standing in the doorway like a deranged mannequin.

"I'm sorry, Rain," Sunshine moaned through Terrance's eager pumps.

Terrance heard Sunshine, but he thought she was simply talking to herself, feeling guilty for what they were doing to each other.

Sunshine tried to push Terrance off of her, but he couldn't stop. He was about to explode, and all her strength couldn't match his.

"Oh, shit! Sunshine, I love you!" Terrance screamed while his dick drained its juices inside her pussy.

To Sunshine's disapproval, her own body began to share an earth-shaking orgasm with his. As both of their bodies jerked and twitched from ecstasy, Rain's body snapped out of it. She charged over to their naked bodies with force, jumped on the bed, and began swinging her tightly balled fists at both of them.

"Y'all some fucking snakes!" she yelled. "I can't believe this shit! Sunshine, you backstabbing bitch! I thought you was cool, but you just wanted my nigga the whole time!" Rain yelled at the top of her lungs.

Sunshine didn't say anything. She was helpless. She balled herself up into a fetal position while Rain landed solid punches all over her naked flesh.

Terrance was mad now. He lifted Rain effortlessly off of Sunshine and threw her on the floor with no remorse. "How the fuck did you get in here, bitch? Did you break in my crib, you psycho bitch? I'm calling the feds on your ass!" Terrance yelled.

Just then, Cathy and Brian charged into the room. After hearing all the loud yelling, they knew that their cover was blown.

"You're not going to call no damn body, except for Jesus to save your ass, nigga," Cathy said.

"Sunshine, put your clothes on, and y'all get out of here," Cathy ordered. She reached into her purse to get her gun ready.

Terrance looked all around him, from Brian to Rain to Cathy, and then to Sunshine. That's when he realized that he had been set up. He didn't have time to think about how stupid he had been. The only thing he had time for was protecting himself.

Terrance quickly reached for his handy .45, equipped with a silencer, from under his pillows. Then he quickly snatched Sunshine's stripped body and pressed it up against his.

"You move too slow, bitch. I can't believe I was going to make your ho ass my woman," he said to Sunshine. Terrance placed the silver barrel to Sunshine's temple and said, "Now I want all you bitches to get the fuck out my crib, crazy bitches!"

By then, Cathy had also retrieved her gun from her purse. It was only a matter of who would bust off first. With Sunshine being held hostage, it put Cathy at a disadvantage for now.

"You need to put that thing away and stop playing with me," Brian said to Terrance.

Terrance pointed the gun in Brian's direction. "Shut up, bitch! I will put my gun away when you and your crew is out my damn crib!" he yelled, ready to blow Brian away if he had to.

"Okay, damn!" Brian said. "But I was talking about that thing," he said, pointing to Terrance's dick, which hadn't completely lost its erection.

"This is not the time to be funny, Brianna. This nigga has a weapon and he will use it," Rain warned.

Cathy took advantage of the situation and slowly raised her arm, pointing her nine millimeter to Terrance's head.

Terrance saw her every move. He swiftly turned to aim his gun at Cathy and pulled his trigger before she could pull hers.

Brian saw it coming. He dove on top of Cathy, just in time to catch her bullet right in his back and through his chest. Brian perished immediately.

Sunshine began to scream in horror. Terrance released her body and tried to run out of the bedroom to get free. From the floor, Cathy raised her free arm and with perfect aim, shot Terrance right in the head—but not before he got one last shot off. His body slumped over halfway out the doorway. Now it was Rain's turn to scream.

Cathy tried to roll Brian's lifeless body off of hers, but he was too heavy. "Rain, please help me!" Cathy screamed.

Rain ran over and freed Brian's dead weight off Cathy. As Cathy stood, blood began to leak from her chest. Terrance's last shot had pierced Cathy's heart before his own lights went out for good. Cathy fell to the floor, and Sunshine and Rain were left in the midst of a massive blood bath, three dead bodies surrounding them.

Sunshine was still on the bed and traumatized, deep in shock. She was incoherent as Rain ordered her to get up and get dressed. She was so gone that, much to Rain's dismay, she had to put her clothes on for her. Rain tried not to let the previous sight of Sunshine love-wrestling with her man get to her. She tried not to let the horrid sight of Terrance's finished body distract her. Rain tried to blank out Cathy's and Brian's murdered bodies as she had to trip over them to get out of the bedroom.

Dragging Sunshine out with her proved to also be a difficult task. Rain let her fall to the floor and eventually had to smack Sunshine's face several times to bring her back to reality.

"Sunshine, get a grip. We've got to clean this place up!" Rain shouted.

Sunshine stood up, still dazed but trying to do as she was told. When she got up, she moved at a much slower pace than Rain.

Rain scurried around the whole apartment, wiping away all traces of their presence. She threw the Remy bottle and the empty glasses off the balcony, deep into the woods. She removed the rented video from the DVD player and put it back into the plastic bag that Sunshine had brought with her.

While Rain worked her way around the apartment, Sunshine looked in Terrance's bedroom closet to find something to wipe their fingerprints off the doorknobs. She picked up the first thing she could find, which was a Tupac T-shirt that lay on top of a pile of dirty clothes. That's when Sunshine also spotted all their shopping bags from Pentagon City. They were stacked up neatly in the corner of the closet. Posted right next to the bags, Sunshine noticed a huge safe with a combination.

"Rain, come here!" she hollered.

Rain ran into the bedroom with Terrance's cordless phone clung to her ear.

"Shut the fuck up," she whispered with her fingers up to her lips. "I've got 911 on the line. They've got me on hold."

Sunshine hushed her voice into a whisper. "Sorry." Then she pointed to the bags for Rain to see.

"Take that shit out to the car. All this shit ain't go down for nothing," Rain muttered.

Sunshine dropped the T-shirt she was holding and picked up two armloads of bags. Rain opened up the front door for Sunshine to help her out, making sure to wipe the doorknob off, so as not to leave fingerprints of her own.

Rain wiped all the doorknobs inside the apartment while she informed the officer on the line of Terrance's address, so they could send some help.

"Would you like to leave a name?" the dutiful officer asked.

"Hell no!" Rain said and hung up the phone.

Sunshine came back inside just in time for Rain to hand her the last of the stolen items.

"Hold up for a minute," Sunshine said. She ran back into the bedroom to Cathy. She kneeled down and pulled Cathy into her arms. Sunshine placed soft kisses on Cathy's face. Tears fell from Sunshine's eyes, as she could still feel the loving warmth emanating from Cathy's corpse. She didn't want to let go.

Rain had to drop everything that she was carrying to go help Sunshine. She was crying and trembling so hard that Rain had to pry her off of Cathy.

"Please, Rain, we've got to take her with us! We can't just leave her here," Sunshine cried.

"She'll be okay, Sunshine. She's better off here. Help is on the way. But we've got to get out of here before they come," Rain said. "Come on, Sunshine, get up!"

Sunshine was relentless. She squeezed Cathy tight one last time, and then stood up slowly to leave. Rain pulled Sunshine away, trying to get her to hurry up. They could hear sirens coming from a distance.

"Let's go, Sunshine! Come on!"

They grabbed the rest of their bags and slid out of the apartment before the authorities could identify them. Once they were outside, Rain double-checked to make sure that no one had noticed them. Fortunately for them, the bystanders hanging around were so engrossed in their own dealings that they didn't even notice the two fleeing the scene of the crime.

Sunshine and Rain threw all the bags into the car, trying to appear as casual as possible. They hopped in the front seat, with Rain on the driver's side. As they pulled out of the complex, they saw two police cars drive into the parking lot and stop in front of Terrance's building. Rain casually drove off the scene without looking back

Sunshine was a wreck and cried uncontrollably all the way home.

SIXTEEN

Although the house was filled with all kinds of fly decorations, jazzy portraits, and cozy furnishings, it felt as empty as air when Sunshine walked inside. Sunshine and Rain sat on the hallway steps in silence. Sunshine couldn't fathom the thought that there was no more Cathy. If she hadn't seen her shot and killed before her very own eyes, she would've expected Cathy to come walking up right behind them, laughing and carrying on as if nothing had ever happened.

Sunshine didn't want to accept this kind of pain. Not again. She didn't know how she would be able to stay even one night in this house where she had shared so many special memories when it was just her and Cathy. Although their memories were short lived, they were priceless, and it was inconceivable that it had all come to such a bitter end.

Rain was also caught up in her own world. She was trying to focus and maintain, but just thinking about her life's events, leading up to now, seemed sadly disastrous. It was as if everything she touched ended up fucked up in some kind of way, and as though she wasn't meant to have anything worth holding on to. With both her mother and father dead, her little brothers gone, Terrance dead, and now Cathy dead and gone too, who could she run to? Rain began to feel sorry for herself because she didn't have anyone left. What would become of her now? Would she merely just be a pass-around package, going from one foster home to another, until she turned eighteen and had to fend for herself? Hell no. Rain couldn't see that happening. She needed stability, something she could call her own for once in this life.

Rain thought about Terrance's safe that was still inside the Camry. She looked over at Sunshine, who looked near death herself. A clear, vivid picture flashed into her mind of Sunshine and Terrance's trembling bodies sharing what seemed to be the ultimate orgasm. That was supposed to be her lying underneath Terrance, exchanging fuck faces.

Rain had to shake it off, because the dominating feeling of a severe ass whooping was becoming very hot and tempting. Rain managed to control the raging sensation to throw bountiful blows all over Sunshine's deceitful body. Odd as it may seem, something within Rain's soul told her not to react on her vicious thoughts. If it had been anybody else, she would have unleashed the tiger, but lucky for Sunshine, Rain had a little compassion in her heart for the girl.

Sunshine looked into Rain's eyes and accepted the look of betrayal that reeked out.

"Rain, for what it's worth, I truly am sorry. I don't know what came over me today. I'm not going to sit here and blame it on the liquor I drank, or the weed I smoked. Everything I did was truly on me, and I take full responsibility. All I can say is that I'm sorry," Sunshine cried on.

Before Sunshine could finish her sob story with a predictable, teary ending, Rain cut in. "Listen to me, Sunshine. I hear what you're saying, but right now we've got some more important shit to tend to. What's done is done." Rain wasn't trying to hear the rest of that bullshit Sunshine was about to say. They both had to get over it.

Rain stood up from the step where they sat. "Meet me back in Cathy's room. I'll be right back," she told Sunshine. Rain walked out to the car and came back minutes later, carrying Terrance's safe in her arms. She dropped the heavy safe on Cathy's bed, in front of where Sunshine sat.

"I'm going to find a way to get this thing open, and you need to start looking around this room to see where Cathy might hide her money," Rain ordered. "Two things for sure: I'm not going to continue to be state's property, so I definitely got to get the fuck away from here, and I damn sure ain't leaving broke."

Rain began to play around with the knob of the safe. First, she tried using easy codes to see if Terrance was foolish enough to set a code as simple as 1-2-3 or 7-7-7. After several attempts, she realized that she wasn't going to get it open that way.

"I'll be right back," Rain said to Sunshine. She jumped off the bed and ran out of the bedroom.

Sunshine got off the bed and began to search throughout the room for a spot where Cathy might hide her money. Sunshine wasn't even sure if Cathy had any money stashed like Rain assumed, and if she did have money, it couldn't possibly be much.

Sunshine lifted up the mattress. She didn't find any money, but she did find several unused condoms, a vibrator, and a small book that apparently looked to be Cathy's diary.

Sunshine began to feel uneasy about the idea of going through Cathy's personal things. It didn't feel right, like she was violating her in some kind of way. She briefly stopped her search, put her hands together, and looked up toward the sky. She pleaded out loud for Cathy to forgive her.

"Cathy, you know I love you, and I would never do anything to disrespect you. I know that you want me to have what I'm looking for. Lead me to it."

Sunshine allowed tranquility set in while she continued with her search. She was careful to fix and put everything as she had found it once she was finished. Sunshine looked inside every dresser. She checked in the file cabinets, underneath the carpet, and inside every pocketbook. She also looked inside the walk-in closet.

After ten long minutes of looking throughout the entire bedroom, she was going to give up. Then she noticed a small opening in the lower part of the wall, inside the closet. Only a smart eye could have noticed it, because it was conveniently disguised, hidden right behind a dirty clothes hamper.

Sunshine pushed the hamper to the side. Butterflies began to spread their wings in her heart as she pried the covering open with her fin-

gers. Inside the dark opening, she saw the pipe-
lines which led to Cathy's bathroom. They were
covered with dust and cobwebs. Underneath the
pipes, Sunshine noticed a plastic laundry bag
crammed in an opening. She didn't hesitate to
rescue the bag from its hiding place and drag it
into the open.

Sunshine sat frozen for a minute. Although
she had asked Cathy's spirit to guide her, she
still felt like a criminal, even before looking at
what was inside the laundry bag.

"Well, don't just sit there. Open it!"

Sunshine's chilled body almost burst into
cold ice chips at the sound of the voice. For a
quick instant, she thought it was Cathy's ghost,
until she turned and saw Rain standing at the
entrance of the closet.

Sunshine did a double take closely at Rain.
Rain stood firm, masked with a face shield,
wearing a heavy pair of safety gloves, and holding a huge chainsaw with both hands.

"What's all that for?" Sunshine asked with
curiosity.

"Girl, this old thing," Rain joked. "No, for
real, though, this getup is about to get us paid. I
found it outside in the garage," Rain explained.

Sunshine sealed the opening to the pipeline
back up and placed the hamper back in front

of it like nothing had happened. She pulled the load with its contents beside the bed.

Rain set down the saw for a minute to place the safe onto the floor beside the bag. Both girls stared with admiration at the two concealed objects, ready to reveal the possible valuable treasures.

Rain picked up the ever-ready chain saw, pulled back the chain, and said, "Here goes nothing." The motor sounded, and Rain began slicing away at the metal, driving its force impeccably, until it reached its center point. Electrical sparks and fire drizzled as she diligently proceeded on.

Sunshine had to stand back as Rain chiseled on. The piercing sound of the mechanical engine from the saw and the determined, thundering heartbeat eventually brought forth the expected treasure to behold. Once the safe was split in half, Terrance's life savings were uncovered.

"Jackpot!" Rain screamed. She felt like she was hallucinating while she carefully examined all the hard-earned drug money that Terrance had stacked.

"Damn! I thought my nigga was small time, but he was bigger than a trigger!" Rain boasted. "Now it's your turn," Rain said to Sunshine, pointing to the unopened laundry bag.

Sunshine was relieved her effort wasn't going to be as great as Rain's had just been. Sunshine effortlessly unzipped the plastic laundry bag and unraveled a hefty load of dirty money. Bundles of dead presidents stared them right in the face.

Sunshine and Rain were both in awe of the green beauty of their newfound riches. There was so much wealth in the room that it temporarily erased all traces of guilt, sadness, anger, and dishonesty. The atmosphere was replaced with dreams, happiness, ambition, and power. There was so much money surrounding them that they didn't even bother with counting it out or dividing it evenly. Each one simply claimed the pile that was closest to her. Sunshine scooped all her Benjamins into the laundry bag, while Rain stuffed her stash into one of Cathy's MCM tote bags.

Sunshine and Rain both realized that eventually the authorities would have to come to the house to investigate, once they identified the dead bodies in Terrance's apartment. Rain stood up to clean the mess from the broken safe. Sunshine went to grab a trash bag so that she could help discard the shattered remains.

"I'm going to throw this shit in a lake somewhere. That way can't nobody point their nasty little fingers at us," Rain said.

Rain knew she had to get rid of any evidence linking them to Terrance's apartment if they were going to have a clean getaway.

"Would you like for me to ride with you?" Sunshine asked.

"Nah, I'm going to ride out and get rid of this myself. I don't need no company," Rain answered. "When I get back, I'm not staying long enough for none of them fake-ass social workers to come and get me. They won't get this young girl to be another one of their orphaned statistics," Rain fussed. "I'm going to take all this money and get the fuck out—do some big shit for myself. Just like you, I don't have no family to turn to, so I'm going to do me," Rain said daringly. "I don't expect for you to be here when I get back, Sunshine," Rain said.

She wanted Sunshine to understand that she didn't want her to follow her wherever she ended up. This would be their separating point, with no hard feelings in the mix. Maybe if things had gone down differently, they could have still flown the coop together, but Rain wasn't going to allow herself to get stationed with someone who she couldn't even trust. The fact that Sunshine had fucked Terrance would always eat at her brain like a tumor. Rain didn't get down like that.

Rain looked at Sunshine, who sat still, with her legs crossed, wearing a clueless expression on her face. Rain began to feel sorry for her.

"Why don't you call Diego, Sunshine? That nigga is really feeling you. Spend some of that bread on his ass and make him your nigga," Rain said.

A warm smile escaped from Sunshine's lips at the mention of Diego's name. She hadn't even given him much thought after all the madness had happened. Rain was right. It wouldn't hurt just to call Diego.

While Sunshine busied herself calling Diego, Rain left to dispose of the trash bag and all its incriminating contents. She made sure to take her money with her. Not that she thought Sunshine would take it, but shit, she hadn't thought she would end up fucking Terrance, either.

Sunshine felt nervous when she heard Diego answer the phone. "Hello, Diego. It's me, Sunshine. Are you busy right now? I really need somebody to talk to," Sunshine said.

"I'm never too busy for some Sunshine," Diego answered smoothly. "What's going on? Are you okay?" Diego asked.

"I'm okay, but I would be better if you could come and get me," Sunshine said.

"Just give me your address and I'll be right there," Diego said.

"It's not that simple, Diego. I need a place to stay," Sunshine said.

"Well, how about you give me your address, and I'll be on my way so we can talk about this," Diego said. "Whatever it is you're going through, we'll work it out," he added.

Sunshine felt more at ease knowing that she had someone to confide in a little bit. Of course she wouldn't give him all the gory details, but something was better than nothing. Plus, Diego sounded so compassionate, unlike Rain, who was ready to abandon her so easily.

Sunshine knew that she had been wrong for making love to Terrance, but she couldn't change it. All she could do now was apologize and try to move on. Certainly she would miss Rain once she was gone; she had grown attached to her in a short amount of time, but this was her call.

Sunshine gave Diego her address and hung up the phone. She thought about calling Ms. Waters but hastily thought against it. Sunshine knew that Ms. Waters would try to make her stay, only to send her to another foster home. Sunshine wasn't in the mood to meet and get to know a whole new family. She just wanted to get on with her life, with no strings attached to anyone, except for maybe Diego.

With Rain gone off on her little mission, Sunshine was able to have a moment to herself to say good-bye to the house and its memories to which she had grown so attached. Before she went upstairs, Sunshine searched around Cathy's room for something small and meaningful that she could keep; something special that she would be able to remember her second mother by. Sunshine already had plenty of pictures of the two of them together, but she wanted something sentimental that belonged to Cathy. She thought about grabbing one of Cathy's dresses, like she had done with Ayanna, but as she looked through her closet, nothing seemed to reach out to her.

Sunshine looked inside Cathy's jewelry box and pulled out a pair of her favorite diamond studs. She held the earrings close to her heart, remembering the many times Cathy had worn them on their nights out at Royals. Sunshine seized the earrings and ran upstairs to her bedroom so she could begin packing. She put only a few of her precious items inside her Louis Vuitton suitcase. She placed Cathy's diamond studs on top of her mother's dress, closed her valise, and went downstairs to wait for Diego on the front porch.

***

When Rain got back to the house, there was no trace of Sunshine's presence. A surprising feeling of emptiness filled her heart as she realized that Sunshine was really gone. She swiftly shook that unwanted feeling and ran upstairs to her bedroom. When she got there, she noticed a white envelope on her bed with her name on it in red ink. Rain picked up the envelope and ripped it open. She took the letter out and unfolded the page. She read the writing aloud:

> *Dear Rain,*
>
> *True friendship is a virtue so strong to behold; Some lies and deception may be hidden or told. Their souls meet, their souls touch, their souls love, their souls lock; and even through unintentional separation, their friendship holds as solid as a rock.*
>
> Love, Sunshine

Rain put the poem up to her heart and was emotionally touched by Sunshine's words. Sunshine had told her she had skill, but maybe she had underestimated just how much. Tears escaped Rain's eyes as she thought about what could have been. She couldn't fight back the pain anymore. Rain let the tears that had always stayed hidden so well fall freely from her eyes. Moments later, her pain turned into anger.

She raised her head to the sky and screamed, "How strong do you want a bitch to be? How much more bullshit do I have to go through to show you that I am official?" When Rain didn't get an answer from her higher power, she wiped away her tears and stood up to make her next move.

While Rain packed her bags, she thought about the endless possibilities. With all her money, she could travel to the end of the world and back if she wanted to. However, Rain just wanted to go somewhere where she could settle down and build a new life for herself until she was old enough to send for her little brothers.

Rain thought about school. She would be a senior this year, and she couldn't just drop out. That would be ridiculous after making it through thirteen hellish years of school. Maybe it would be better if she just got her GED. It was just as good as a diploma, and that way she wouldn't have to find somebody to enroll her in school.

Maybe she would move to New York City. She had heard a lot of hype about New York. Maybe she would venture to California and Las Vegas before she decided on a permanent spot. Shit, her options were worldwide. If she didn't like any of those hoods, she could always go somewhere else. Rain was beginning to feel better. Things were actually starting to feel like they were looking up.

Rain lifted her head back to the sky. "Forgive me for shouting out like that. I was so over-whelmed." Rain knew it was time to get out of there. She left behind the deafening silence, the empty house, and the brief memories of Sunshine, Cathy, and Brian.

SEVENTEEN

FIVE YEARS LATER

"Throw the ball to Mommy, baby!" Sunshine yelled to Little Diego. He threw the basketball to her with all his little-boy might and successfully landed the ball midway to his mother.

"Good boy!" Sunshine commended. She ran to get the ball from the short distance. "Ready! Set! Catch!" Sunshine yelled, and then she threw the ball back to Little Diego.

The small boy spread his arms open wide and caught the flying ball. The force from the ball soaring through the air was more powerful than the small boy could handle, and his whole body toppled over in the grass. Sunshine laughed at her young superstar as he struggled to get back up, never once letting go of the ball.

"I did it, Daddy! I did it!" Little Diego screamed excitedly.

At first Sunshine was confused, but then she turned to look behind her and was glad to see Diego standing there.

Sunshine smiled and gave her husband the biggest hug. She liked to show him big love whenever he entered a room. Little Diego ran up and joined in to make it one big family hug.

"I did it, Daddy!" he cheered.

"That's Daddy's big boy! I'm proud of you, son," Diego praised.

Diego released his family, picked up the ball and yelled, "Now see if you can catch this one from me, 'cause you know your mommy throws like a girl!"

Sunshine laughed at the insult, and Diego winked his eye at her to confirm. Sunshine took that as her cue to just sit on down. She didn't go far though. She walked to their back porch and sat in the lawn chair to watch her two favorite men play ball. She sat back and was pleased to be able to relax now that Diego was home. He would pick up with Little Diego where she had left off.

While Sunshine began to unwind from another busy day of motherhood, she allowed the cool fall breeze to accommodate her. She watched with interest as her pair of Diegos fooled around with the ball.

To Sunshine, the picture looked perfect from the outside, but on the inside, the portrait wasn't original. As Sunshine continued to watch them play, she could feel another guilt trip coming on, because deep down inside, she knew it wasn't right to keep such a deep, dark secret hidden from her husband. Diego would be torn apart if he knew that there was the slightest possibility that Little Diego was not a 100% full breed. He was proud, to say the least, to have his first-born be a son who carried his full name.

Sunshine didn't know how to tell Diego that Little Diego may not be his son, especially after so much time. Five years ago, when she moved in with Diego, everything had progressed so fast. When she moved into his apartment, they instantly became the perfect couple. Diego lived up to every word that he preached. They did all the things that lovers do. Sunshine would accompany him to all his late-night concerts. She would even write some of the band's material. They double-dated a few times with some of the other band members. They would go to see all the latest movies, plays, and shows that came to town, and even some out of town. Sunshine hadn't planned on living with Diego that long, but love wouldn't allow her to move on.

Two months into the relationship, Sunshine still hadn't seen her period. When her pregnancy test came back positive, she realized then that the baby very well could be Terrance's. Diego didn't know anything about Terrance.

Sunshine had been very convincing when she told Diego that he was her first lover. Diego was honored by that, and he would be mortified at the thought of another man making love to his precious Sunshine.

However, every day, Sunshine was ashamed by how much Little Diego favored Terrance. The long, slick plaits that fell to his neck reminded her more of her first lover than ever. Sunshine couldn't count how many times she thought about telling Diego the truth. She thought about it in the early morning while they ate breakfast, late at night during dinner, even while making passionate love, but it never felt like the right time. She knew that once the truth was told, Diego may want to divorce her and sell their beautiful three-level home that they had built together. Sunshine couldn't let that happen. She would keep the truth concealed from him forever and endure a million guilt trips before she would lose the love of her life and mess up their happy home.

The phone rang and brought Sunshine out of her deep thought. She stood up to go answer the phone.

"Hello?" Sunshine answered cheerfully.

Click! The caller hung up instantly at the sound of her voice.

Sunshine was irritated by the phone call. She checked the caller ID, and as usual, it read CALLER UNKNOWN. Sunshine wondered who was constantly playing on their phone. The caller never said anything, and nothing could be heard in the background. At one point, Sunshine went as far as getting their number changed and unlisted, but the determined caller still found a way to get the new number.

Sunshine put her aggravation to the back of her mind for the time being and decided to get ready for her weekly bible study. Since Diego spent a majority of his time out of town, promoting his band and trying to get them higher exposure, church had become Sunshine's best friend. She and Little Diego went every Sunday for the Lord's message, every Tuesday for choir practice, and every Wednesday for bible study.

Sometimes Diego would attend if he had time. Tonight he wouldn't be going because he had band practice. He had been out all day, passing out flyers for tomorrow night's show. Sunshine missed the days when she was able to escort him to these events, but Little Diego couldn't watch himself, and there were very few people who they trusted to watch him.

Sunshine walked upstairs and ran some warm water in the tub for her bath. While the water ran, she searched in her closet for a casual outfit to wear. Her selection was endless, and she even still had clothes with the tags attached. She pulled out a sky blue pantsuit similar to the one she had admired years ago that Ms. Waters had worn.

She smiled as she laid the outfit on the bed and thought about Ms. Waters. Once she had turned eighteen years old and had known that she was completely out of social service's system, she had called Ms. Waters to let her know that she was doing fine.

Their conversation had lasted for over an hour while Sunshine brought Ms. Waters up to date on all her current events. She told Ms. Waters that she had heard about Cathy's unfortunate death and was so messed up behind it that she just ran away.

Ms. Waters didn't think anything of her partial lie; she took it in like the truth. She would call all the time to check in on Sunshine and Little Diego. Sometimes they would even ride to church together. When Sunshine had asked her if there was any word on Rain Concise, Ms. Waters said she hadn't heard anything, but that she would check into it.

Sunshine thought about Rain all the time. She missed her spunky attitude, her sharp tongue, and her strong "I don't give a fuck" nature. Although she had met a lot of new friends in her church, she didn't connect with any of them like she had with Rain. Rain was real, and Sunshine had to admit that there weren't too many official females left that she could put on her level.

Sunshine wanted so badly for Rain to see Little Diego so they could compare notes. Surely by now, after all this time, Rain would have gotten over the fact that she slept with Terrance. Sometimes Sunshine thought about hiring a private investigator to find Rain, but she never did, afraid of what she might find.

She stepped into her warm bath and closed her eyes. This was her favorite part of each day. Usually she would light candles and spend some quality time with herself, but this evening she didn't have any extra time, as she still had to make dinner and get Little Diego dressed and ready to go before they left for bible study.

Sunshine couldn't wait to get to church and be around her church family. Church always made her feel whole, when nothing else did. Even Little Diego loved to go. He didn't fall asleep like most children did. Sunshine thought he would grow up to be somebody's preacher or something because he already seemed filled with the Holy Spirit.

While Sunshine got dressed, she could hear her two boys racing up the steps. They sounded like a herd of elephants coming after her. She was in the process of pulling up her g-string when Diego charged through the door. Little Diego must have gone in his own room, because she did not see him behind Diego.

"Got damn!" Diego said. "Who are you, and what have you done with my wife?" he asked while staring at her bare breasts enticingly. Fortunately, pregnancy had not done a thing to deflate Sunshine's breasts, and they still stood nice and firm, just as they had before. Diego closed the door behind him and decided to take full advantage of the situation.

Sunshine saw the wanting look in his eye and felt sorry to have to bat him down. She did not like making love before service. Husband or not, he would have to wait until she felt right and ready.

"Baby, you know I'm on my way to church," she said.

Sunshine did not have to say another word. Diego understood only too well. He knew that Sunshine didn't play that "messing around before church" mess.

He walked up to her, kissed her innocently on her cheek, and said, "Well, I'll be taking a cold shower to calm my main nerve until you get back."

Sunshine laughed and put her bra on to conceal any further temptation from him. She put on her robe and went downstairs to prepare a quick dinner.

"Mommy, Mommy, can I wear this to church tonight?" Little Diego yelled. Sunshine looked at the denim jeans and Batman T-shirt that her son had picked out all by himself. She was pleased to see that it actually matched.

"Yes, baby, you can wear that," Sunshine answered.

As Sunshine began to prepare dinner, the telephone rang. The caller ID read UNKNOWN CALLER, just as it had earlier. Sunshine thought about ignoring it this time, but picked it up out of curiosity anyway.

"Hello?" she said into the phone.

"I got it, baby," Diego said from their bedroom phone.

Sunshine hung up the phone, but she was even more curious as to who the caller was on the other end.

Sunshine was in a daze. She could have sworn that she had just heard another woman's voice on the other end of the phone.

"Mommy, what are we eating for dinner?" Little Diego asked, interrupting Sunshine's thoughts. Sunshine had almost forgotten that he was still in the room.

"Mommy's making some hot dog sandwiches tonight, baby, so we can hurry up and get out of here."

"I don't want any mustard on my hot dog, Mommy. Mustard is nasty," Little Diego informed her.

"I know, sweetheart, Mommy's not going to put any mustard on your hot dog. Okay, now go run upstairs and wash your face so I can put your clothes on," Sunshine said.

Little Diego ran back up the steps to do as he was told.

Sunshine thought about picking the phone back up to see who Diego was speaking to; however, she didn't want to be sneaky like that. She would simply go upstairs and ask him who the woman was.

Sunshine turned down the boiling hot dogs and ran upstairs to question her husband. When she walked into the room, Diego was laughing and carrying on with his conversation as if he didn't have anything to hide.

"If you're singing tomorrow night, then I quit," Diego joked.

Sunshine suddenly felt foolish. Apparently, he was just talking to someone about business.

Sunshine took off her robe and slipped on her clothes. Diego was still talking to the woman, making plans for tomorrow night's show. Sunshine was beginning to get a little jealous.

"Can't you make these plans tonight at practice? Dinner is ready and we should go downstairs and eat," she said.

"Okay, Charmaine, I'll talk to you in a little bit. My family and I are getting ready to have dinner. Okay, bye-bye."

"Why does Charmaine have to call you from a blocked number?" Sunshine asked as soon as he hung up the phone.

"I don't know, baby. Maybe she's calling from her cell phone," Diego answered.

"Well, how come you have to make plans with her, and not James or some other guy in the band?" Sunshine asked.

"Oh, baby, come on. I know you're not thinking that I'm messing around with her," Diego said.

Sunshine realized how pathetic she seemed, and walked over to embrace Diego. "I'm sorry, sweetheart. I guess since we don't spend as much time together like we used to, I just thought maybe . . ." Sunshine couldn't even finish her thought.

"Well, you need to stop thinking crazy, Sunshine. I love you, and only you." Diego wrapped his arms around Sunshine and began to taste her lips with hunger and desire.

Sunshine felt herself beginning to weaken to his touch. When Sunshine didn't hold back, Diego started to grind his hips against hers. She could feel his erection growing hard against her, even through the baggy jeans he wore. Sunshine's neatly pressed pantsuit was on the verge of getting wrinkled while Diego laid her across the bed and began to sexually attack her.

Just then, Little Diego barged through the door.

"Mommy, Daddy, how do I look?" he asked. He had gotten dressed without any help from Sunshine.

Diego rolled off Sunshine, and they both laughed.

"You look heavenly," Sunshine answered. "And you look like the devil," she said teasingly to Diego. Sunshine stood up and wiped the merging wrinkles off her clothes. "Let go eat, Diego."

The next morning, Sunshine woke up extra early to the phone ringing non-stop.

"Get the phone, Diego," she said in a groggy voice and fell right back asleep. Seconds later, the phone rang again. Sunshine growled with irritation and rolled over to answer the phone herself. She was surprised to realize that Diego wasn't in the bed with her.

He must be using the bathroom, she thought.

Sunshine picked up the phone. "Hello?" she answered in her early morning voice.

"Hello, can I speak to Sunshine?" the woman asked.

"This is me," Sunshine said.

"Damn, you sound like shit!" the woman said.

Sunshine was waking up now. "Who is this?" she asked. The voice sounded familiar, but she couldn't quite make it out.

"It's your sister, dammit! Wake up!"

"Who is this, Vashti?" Sunshine said, guessing it was Little Diego's godmother.

"No, bitch. It's your sister, and I'm on my way over there, so get up and get dressed."

Click! The phone was dead.

Sunshine didn't know who the woman was, but she got of bed and went to the bathroom to splash some water on her face. Maybe it was a crank call.

It took her a minute before she realized that Diego wasn't in the bathroom. Maybe he was downstairs. She crept quietly downstairs so she wouldn't wake little Diego, because once he was awake, the day had officially begun, and it wouldn't be over until he was asleep later on that night.

Sunshine tiptoed around the house in search of her missing husband. After searching the entire house, she realized that he wasn't home. This was turning out to be a crazy day already. Where was Diego? And who was the mystery caller who had awakened her to this mess?

Sunshine went back upstairs and crawled into bed. She lay awake for a few minutes, wondering where her husband could be.

Did he even come home last night? she wondered. She had been sleeping so hard she didn't know the difference. Maybe he just went out for an early morning jog. Sunshine relaxed her nerves and could feel herself about to doze off when she heard the doorbell ring. She looked at the alarm clock and saw that it was six in the morning.

"Who could be ringing my doorbell this time of morning?" Sunshine said to herself.

Maybe Diego forgot his key, she thought as she put on her robe. She checked on Little Diego before she headed back down the steps. Seeing that he was still asleep, she went to go unlock the door for his father.

Sunshine yanked the door open and was shocked to see Rain standing right in front of her. Sunshine stood frozen for a moment, trying to make sure she was seeing right.

"Okay, Sunshine, Kodak moment is over. Can I come inside, or do you want to frame me?" Rain asked.

Sunshine opened the door wider and stepped to the side to let Rain in. "So that was you on the phone earlier?" Sunshine asked, knowing it was.

"Every drip drop," Rain said.

Sunshine looked Rain up and down real hard with astonishment, taking in all her new changes. She was even more beautiful than before. Time had definitely done her well.

"You cut all your hair off," Sunshine said, checking out the short haircut she sported. It reminded Sunshine of the way Cathy used to wear her hair before she died.

"Is that all you have to say to me after five years? I know you can come better than that," Rain teased.

"I'm sorry. You look gorgeous," Sunshine said.

"So do you," Rain replied.

Both women opened their arms wide and took each other in. It felt like days had passed before either one could let go of the other. Sunshine let go first.

"Where have you been? And what you been up to all this time? How did you find me?" Sunshine asked.

"That's better," Rain said. "Well, for the past seven months, I've been trying to hunt your missing ass down. When I said we should go our separate ways, nobody told you to drop off the face of the earth," Rain scolded. "But before that, I was on a mission, traveling all around until I got bored. I've been to Florida, California, Hawaii, and Jamaica."

'Wow!" Sunshine said.

"Tell me about it," Rain said. "Last year I tried to settle down in California. My little brothers are living out there, but they be doing their own thing."

Sunshine was happy for Rain. She seemed more mature, almost like a real woman.

"For a long time, I tried to get you out my head, but I never could," Rain said. "No matter how many Rastas I smoked with, or how many bitches I sipped with, I couldn't stop thinking about your ass," she added.

Rain's facial expression suddenly turned serious. "Is there somewhere where we can sit down and talk?" Rain asked.

"Yeah, come in the kitchen. I'll make us some coffee. My husband's not home yet, so we can talk," Sunshine said.

Rain followed Sunshine into the kitchen. They sat across the table from one another, exchanging glances.

"What's up, Rain?" Sunshine asked. She couldn't imagine what Rain had come all this way for, after all this time to talk about.

Rain got up and grabbed Sunshine and held her tight like she was about to leave for five more years, before she began. Strangely enough, the hug gave Sunshine the chills. When she let go, Rain had tears in her eyes. Sunshine knew it had to be serious.

"Sunshine, I am sorry I didn't come to you sooner. At first I was just being petty, because I was still upset about what happened right before we split up. But then, after the anger wore off, there was no excuse. I was just funning and spending money, living big, but I always had you in my mind."

Sunshine sat quietly, listening intently, still confused by the expression on Rain's face. She didn't know what to expect as she continued to listen.

"Seven months ago, I decided to find you, so I hired a private investigator. Six months ago, she found you and told me that you were married and had a son. When she told me that you had married Diego Sanchez, I couldn't believe that you two had stayed together this whole time. I began calling you then, but I didn't know what I'd say if you answered, so I would hang up and call back the next time I felt the time was right. Not until now did I actually have the nerve to come back and see you face to face," Rain said.

Now Sunshine knew who had been the crank caller all this time.

"I don't understand," Sunshine said.

"Listen to me, Sunshine. I'm about to hit your head with some shit."

EIGHTEEN

"Do you smoke cigarettes? Because you might need one right about now," Rain suggested.

Sunshine was getting mad. "No, I don't fucking smoke! Now stop stalling, Rain, and tell me what's going on!"

Rain sat up from her slouched position on the bed. "Is it okay if I smoke then?" she asked.

"Whatever," Sunshine said. "Just get to the point."

Rain lit her cigarette, blowing her nasty smoke all in Sunshine's face. "The private investigator cost me a pretty penny, and she was well worth the price," Rain began. "She dug up some information I didn't even ask for." Rain opened up a large yellow envelope and took out a sheet of paper. Rain handed the paper over to Sunshine.

"What is it?" Sunshine asked.

"Read it," Rain insisted.

Sunshine looked over the information and observed that it was a copy of her birth certificate, but she still didn't understand what her vital records had to do with anything. Sunshine looked at Rain, wanting some answers.

"This is your news?" Sunshine asked, baffled.

Rain rolled her eyes to the sky. "Don't you get it?" Rain asked, looking at Sunshine as if she were a freak of nature.

"Yeah, I get it. It's a copy of my original birth certificate, but what's the big deal?" Sunshine asked.

"Check out the name of your biological father," Rain said, pointing to the certificate.

Sunshine read the name of her father aloud for Rain's satisfaction. "Name of father, Jimmy Bernard Concise. I still don't get it," Sunshine said.

"Do you get one plus one equals two?" Rain asked sarcastically.

"Sunshine, Jim Concise is my father. Don't you even remember my last name?" Rain asked, bewildered. "This means that you and I are sisters," Rain said bluntly, so that Sunshine could understand completely.

Sunshine read over the birth certificate one more time for confirmation. It was beginning to make sense to her now. She looked over at Rain and saw her in a whole new light. She could see some resemblance the harder she looked. Now

Sunshine understood why she felt so connected to Rain, even while they were apart.

Tears came to Sunshine's eyes. She wasn't sure if it was from the disgusting Newport that Rain had lit, or if it was from the emotional news that Rain had just hit her with.

"This is wonderful news, Rain! All this time I had a sister and I never knew it," Sunshine said.

"A sister and two brothers," Rain reminded her, "and it's no telling how many more of us is out there, the way my father was going."

"Yeah, I never knew our father, but I heard he was a roller," Sunshine added.

"Crazy, huh? Now I wish I would have had the nerve to come back sooner," Rain said.

Both women sat in silence for a minute before Rain said, "Yeah, so how's it being married with a kid and the whole bit?"

Sunshine smiled and said, "It's been great. I have a wonderful life now, but to tell you the truth, I had always felt like something was missing. I could never pinpoint exactly what it was. Now I feel like it all makes sense." There was another pause. "Thank you for coming here."

"Yeah, well, I figured you deserved to know." Rain attempted to make light of Sunshine's heavy emotions. "Plus, I wanted to come back around the area to see my old haunts. Not a bad place you got here, huh?" Rain began to ramble.

"Yeah, thanks. Where are you staying while you're here?" Sunshine asked.

"Not sure yet. I'm not even sure how long I'll stay. I didn't really have much of a plan after telling you about this," Rain confessed, a little surprised at her own bewilderment. Even though she had known that Sunshine was her biological sister, Rain felt like the reality of it all was finally sinking in. Now that she was looking at Sunshine, sitting in Sunshine's home, thinking about Sunshine's family, Rain's eyes actually began to tear up.

Sunshine just leaned over and said simply, "Why don't you stay here with us? I'll introduce you to your family."

But Rain had more to tell. She wasn't ready for this part of the conversation. She thought she could handle it, but now that she was face to face with Sunshine, it was harder than she had expected. Rain looked deep into Sunshine's eyes as her own eyes filled with tears. She grabbed both of Sunshine's hands and decided to just spit it out.

"Sunshine, Diego is gay. He used to fuck with Brianna, and now he's fucking around on you with a switch bitch named Charmaine," Rain spat.

"What? Uh-uh, now you're talking crazy, Rain. There is nothing gay about my husband, and what on earth is a switch bitch?" Sunshine asked.

"A switch bitch is a man switched over to a bitch, and if you don't believe me about your husband, check this out," Rain said. Rain pulled over a dozen photos from a different envelope and sprawled them all across the table for her to view.

Sunshine picked up each picture one by one and was horrified by what she saw. There was no denying that the man in the pictures was Diego. Almost every picture was explicit in Sunshine's eyes. Diego was making out with Charmaine, right out in public, as if he didn't wear her ring. Then there were pictures with Diego from way back in the day, hugging all over Cathy's son, Brian, like they were first lovers. She didn't know who she should be more upset with: Diego's lying, cheating, gay ass, or Rain for ruining her life.

Sunshine threw the repulsive pictures to the side and put her hands over her face to hide the humiliation she felt. Her body began to shake and tremble uncontrollably, as the sight of each picture flashed in her thoughts.

Rain reached over to console her, but Sunshine resisted her touch. She pushed her away and screamed, "Get off of me!"

She no longer cared if she awakened Little Diego. She didn't care if she woke the whole damn neighborhood.

Rain sat still and honored Sunshine's wishes. She had already prepared herself for Sunshine's reaction.

Sunshine got up from the table. She couldn't be confined any longer. She needed to get some air. She ran out of the room and out the door, flying like the wind, away from Rain and away from those filthy pictures that she had brought with her.

Rain sat at the table for a long moment, allowing Sunshine to express her entitled tantrum in peace before she went after her. Rain picked up her evidence and put it back inside the envelope. Little did Sunshine know that this was as hard for Rain to tell her as it was for her to comprehend. What was even more fucked up was that she hadn't gotten to the worst part yet.

Rain went outside to find Sunshine and to make sure she wasn't doing anything extreme, like roaming around outside with her nightgown on, scaring innocent people. She found Sunshine huddled on the back porch, staring blankly into the rising sun. Rain took a chance and approached her.

"Come on, Sunshine. Let's go back inside. It's a little chilly out here for you to be wearing that skimpy outfit." To Rain's surprise, Sunshine got up and followed her in the house.

They went in the kitchen, and Sunshine sat at the table, while Rain searched the unfamiliar cabinets for some coffee. The cabinets were loaded, but Rain didn't see what she was looking for. She didn't bother to ask Sunshine, as she still seemed to be trying to adjust to the news.

Rain decided to give up on the coffee and took a seat next to Sunshine. Sunshine must've secretly known what Rain was trying to do, because she stood up and went directly to the one cabinet Rain had missed and took out a huge container. She moved like a snail as she began brewing the coffee in the coffeemaker.

Then she slowly turned to Rain and asked, "There's more, isn't there?"

Rain put her head down in shame, as if she had been the one caught cheating. She knew this was going to be hard, but damn, did Sunshine have to look sadder than a giftless child at Christmas?

Might as well get the last of it over with, Rain thought. She lifted her head back up to face Sunshine.

"Sunshine, sit down," Rain ordered.

Sunshine sat back in her seat, still wearing the depressing expression on her face.

"Sunshine, when you left Cathy's house the last time I saw you, I was looking through some of Brianna's things, and I saw a prescription for AZT."

Rain waited for a reaction. "So, what does that have to do with me?" Sunshine asked nonchalantly.

"In case you don't know, AZT is a prescription for patients carrying the HIV virus. I'm not saying that you have HIV, but it's no telling how long Brian had it, and he could have given it to Diego, or shit, maybe Diego even gave it to him—which means one of them may have given it to you or even my nephew. When is the last time you had an HIV test taken?" Rain asked, concerned.

Sunshine thought about it for a second. "I had one while I was pregnant with Li'l Diego, and it was negative," Sunshine answered.

"But that was over four years ago, right?" Rain asked, trying to calculate the years it had been.

"Yes, it was about that long ago," Sunshine answered.

"Sometimes it takes a while for the virus to show up in your system, so we need to get you tested again, to make sure you're still healthy," Rain suggested.

Sunshine didn't seem to take the news as hard as she took Diego cheating on her. Maybe because the last *HIV* test was negative. Or, maybe she wasn't ready to face the thought that the very disease that had stolen her mother away from her would be the same one to take her from Little Diego.

Rain knew that she had to get her big sister away from the house and away from Diego's unfaithful ass.

"What am I supposed to do now?" Sunshine asked Rain, looking for answers since she had all the facts.

"Pack your shit, and you and Little Diego come move with me to my house in California. There is plenty of room for you and Little Diego there. You could go to school and find out what it takes to be a professional music producer," Rain went on.

"Are you serious?" Sunshine asked. "How can you expect me to just pack up and leave with you to another state without even talking to Diego first?"

"Fuck that nigga! But if it's really important for you to talk to his dick-sucking ass, then just call him. I'm more than positive he's with Mr.

Charmaine. Why else wouldn't he be here this time of morning with his lovely wife and kid?" Rain asked, not really expecting an answer.

Rain stood up to finish the coffee that Sunshine had started. She made Sunshine's like she made hers, with lots of sugar and little cream. She set the hot mug in front of Sunshine and watched as she began sipping non-stop, showing that her taste buds agreed with the flavor.

Sunshine set her cup down after a long moment of silence. "I'll wait for him to come home, because I don't have a way to reach him," Sunshine said. She was almost sorry as soon as she said it.

Rain went into her bag of tricks and pulled out a sheet of paper with all of Charmaine's information printed out. Her full, real name, which was actually Jermaine Washington; her address, social security number, date of birth, and all of her phone numbers.

Sunshine almost wanted to laugh. "You must have given your private investigator some wonderful head for all this info."

"Hell yeah. She even told me when you had your last menstruation," Rain joked back. It felt good to see Sunshine put a smile on her face. "So what's up? Are you gonna make the call to see if your precious dick-sucker is there or not?"

Sunshine shook her head. She knew it was going to be a crazy day, but this was too much.

"Do you have a cell phone on you? I don't want to call from the house phone," Sunshine said.

Rain went into her purse and handed Sunshine her phone with no problem. Sunshine took the phone but hesitated for a second before dialing. She took a deep breath, exhaled, and then began dialing.

The phone seemed like it would never stop ringing. Then finally, someone picked up on what felt like the thousandth ring. Sunshine could hear someone tussling with the phone, as if they were having a hard time getting it together.

Sunshine's heart began pounding so hard that it could probably be heard through the phone. It almost went through the phone when she heard her husband say, "Hello."

When Sunshine listened harder, it sounded as if someone was in the background moaning. That's when Sunshine put it all together. Diego was in the process of making love at that very moment. That was what took him so long to answer the phone, and that was why he had such a difficult time doing it.

A flash came into Sunshine's mind of the many times they had done the same thing, answering the phone in the middle of making passionate love and trying to maintain a decent conversation at the same time. It was funny to her then, but it wasn't funny now.

Sunshine stopped reminiscing and stopped stalling. She knew the truth for certain now.

"Diego, I'm leaving you. I'm taking our son, and we are moving out. You can have all this shit. The house, the cars, and your name; all that can be replaced. I'm filing for a divorce."

Sunshine hung up the phone without waiting for a response. She headed upstairs to wake Little Diego. While she packed their clothes that they would take with them, the phone rang non-stop, but Sunshine didn't bother to answer it. She knew it was Diego calling, trying to fill her head up with more lies.

Rain helped Sunshine put the luggage into her truck, and the three of them headed down the road toward the airport. Sunshine felt an overwhelming peace the farther away they got from the house that was built on nothing but lies and deception. This new beginning felt different, like this was how it was supposed to be.

Sunshine thought about the HIV test she would have to take once she got settled in

California, but no matter what the outcome, she would live the rest of her life to the fullest and raise her son the best way she knew how, just as her own mother had done. And no matter what, she would always remember to keep her face to the sunshine.

She looked over at her little sister, and tears of joy flowed down her face for the love she felt for her. Rain had come back for her, and now they would build a new life together, with no more deception or lies, just Sunshine and Rain . . . and Little Diego.

Nothing in this life is promised to you;
Not fame, not fortune, not life, it's true.
You have to be strong-willed in all that you do;
You've got to hold tight when trials come at you.
Treat every day of your life like one to behold;
You must not be misled by all the monies and gold.
Friends are few, and you must select with care;
Relationships hurt, my people, you had better beware.
When true love is found, you must treat it with care;
Be true to the game still when life is unfair.
Believe in no one but yourself and your God;
and you will be way ahead of this game we call life,
until the play of your ending.

                                        SUNSHINE